W9-BRV-732

Final Approach

Final Approach

Rachel Brady

Poisoned Pen Press

Poisoned Pen Press

First Edition 2009

10 9 8 7 6 5 4 3 2 1

Library of Congress Catalog Card Number: 2009924186

ISBN: 978-1-59058-655-6 Hardcover

Poisoned Pen Press
6962 E. First Ave., Ste. 103
Scottsdale, AZ 85251
www.poisonedpenpress.com
info@poisonedpenpress.com

Printed in the United States of America

For Myrna and Deb,
who showed me the joy of reading for fun.

And for Tey, Jill, Lindsay, and Sam,
who bring so much joy to everything else.

Acknowledgments

They say it takes a village to raise a child. The same may be true for writing a book.

Dave Finney, Jon Matherne, Chad Randall, Mike Pace, Ray Beyer, Elizabeth Greczek, Shannon Miller, Lisa Cervantez, Randy Williams, and Chuck and Dee Akers humored what were probably a few too many questions. These folks have very cool jobs and I thank them for talking shop.

Linda Harris Dobkins, Carl Vonderau, and Gordon Aalborg steered me through early drafts. When I stumbled into a confusing new world called Publishing, Victoria Skurnick took good care of me. The amazing team at Poisoned Pen Press—Robert Rosenwald, Barbara Peters, Annette Rogers, Jessica Tribble, and Nan Beams—warmly guided me through the final stretch and gave the book a home.

Friends Jill Finney and David Hansard will always stand out when I remember working on this novel. Jill encouraged. David inspired. Neither may ever know how much.

Throughout, my family tolerated a wife and mother fused to her laptop. Tey, Jill, Lindsay, and Sam—thanks for understanding when my thoughts were away in a story.

To all these incredibly supportive people, thank you for being my village.

Chapter One

Jeannie found me in the ladies room, standing in mountain pose, trying to breathe like my yoga teacher.

"Jesus, Emily. Look at you." She smelled floral and cheerful but sounded grim.

I didn't have to look in the mirror to know why. My mascara had been wiped away and I knew my eyes would still be pink and glassy. I closed them and took another three-part breath.

"Richard's in the lobby," I said. "Don't make me talk about it."

"He can't see you like this."

Inhale. "Then fix me, please."

Exhale. "And bring me some of that perfume."

I opened my eyes in time to see her give what was meant to be a reassuring smile and pull open the door.

"Be right back," she said.

As her Guccis tapped down the hallway, I realized what her smile actually said: "Sucks to be you."

I checked my eyes in the mirror, first straight-on, then from the sides. They'd begun to whiten up and were less puffy. When Jeannie was finished, there'd be no evidence of my breakdown.

She was back right away with an already-unzipped handbag from which she produced concealer, lipstick, mascara, and eye shadow in a single swipe.

"Close your eyes."

I did what she said and she tugged, brushed, and blotted. Her work was gentle, but fast.

"Relax your jaw. Like you're dead."

I watched her eyes while she dabbed lipstick around the corners of my mouth. There were fine lines in her porcelain skin, but nothing I'd have spotted if I weren't inches from her face. Jeannie could conceal anything; she was like a cosmetics wizard.

She snapped the lid onto her lipstick and suddenly, it seemed, we were enveloped in a cloud of perfume.

"Walk through this," she said, spritzing the air between us again.

"There." She opened the door. With her free hand she pulled me by the wrist and shoved me into the corridor. "See him now, before you think."

"But—" I never even got a look in the mirror.

"Go."

Through the closing door, I saw her turn to the counter to collect her things. There was nothing left to do but what she'd said, and I knew as soon as I rounded the corner to the lobby that four years hadn't been long enough.

The receptionist looked up from her monitor and nodded when I passed. Richard was the only other person there, absorbed in some article in *The Plain Dealer*. A cheap Styrofoam coffee cup looked small in his hand and I watched him take a sip before I let him know I was there. There were gray streaks near his temples that I didn't remember, and his shirt was wrinkled. It was easier to look at his clothes than his face, and I didn't like that.

"Sorry, Richard. I was with someone."

He stood and dropped the paper into his chair. "I'm so glad you still work here."

When he extended his hand, I considered snubbing him, but couldn't. So I shook it.

I focused on three-part breathing but tried to be inconspicuous about it. Richard lived in Texas. I couldn't imagine what he wanted or why he'd come fourteen-hundred miles to get it in person.

"You might have started with a call."

"But I thought I'd have better luck in person. Forgive me for being this direct, but I'm here because I could use your help with a case."

He was being direct to skip the awkward small talk and avoid what could become a possibly volatile tangent.

"You think one of our nerdy chemists snuffed his wife for the insurance? Want me to do a little inside fact-checking for you?" I crossed my arms and gave my best "Duh" look.

"Not quite. I don't need an insider *here*. I need help from a skydiver and you're the only one I know."

I couldn't remember ever talking hobbies with Richard, so his request was not only insulting, but creepy.

"You're working a case in Cleveland?"

He turned around, to a briefcase I hadn't noticed, and produced a plane ticket. "Houston."

I shook my head. "Sorry, no. Try USPA."

"US-what?"

"United States Parachute Association. This isn't for me."

Richard tapped the ticket in his hand and stared at me until it became uncomfortable. I hated being bullied so I stared right back and added a little squint for good measure.

"Sure," he finally said. "I could find other skydivers. How many will care as much as you?"

"There's your problem. I don't care."

"It's a missing kid! Focus on a terrified little boy…Imagine his mom, wondering if he's alive. Tell me I'll find another person, much less another skydiver, who'll care about that like you."

Care about that like me. He meant "identify with" that like me, but wouldn't say so. He didn't have to—he knew I couldn't *not* become involved, even if it meant putting my mental health on the line all over again. I was being manipulated, and we both knew it. The jerk.

Chapter Two

I'd never gotten very good at winter driving, but I managed. By February, sounds of snow crunching under tires and wipers scraping ice were as familiar as the voices on my morning radio show. Like most northern Ohio winter days, the sky was overcast and dumping snow. Flakes the size of dimes sank heavily and swiftly, the way real dimes fall through fountain water. I imagined I was in a high school play, that the snow was a stage effect, and that thousands of pimply faced teenagers were in overhead rafters shaking boxes of this crap down on my car. I hate winter.

I drove home from work that morning, struggling to control my car and the emerging situation with Richard, who'd apparently reinvented himself as a private investigator. This wasn't our first brush with a missing kid. We'd met after my friends' son disappeared. Richard worked their case; he was a cop then. Their boy, Mattie, came home, but justice wasn't served to the man who'd snatched him. I'd always suspected Richard had a hand in getting that guy off.

My wipers pushed aside a fresh coat of flakes and my house came into view on the other side of the wet, streaked windshield. Four stark elms cloaked in a thin layer of ice jutted out of my desolate yard. In warmer months, they shaded my place. That day, they looked like a strange weather experiment someone had left on my lawn as a prank. I pulled into my driveway, past a snow-capped mailbox still marked for "Jack and Emily Locke," and pressed the button to raise my garage door.

The dashboard clock said 10:47 a.m. In the two hours since my ladies room meltdown, I'd managed to speak face-to-face with both Richard and my group manager, Peter "The Abominable" Bowman—undertakings that, each alone, could dampen a day. Doing both in one morning had annihilated it.

I parked in the garage, scooped up my purse and scarf, and headed toward the house. My phone was ringing on the other side of the wall. I squeezed between my front bumper and recycle bins and made it over a pile of old newspapers before catching my toe on a box and stumbling. The contents of my purse clattered at my feet.

I swung open my kitchen door and lifted the cordless from its wall mount. It was Jeannie.

"You sound frenzied," she said.

"I had to run to catch the phone." I headed back to the mess in the garage.

"How'd it go with Bowman?"

"I told him I needed some discretionary leave."

"And?"

Next to my car, I knelt to collect my spilled things and dump them back into my purse.

"You know Bowman." I palmed my compact and car keys off the freezing cement floor. "He's not okay with any absence unless your entrails are dragging between your feet."

"But you're home now, so you worked something out."

"I told him it was only for a couple of days and reminded him I haven't taken leave for years."

"Did he ask why you're leaving?"

"I said it was personal."

My lipstick had rolled behind the hot water heater, and when I saw the spider webs and dusty funk back there I decided to abandon it forever.

"Mmm," Jeannie said. "What was your concession?"

"What do you mean?" My purse back together, minus the lipstick, I stood and went back inside.

"I know he didn't let you walk out of there with a pat on the back and tell you to enjoy a few days off."

She knew him better than I thought.

"I said I'd work remotely." I headed for my hallway. "Laptop's in the car. I'll lug it down there with everything else."

I tugged the rope that hung from my hallway ceiling and extended the folding ladder to my attic. Its hinges were stiff. They squeaked when I stepped on the first rung.

"Down where? Where are you going with Richard Cole?"

I tried my best southern drawl. "Texas, *y'all.*"

An empty backpack and three stuffed Christmas bears careened past my shoulders and landed on the hallway floor.

"What are you doing over there?" she asked. "It sounds like you're in a washing machine."

"Packing," I grunted, and eased an unwieldy American Tourister down the ladder.

"When are you leaving?"

I made it to the floor and glanced at my watch. "About ninety minutes."

I hurled the fallen attic artifacts back upstairs and returned the ladder to its loft.

"What's he want you to do in Texas?"

"That's the weirdest part. He wants me to skydive."

"Why?"

I dragged the bag-on-wheels to my bedroom and flung it onto the unmade bed.

"To check out a drop zone near Houston." I rummaged through dresser drawers. "It has to do with his case and he needs somebody who can fit in. He was about to explain it all when Bowman walked by and asked me for 'a word'. There was only time for Richard to pass me a plane ticket and promise more details on the flight. Now you know as much as I do."

She was quiet.

"At least it's warm there," she finally said. "You might see some sexy cowboys. Maybe you'll meet the Marlboro Man and he'll whisk you away to Me-he-co."

"Me-he-co?" I opened my top drawer, distressed to find only two pair of clean underwear. "You sound like Speedy Gonzales on Prozac."

"You're funny now. Spend a couple days with Richard and you'll be the one on Prozac. I don't think this trip's a good idea."

In my master bath, I unplugged my hairdryer and grabbed a cosmetics pouch from under the sink.

"I don't have time to get into this now. I'll call you from the road."

"Don't let him call the shots," she said, and hung up.

The last items I shoved into my suitcase were an assortment of skydiving tees and a couple pairs of shorts. Then I opened my closet, where my skydiving gear was hibernating for the winter.

Plenty of my friends jump after there's snow. But they're fools. When ground temperatures reach the fifties, at altitude it's in the thirties. That's cold enough for me to hang it up for the year. My last season ended in October, so there was dust to brush off my gear bag.

I hoisted the forty-pound sack onto my shoulder and dumped it next to the suitcase on my bed. I unzipped the compartments and checked that all the miscellaneous must-haves were inside—goggles, gloves, tube stows, rubber bands, and pull-up cords. My jumpsuit and helmet were there too, under my logbook. I pulled the logbook out and flipped to the last entry:

Jump No.:	686
Date:	Oct. 9
Place:	Northern Ohio Skydivers
Aircraft:	Super Otter
Equipment:	Sabre 120
Altitude:	14,000 ft.
Delay/Total Time:	65 sec. / 11 h, 3min, 7sec
Maneuver:	4-way with Mike, Walt, and Jerome
Description:	Launched the exit. Went to crap. Built 1st and 2nd points. Turned for the 3rd point, a bipole, but never got it. Breakoff at 3000 ft. Pop up landing over the peas.

I snapped the book shut and tossed it back into the bag. It reminded me of another log, my old journal. I hadn't looked at it since my last entry, which now seemed so long ago and yet so relevant. It was buried under old cards and photos in the bottom drawer of my desk. I pulled it out and ran my fingers over the ratty cover and twisted binding, tempted to open it, but short on time. I tucked it under my arm and returned to the bedroom, where I dropped it into my gear bag with the rest.

The parachute system itself, or rig, was safely cocooned inside the gear bag too, dominating most of the space.

"Good to see you, old friend," I muttered. I pulled the gear bag's zipper shut, slipped my arms through its backpack straps, and heaved it onto my back. Then I rolled my bag-on-wheels across the living room, wondering what I'd forgotten to pack.

◇◇◇

When I found my gate at Cleveland Hopkins, Richard was waiting in the chairs. The terminal smelled like hot dogs and popcorn. Two little girls in matching dresses wove under and around velvet ropes that cordoned the boarding area. I did a quick side step to avoid bumping into one of them, then felt a pang watching them play.

Richard leafed through a thick file on his lap and scribbled notes on a legal pad.

I took the seat beside him. "Heavy reading."

He looked up from his file and seemed surprised to see me. His eyes were slightly bloodshot. That was either new or had escaped my notice earlier at the office.

"I don't have much to go on, but I'll show you what I have on the plane."

He paused and added, "I want to thank you—"

An airline rep on the loudspeaker announced the first round of boarding. I used her distraction to pretend not to hear his thanks. I wasn't in the mood to let bygones be bygones. Instead, I followed him toward the boarding line and glanced out the windows. It was bleak as ever and still snowing. We'd be lucky if our plane didn't fall out of the sky like a hundred-and-fifty-thousand pound Popsicle with wings. The line inched forward, and Richard and I obediently blended into the herd.

I remembered my last trip to Texas, when we'd first met. Little Mattie Shelton was missing then. *Please let this trip have a better ending for the family involved.*

Chapter Three

Our flight was full, and the cabin too warm. We'd barely received the safety spiel and located the nearest exits when Richard set his briefcase on his lap, popped its locks, and pulled out a folder.

"Eric Lyons is my clients' son," he said without looking at me. "He and his wife divorced after Christmas."

So much for small talk, I thought.

"They shared custody of their boy, Casey. Eleven months old." He passed me a thin stack of photos. Casey was a cherub sprouting dark curls, adorable dimples, and a wide smile with four budding teeth.

"The arrangement was amicable until last week," he continued. "Karen, the ex, took a job in Louisiana. Told police that when she asked Eric to go back to court to change the custody order, he got upset—afraid he'd never see the boy."

"Change the order?"

Richard nodded. "Otherwise she couldn't relocate more than a hundred and fifty miles away. Then Friday night, Casey disappeared from his mom's home. No forced entry."

I shot him a quizzical glance, but he wouldn't look at me. He paged through his folder and dumped more facts, like an information waterfall.

"In her police report, Karen noted she didn't change the pass code for her security system when Eric left. And, since Casey's disappearance, Eric hasn't returned to his apartment. Naturally, police suspect a parental abduction. But my clients are sure they're wrong."

We accelerated down the runway. Richard swallowed, then brushed his nose nervously, and I suspected his verbal deluge had more to do with self-distraction than with filling me in.

"You okay?" I asked.

"Fine."

"Not a fan of planes?"

He didn't speak or look at me, just shook his head.

I begrudged his intrusion into my life, and couldn't resist twisting the knife a little.

"I love planes."

He didn't bite. If I'd known ahead of time that he was afraid to fly, I'd have figured a way to stick him with my window seat.

Our wheels touched off and we ascended through spotty clouds. I peered through the window at the snowy landscape below.

"On jump runs, we go to fourteen thousand feet," I said. "Much higher, we'd need oxygen masks. Much lower, we'll complain we're not getting enough altitude for our money."

I turned from the window back to Richard. "What's our cruising altitude today? Thirty, thirty-five thousand? That'd be about two minutes of freefall, Richard."

He swallowed again and nodded. When he stole a glance at the puke bag in the pouch in front of him, I decided against taking this much further.

I switched gears. "Do you believe the parents?"

His eyebrows twitched. "I never met Eric. I'm taking their word."

A baby in the front of the cabin cried out, and I ached for it.

Richard continued, "If Eric didn't take the boy, police are wasting valuable time."

I heard his words, but my attention had shifted to the crying in the front of the plane. Most passengers worry the fussing will be everlasting. My take is that there isn't much about young kids that's everlasting. If I could hear my daughter's noises again—any of them, good or bad—you can bet I'd listen up in a heartbeat.

Richard was still talking. "If somebody else has Casey, the sooner that trail is picked up, the better. So it doesn't really matter who I believe. I'm one more person looking for this kid, and that's enough for me."

I wondered whether his devotion could be some sort of penance. Was he making up for the mess he'd made of the Shelton case? Or was he trying to gain back my trust so I'd give him my full effort?

"What do you know about Karen Lyons?"

"Only what's in her report. She woke up late on Saturday morning and knew right away something was wrong. It was 7:45 and Casey hadn't woken her up yet. When she checked his room, he wasn't in the crib."

I flashed on a similar event in my own past, and my chest felt like it was being squashed. The scenario Richard described—an intruder slipping unnoticed into a protected home and targeting its most vulnerable occupant—was personal. I'd lived it, and Richard knew that. I resented him for pulling me back into an emotional viper pit, and when I looked at him this time I could feel my face was flushed, and it wasn't from the heat in the cabin.

His eyes leveled on mine. A confrontation was brewing, but neither of us would initiate it. I avoided it because it was too painful. I figured Richard avoided it because he was a coward.

A flight attendant's call bell sounded, and Richard jumped. His fingers fumbled across his lap until he found his seatbelt buckle, then he pulled the belt tighter. He took a slow breath.

He added, "No prints were lifted from the home. The family hasn't been contacted. No ransom demands, threats...nothing. HPD canvassed the neighbors and are looking for Eric's vehicle. But the Lyonses think police are barking up the wrong tree. They're worried sick about their son and grandson."

I remembered Keith and Nora Shelton, my friends from Cleveland, and the extra investigators they'd hired when Mattie disappeared.

"Why do you suspect a skydiver?"

"Couple things," he said, tugging at his folder again. He opened it and searched its papers until he found a 5"x7" color print of a paper chit. Its ink had run and the text was partly smudged, but I recognized it.

"A jump ticket," I said.

I'd used my share of jump tickets, but that was the first time I'd seen one photographed and enlarged, looking like evidence. It was weird.

Richard said, "This was in Karen's landscaping. Police bagged it, but don't think it's related. It could have come from anywhere, maybe blown across the neighborhood from someone else's trash. It could have been stuck in the mulch for days or weeks. Karen didn't recognize it, and neither did her neighbors."

The plane lurched and Richard reached to turn the overhead knob for more air conditioning.

"Getting warmer in here," he mumbled.

"What else do you have?"

He shrugged. "A gut feeling. Someone gave me the slip at that drop zone yesterday. I interviewed the owners, staff...a few regular jumpers. Friendly people mostly, but a tight-lipped bunch. One employee agreed to talk to me, but left before I got to him. That seemed odd."

I thought about the tight-lipped part and believed it. Skydivers are a tight group, period. Protective of each other, and probably chattier with new jumpers they've just met than with the non-jumping postmen they see every day. "Okay. What else?"

"That's it."

"You came to Cleveland, got me on a plane to Texas, put me in deep water with my boss...because of a gut feeling and a ticket in this lady's shrubs?"

We lurched again and Richard hesitated. "Emily, sometimes whole cases are broken because of one tip, one clue. Nobody's following up on this one. What if it's important?"

I didn't answer.

Doctor Hess, my graduate student advisor, came to mind. He popped into my brain the way Cinderella's fairy godmother popped into her garden the night of the ball. I remembered advice he'd offered in a lecture years before: "When you're problem solving with a team and somebody has an idea," Hess had said, "separate the idea from the person talking, because once in a while a jackass might come up with something useful."

I thought, Hess, this one's for you.

"It's not trash," I said. "If you aren't going to use tickets, you cash them back in. Did the police visit the drop zone?"

"I'm sure they did, but I'm not privy to that investigation. I asked about the ticket when I was there yesterday, but they can't trace who bought it. It's not marked with a date or number or anything."

"They can't trace the buyer specifically, but they could have helped you narrow it down. Jumpers sign waivers. If the ticket isn't older than a year, when waivers expire, the owner's name is in the drop zone files somewhere. Granted, you'd turn up the names of all the jumpers who've gone through there in the last year...probably a long list."

Richard didn't answer, but a purposeful tilt of his chin told me he was digesting the information.

I continued. "Also, only licensed skydivers buy tickets. Students don't use them, so that eliminates some of the clientele."

I considered the context of the ticket and added, "If I were visiting a drop zone and didn't use all my tickets, I'd cash them in before leaving. But, if it were my home DZ, the place I jumped most of the time, I'd save them for next time. Since whoever bought that ticket left with it, I bet it was a regular, somebody who knew he'd be back."

I looked at the picture again. The ticket was the size of a business card and looked like it was generated from a desktop printer. Some of its characters were blurred, I assumed from its stay in Karen Lyons' mulch bed.

ULF CO ST SK DIV NG
$17

"Gulf Coast Skydiving," Richard read out loud, filling in the smudged characters. "A mom and pop operation about ninety minutes south of Houston. Your home for the next few days."

"What do you want me to do?"

"Introduce yourself and make friends. Tell me who seems unusual. Find out if anyone's left town recently. Does anyone have trouble with the law? That sort of thing."

"You're not coming with me?"

"I was there already, asking questions. If somebody there is involved, or somebodies, it's better they don't know you're with me."

I cringed. "I'm not 'with you,' Richard."

He took back the photograph and closed it in his briefcase hard enough that the tray table under it bobbled.

Awkward silence followed. Cold-shouldering is worse on an airplane because you have to sit so close.

I pouted. He ignored me. He reached for a magazine in the seat back and thumbed through a few pages before giving in and speaking first.

"I'll think about how we might get a look at those waivers. But, until we can get names, I'd like to work on faces. We'll—"

A mild patch of turbulence cut him short.

When it passed, he started over. "We'll hide a camera on you and then show pictures of the jumpers to Karen Lyons. Maybe she'll see a familiar face."

"I'll be in and out of a jumpsuit all day. Anything I wear will get covered up or hurtle toward earth at a hundred-twenty miles per hour. What kind of hot shot camera do you have?"

Richard slumped. He tapped the rolled magazine in his palm. I enjoyed watching him re-plan because re-planning meant his first idea had been wrong and it felt good to make Richard be wrong. But then I felt a little guilty, since I knew all along his scheming would be unnecessary.

"Relax," I said. "Skydivers are hams. The most subtle way to take pictures is to tell them to say 'Cheese.'"

After that, we didn't talk much. Richard leaned his head back and closed his eyes. His face looked gray.

I thought about what was in store for me at Gulf Coast Skydiving. Would I fit in as easily as I hoped? Could I be a convincing liar? And how well could I judge people, anyway? The last question worried me most, considering who I was sitting next to.

Chapter Four

In Houston, Richard put me up in a hotel near his office. He made arrangements by cell phone on our way from the airport, dropped me off at the entrance, and told me he'd come back first thing in the morning for a working breakfast. Then he peeled out of the hotel drive so fast you'd think I was a bucket of festering biological waste.

It was four o'clock Central Time. Going home to an empty house back in Cleveland was no treat, but checking into an empty hotel room was worse. I was already lonely and bored, wondering how to pass the rest of the day without a car to explore town. Movie channels would offer no relief. There could be nothing showing I hadn't already seen in four years of spending Friday and Saturday nights alone on my couch.

I checked in and found my room. With the day mostly over, the responsible thing to do would be to work on Bowman's monthly reports, but what I really wanted to do, although I wasn't sure why, was have a look at my old journal. The record from *then*—when I still believed Richard was a good guy, there to serve and protect. I pulled it from my gear bag, and stared at its worn cover. I'd stopped journaling years ago, when it seemed little in life was worth remembering anymore.

I sat on the edge of the neatly made bed and thumbed to the day I'd first met Richard, back when life was good and my family was alive. He was a cop, answering a call. I was traveling on business, killing time. Funny how life tosses folks together.

◇◇◇

April 8—11:30 a.m.

Asphyxiating from bus fumes

I'm curbside, at Austin Bergstrom airport, waiting for the bus that will take me to my rental car. Tried to call Jack and see how he's faring as a single dad (frightening prospect) but nobody's home. Annette is probably eating a Dairy Queen Blizzard for lunch, his treat.

It's Sunday. Conference starts tomorrow. I read in the paper about a state record they hope to set at a local drop zone today. Figure I'll head that way, grab lunch, and go watch. If my bus ever comes.

April 8—8:21 p.m.

Austin police station, waiting room chairs

Never made it to drop zone. Ended up here instead. Still reeling from coincidence.

Five miles from the drop zone, I pulled over for carry-out and found Mattie Shelton belted into a plastic high chair at a table with strangers. Sudden change of plans.

I stepped out of line, seated myself at a corner table, and stared. I thought about how long Mattie had been missing, and how long it had been since I'd seen him. By my calculations, it'd been three weeks since his abduction, and two months since I'd seen him. Our last visit was when Nora turned thirty.

Three people were with him—a couple and another man, all dressed nicely. It looked like a young family out for Sunday lunch, except the extra man was shuffling folders and taking notes.

I reached for my cell phone, but thought better of it. No sense making an ass of myself. I've confused people before, called them by the wrong name. Not the best with faces, especially baby faces that change so much, so fast. What if I had the wrong kid?

So I got up and walked toward his table as if headed to the restroom. I stopped to admire him, and this brought lots of information from the woman standing in as Mom: the baby was about to turn one, a good eater, and a shameless flirt. His favorite character was Thomas the Train and he loved to be outside. She called him Ben. That was freaky.

I said hello to "Ben," took a tiny, ketchup-coated hand in mine, and gave him a little baby handshake. I found what I was looking for on the inside of his wrist, a small hemangioma. Nora had told me once that the little strawberry birthmark would disappear on its own in the next few years.

I wanted to take him from the high chair right then and run for my car. But I collected myself and moved on.

The hallway with the restrooms was far enough from the table to be out of earshot and still allow a view of Mattie. I used my cell to call the police, told what I knew of Mattie's disappearance, added that I'm friends with the Sheltons, and finished with how I'd checked the birthmark. The dispatcher said to stay put; a patrol car was on the way. We hung up.

A waitress brought the check to Mattie's table and I panicked when one of the men pulled out a credit card. How to keep them there? I shoved open an "Employees Only" door, found the manager, explained, and convinced him to stall their credit slip. He left to take care of it, then joined me by the front door. We watched for police, but I couldn't see Mattie's table anymore. It was behind a salad bar partition.

The manager noticed my Indians jersey and asked me about Cleveland, which I thought ridiculous, considering everything going on. Turns out he knew folks in Shaker Heights. I figured he was trying to calm me down. He had a UT ring and a cursive "T" tattooed on his wrist, both potential topics for small talk, but the first cruiser pulled into the lot faster than I'd expected and I was off the hook.

I introduced myself to the officers when they walked inside. One went around the corner to Mattie's table. The other waited near the manager and me. Standing by a cop made me as nervous as driving in front of one. He asked for my story.

A second cruiser pulled in.

I heard the officer in the dining area introduce himself to the people at the table and ask about Mattie. There was no way to talk to one cop and eavesdrop on the other. But, the cop with me seemed equally curious about what was going on behind the salad bar. The manager too. We all stood there, straining our ears like dogs. At first we only heard a little of what was said, but voices at the table grew louder, more agitated. Mattie fussed, and finally the rest of the dining room fell silent while everyone watched the drama. The couple sounded confused and indignant. They got defensive. My officer buddy moved into the restaurant to help his partner.

That's when the policemen from the second cruiser came inside. These were plain-clothes guys. Detective Frank Morgan was big as a tree and smelled like Old Spice. His partner, Detective Richard Cole, was in his early forties and had the same concerned look that Father Denny used to have when I'd see him for confession in high school. They told me they had questions for me. I had questions too.

That was seven hours ago. Since then, the detectives and I have done oodles of talking. I've had entirely too much bad coffee. I've memorized the graffiti in the bathroom. There's a shaky guy sitting across from us who shares a random Bible verse with me every twenty minutes. I think he's with the hooker they brought in right before the desk sergeant's Little Caesars order arrived.

Mattie's waking up! More later.

April 9—1:05 a.m.
Days Inn, Austin

Too wired to sleep, so will finish getting this down. Keith and Nora made it to the station and were reunited with Mattie tonight. I'll tell it in order so I won't mess it up.

At the restaurant, I'd started to fill in details for the detectives when the other officers brought the couple toward the door. No handcuffs, only stern faces on the cops and desperate explanations from the couple. The woman seemed shocked and was crying. Her husband was irate.

Mattie, in the arms of one of the policemen, squirmed and reached for the woman. The officer carrying him wouldn't hand him over, and Mattie's outstretched arms and wriggling upset this woman even more. I asked whether I could hold him, and the officer told me, "Not yet, ma'am," and whisked him past me, out the door.

Morgan and Cole asked me to follow them to the station to give a statement. Confused, I asked about the second man from the table. The detectives and the patrolmen had a brief discourse outside, and when Morgan and Cole returned, I learned that, whoever the second man was, he was gone by the time my call had been answered.

But where did he go? And when? I'd watched all of them at their table during my call and was standing at the exit after that.

I described the guy and the three of us searched the restaurant without luck. The place had video surveillance of its parking lot though. It showed a hurrying man, in clothes like I remembered, leaving through an employee entrance. His face was grainy, but I felt pretty sure it was the guy. He got into a dark pick-up and booked it out of the lot. Morgan rewound the tape, paused it, and wrote down part of a license plate number.

I called Nora on my cell while following the detectives to the police station. I started with, "I found Mattie!" and never got around to the nuts and bolts of how that happened. She was hysterical. Listening to her carry on, my eyes started tearing so badly I had to keep wiping them so I could see the road. Keith picked up on another extension and asked questions that made me feel useful. Am I sure it's him? Where did I find him? Does he look mistreated? Who has him now? He gave his cell number and said they'd be on the next flight to Austin. I heard keys jingle in the background as he said it. I promised to call them with more updates and the street address for the station as soon as I knew it. And I promised to stay with Mattie.

When we got to the station, Mattie was undergoing a physical exam in a private room but I was told I could be with him shortly. I'm not sure how cops divvy up their questioning, but apparently Cole got me and Morgan got the "parents." He led them to an office and I watched as the crying woman collapsed into her husband's arms. I think she said "we were so close" right before Morgan shut the door.

Cole sat me at his desk with a small stack of statement forms and told me to write about my experience using as many continuation sheets as I needed. It took fourteen hand-written pages.

Next, it was off to a computer station where I used special software to create a likeness of the mystery man. It wasn't perfect, but gave the detectives a start.

Meanwhile, Keith had been in touch with the Austin PD and asked that I be allowed to stay with Mattie until he and Nora arrived. Keith's company has a corporate plane; his VP was happy to help any way he could. They traveled on a private flight and would arrive at the station in a few hours.

Finally, I got the little guy. When I scooped him into my arms, I imagined how this would feel to Nora and Keith when they got to hold their baby again. As soon as he settled into my lap, I dialed them. When Nora answered, I said, "I have somebody here who wants to talk to his mama," and got teary again.

After our call, the hard part started. The station is no toy land, and I wasn't allowed to leave with the baby. Entertaining a toddler for nine hours in a police station was...well, shitty. But what are friends for?

Detective Cole walked up with two Dr. Peppers and a carton of milk in time to see Mattie try to decapitate me using my necklace. I searched my purse for something safer and came up with a library card and the keys to the rental. What he really wanted was my lipstick. I made a mental note to tease Keith.

Cole noticed my parachute pendant. I pulled a picture of Annette from my wallet and explained why I quit skydiving. He produced his own photo of two cute kids, the reasons he sometimes worries about being a cop.

He went back to work and Mattie and I were relegated to the waiting room chairs. Keith and Nora burst through the doors around 11:30 p.m. and I've never seen parents look worse or better.

◇◇◇

Even after so much time, those memories were sharp.

My cell phone rang, muffled within the bowels of my purse, and jolted me back. I sniffled and brushed away tears. When I answered the phone, I tried to sound normal.

"Where are you?" Jeannie wanted to know.

"In a Houston hotel." I crashed backward on the bed with my feet hanging over the edge of the mattress. My eyes closed involuntarily.

"Is Richard there with you?" she whispered.

My eyes popped open. "Of course not."

"What's going on?"

"What's going on is, this is a mistake," I said. "The only reason he wants to explore the drop zone angle is that police found a jump ticket in some lady's bushes."

I thought of the staff member who'd evaded Richard's questioning, but left that part out. I stared at the swirls on the ceiling.

"What about you?" I said. "What's going on there?"

"Sure, I'll get that ready before I leave. No problem."

I knew the cover. She'd called from her desk at work—and had been busted.

"Talk to you later," I sighed.

I tried to concentrate on the BioTek work I owed Bowman, but Richard's case was distracting. After forty-five minutes, I closed my laptop, changed into running clothes, and left to explore the city on foot.

I started east at an easy pace, toward what I thought was downtown. Traffic often moved slower than I did, and for blocks I passed only apartments, strip malls, and donut joints. But within a mile, establishments like the Taco Cabana and local pregnancy crisis center faded off the landscape, replaced by more upscale businesses like leather vendors and gourmet smoothie shops. High rises in shades of green and blue loomed ahead and, even though it sure looked like downtown, signs said otherwise. I'd found the Galleria.

On Post Oak Boulevard, I passed Williams Tower. The building reminded me of a 1920's skyscraper, except that it was fronted with glass, and it was so tall I stumbled when I tried to look up at it. Ahead, a series of ornamental silver arches spanned each intersection. Running beneath them felt like going under a bunch of chrome rainbows. The effect was too over-the-top for my taste, but at least there were no creepy men leering at me like in Cleveland. Instead, the quizzical looks from suited businessmen and swanky women seemed only to ask why I'd reduced myself to public exercise.

I continued in the shadows of parking garages and high-rise offices, and each time I spotted a luxury hotel—they could be found in any direction I looked—I wished Richard had put me up in one of those suckers instead. The air quality in Houston was disgusting, I realized, but at least none of the cars had chains on their tires. They didn't seem to rust, either. Without salted roads, even older models still looked strangely new. On two occasions, I noticed "Don't Mess With Texas" bumper stickers.

My new environment was certainly interesting, but even fancy landscaping and posh architecture couldn't take my mind off the reason for my visit. At the drop zone, I'd meet potentially dangerous people. I had no undercover experience, no reason to believe I'd be any good at my assignment. I was a thirty-two-year-old burned out chemist, for Pete's sake, not a swashbuckling private eye. My imagination went haywire, conjuring wild cloak and dagger scenarios. I ran faster, imagining myself a tough she-woman like Jaime Sommers, Sydney Bristow, or Xena.

When I finally got back to the hotel, sweaty and spent, my GPS watch reported a distance of 4.2 miles. That warranted overpriced cookies from the mini-bar. I headed upstairs to claim my reward.

Chapter Five

Tuesday morning, the only indication I was in the right place was a faded wooden sign nailed to a post that said "Gulf Coast Skydiving. Howdy, Y'all!"

With an impressive lack of verbiage, Richard had pushed a Houston area map and a set of car keys across the breakfast table at my hotel. The car was his teenaged son's. It was my loaner. The map led to the drop zone, about seventy miles south of Houston, six miles from the Gulf of Mexico.

I eased onto the dirt road and watched a plume of dust rise behind me in the rearview mirror. Ahead, down a half-mile stretch of pitted dirt road, a compound of small airport hangars was clustered in a field. I grew anxious thinking about what and who I would find.

Private planes were tied down between hangars, but the place looked otherwise deserted. I figured the owners of the little planes must be weekend hobbyists, busy today at work.

Then a Cessna came into view, making a final approach to a grass runway. It dropped out of sight behind hangars at the end of the drive. I checked the sky. Four parachutes swirled overhead.

The road dead-ended in a grass lot next to the largest hangar. Enormous sliding doors, large enough to pull a plane through, were wide open on both sides. I looked straight through the building to the landing field behind it, where orange windsocks flared sideways, then flopped beside their posts. The Cessna was taxiing back.

I parked next to a dusty Mustang with a license plate that said SKYD1VR and got out of the car.

It felt good to stretch. I pulled my gear bag from the backseat and was about to head for the hangar when I had a shameful thought. My chances of befriending jumpers, at least the men, might improve if I took off my wedding rings. I slipped them off and shoved them deep into the pocket of my jean shorts. The naked sensation on my finger felt dishonest, and I longed for Jack. I imagined he'd understand; maybe even scold me for not doing it sooner.

Inside the hangar I found an office, where a friendly looking hippie in his mid-forties was going over student rates with a caller on the phone. He wore a Dave Matthews Band concert shirt, cutoff jeans, and Teva sandals. A skinny ponytail snaked down his back. He winked at me and gestured he'd be a minute, then flipped through some paperwork stacked behind the counter.

I set my gear down and inspected pictures hanging on the office's scuffed walls. One showed silhouettes of a beautiful round formation at sunset. I estimated it as a forty-way. Several photos captured the exaggerated smiles of tandem students in freefall, their instructors giving two thumbs up behind them. A collage showed various jumpers with pie smeared on their faces. I remembered my own hundredth jump from back in the Stone Ages, it seemed. My friends had gotten me with six key-limes, a vanilla crème, and a cheesecake. I smiled, remembering Jack. Later that night, when we'd gone to bed, he'd gotten me with a chocolate pie.

I scanned one photograph to the next. Who in those pictures knew something about Casey?

The man behind the desk hung up. "Thanks for waiting. What can I do ya for, hon'?" His smile was warm; it reminded me of my dad's.

I explained I was new in town and needed a re-pack. Unlike the main canopy, which we pack ourselves, reserves have to be packed by a certified rigger every ninety days.

He shook my hand. "Rick Hanes. My wife and I own this shack. What brings you from out of town?"

"Work." I'd hatched a cover story during my lonely night in the hotel and felt a little self-congratulatory because my burst of foresight was about to pay off.

He leaned on the countertop between us, resting on his elbows.

"What line of work?"

I'd once heard it's best to stick with what you know. "Chemistry."

An eerily silent tabby cat sprung onto the countertop to investigate me. I started petting it.

"That's Otter," Rick said. "Showed up one day and never left." He stroked her under the chin, then turned toward the window. "Who you working for?"

Cat hair began to stick to the palm of my hand.

"NASA."

It seemed easier to function inside a huge, open-ended lie than small, specific one, so I'd selected a fake employer accordingly. For good measure, I'd even Googled the surrounding area and decided on a pretend waterfront apartment on Clear Lake. "I found a cute little place in Kemah, not too far from some great seafood restaurants."

"Excellent!" Rick said. "We have several space nuts here. I'll introduce you."

He tapped a stack of flyers on the counter and explained that a boogie—jumper lingo for a major skydiving event—was planned for the weekend. He was bringing in a couple hot air balloons and a Twin Otter from Tulsa for some special jumps.

In addition to regular weekenders, boogies often attract other regional jumpers. If a skydiver in southeast Texas was responsible for Casey's kidnapping, I thought there was a good chance he'd be at the boogie.

"Let me introduce you to the gang," Rick said, "Then we'll take care of your rig and waiver."

He held open the office door and followed me outside into the expansive hangar, where I met a love-struck young couple lounging on carpet remnants covering the cement floor. They could hardly look away from each other long enough to meet me.

Rick leaned close to me and whispered, “Hot pants,” as we walked outside.

I laughed, and it felt good. Good to laugh, and good to be at a drop zone, where a person can walk into a crowd of total strangers and almost any of them will make room for a newcomer on their dive.

Outside, in alarmingly quick succession, I met three women and four men. I realized immediately my problem linking names and faces would be a severe handicap in my new role as Richard’s operative.

Two names stuck.

The first was Marie, Rick’s wife. She dog-eared a page in a paperback when Rick brought me over. Petite and athletic, she was in her forties like Rick and had a gorgeous tan. She smiled from her perch on a picnic bench and extended a hand toward me.

In the first Texas accent I’d heard on the trip, she said, “Welcome. We need more girls around here.”

Another woman nodded in agreement but was unable to speak because her mouth was full of Fritos. She gave an embarrassed chew-smile and held out her bag to offer some chips, which I accepted. The third woman tossed a cigarette to the ground and smashed it under the toe of her Nike. Marie’s friends were younger than she, but all had bronzed skin, a definite perk to life in the south as far as I was concerned.

Standing next to them were four men, still in jumpsuits.

“I saw you guys when I was coming up the road,” I said.

Rick told me their names, but as soon as the final handshake was complete, the entire list was wiped from memory, save one.

“Scud” had a face that should be in magazines. He used his grip on my hand to pull me into a swift hug, as if he’d known me all his life. I’d met the resident flirt, and couldn’t help but ask about his name.

"It's because of the way he flies that damn Batwing," Marie snickered, referring to his high performance parachute, which handled like a sports car in the automotive world. She said "flies" like "flas." "Crazy fool whizzes through here like a missile."

"Don't believe a word of it, sweetheart." Scud lifted my hand and kissed it. Marie rolled her eyes.

The skydivers carried their gear into the hangar. I followed Marie's gaze and watched Scud trudge away with a slight limp.

"When you gonna fix that knee, tough guy?" she called.

"No sense doing it before the boogie, woman."

She shook her head and opened her book again. "Man's got the sense of a tin can."

I dropped some quarters into a vending machine beside the door and popped open an A&W, eavesdropping while the jumpers went over their dive. They spaced themselves throughout the hangar, laid out their lines across mismatched swatches of old carpeting, and started packing.

I noticed a guitar case in the corner and asked the closest jumper if it were his.

"Nope, that's Vince's. You play?"

I swallowed a sip of root beer. "A little."

"Well, he sure can't," he said, and the others laughed. "Help yourself. He's a good guy. No worries."

I set down my can and unfastened the case's latches. I was surprised to find a Martin inside.

"For somebody who can't play, he sure has a Cadillac in here."

"Whatcha gonna play, sweetheart?" Scud called from across the room, where he was folding the Batwing's cells.

His flirting was relentless, but it went a long way toward breaking the ice and I needed the help. He was also nice to look at, so all the better. I decided I could keep up with him, even though I was years out of practice. There's a certain level of courage gained by pretending to be someone you're not.

"Whatcha wanna hear, sweetheart?" I lifted the guitar and took a seat in a nearby folding chair.

"'American Pie'?" He laid belly-down on the floor and straddled his folded nylon parachute cells. He pressed as much air out of the fabric as he could and began to compress the canopy into an S-pattern.

I played, and Scud sang along badly. We finished while he muscled his canopy into its D-bag and stowed the lines. When the song ended, he shouted across the room, "When are we getting married?" I felt myself blush.

The woman with the Fritos said she was having a mellow day and asked for a ballad. I chose Marty Robbins' "Don't Worry 'Bout Me" and sang that moody, soulful old song while I watched the group finish packing. It was hard to believe any of them could have something to do with Casey's disappearance, but that was a hunch based on intuition alone. As far as facts went, I realized, the only thing I knew with moderate certainty was that nobody so far worked for NASA. I didn't imagine Richard would find that very useful.

Part-way through the song, I glanced out the front doors of the hangar and watched a modern day cowboy approach from the parking area with a sack of fast food in hand. His plain white tee showed off a strong chest and well developed arms, and Jeannie would have said his jeans fit "mighty fine." He walked into the hangar in a pair of dusty, brown boots. A black Stetson hid his eyes.

Jeannie would never believe my luck, meeting two men that good looking in the same day.

The song was over fast; the old ones always are. I kneeled to put the Martin back in its case, and when I stood again I was face to face with the sexy cowboy.

His eyes, still in the shadow of his hat, were cast to the floor. You don't find too many shy people at drop zones.

He spoke with a light accent, softly enough not to be overheard. "Damn, girl," he said. "You made your first million yet?"

I laughed. "Hardly, but thanks." I offered my hand. "I'm Emily."

When he took my hand, the contact was electric. I mean, it was literally electric—we both got shocked. I looked at the carpet beneath us and felt my smile get bigger. When I raised my eyes again, I got my first look at his smile and it was beautiful.

"You have an amazing voice, Emily, and a good way with a guitar too. Name's Vince."

I glanced at his guitar case. "Caught with my hand in the cookie jar."

"My guitar never sounded so good. Was beginning to think something was wrong with it."

I forced my eyes away from his chest, finding irony that such efforts usually go the other way around.

He started to speak again, but Rick brought someone over. It was Billy, the rigger, and I brightened at the prospect of being in the air again soon. I excused myself from Vince, and followed Billy to the office. When we passed through the door, I tried to sneak a final look over my shoulder, but I got caught. Vince tipped his cowboy hat at me and grinned, and then the door snapped closed between us, leaving his image sharply focused in my mind.

Chapter Six

Billy was in no hurry. I followed him into the rigger's loft, a glorified walk-in closet that opened off the drop zone office. When I handed him my rig, he put it beside five others and sat down to enjoy a pinch of Skoal. "Sometime this afternoon," is all he would promise. Even his voice was a slow drawl. His easy smile told me any attempt to hurry him would only make him take longer.

I felt stymied about what to do next. Without gear, I'd have to go back to the hotel or invent a reason to keep hanging around the drop zone. Going back to the hotel wouldn't help find Casey, but making up an excuse to stay seemed dangerous, considering my ineptitude at lying.

A third option was to rent student gear. It wouldn't be pretty—student rigs are like your dad's station wagon—but at least it would keep me at the drop zone for the rest of the day. I paid Rick his thirty-dollar per jump rental fee and he handed me a 170 square-foot Manta in return. I'd be falling from the sky under enough fabric to cover the old Astrodome. I heaved the giant rig over my shoulder and toted it out of the office like a pack mule.

I couldn't find Marie, but managed to line up a jump with her friends. Their names were Linda and Beth. Linda seemed too young and exuberant to be mixed up with anything dark and sinister like kidnapping. Her attentive eyes and infectious laugh gave the impression she was a people-pleaser. She smoothed a wayward ringlet into her ponytail and told us she'd find our fourth. The Cessna wouldn't go anywhere without a full load of four. Otherwise, Rick and Marie wouldn't make money.

While we waited, Beth lit a cigarette, then tossed her lighter onto the picnic table where it landed next to an open issue of *Blue Skies Magazine*. The magazine's pages lifted in the slight breeze, and I was about to pick it up and read the latest news when Linda returned with Scud shuffling behind her.

"Sweetheart!" I said.

Beth took a drag off her Newport and turned her head to exhale.

Scud's legs were still in his jumpsuit, which was now only partially zipped. He'd taken his arms out of the suit and tied its sleeves around his waist like a jacket. He wore a faded No Fear shirt underneath.

"Wouldn't miss this," he said, ogling the three of us in turn.

"We're on a twenty minute call," Linda said. "Let's dirt dive."

We practiced the dive on the ground, rehearsing maneuvers we'd try in the air. Each time I took someone's arm or leg gripper, I had the uneasy feeling I might be hanging on to somebody involved with the abduction. And each time one of them joked or smiled, I switched to feeling like a nitwit for suspecting decent people. How did the pros tell good guys from bad?

I spotted two men I didn't recognize near the Coke machine. They watched us line up at the Cessna. One was a heavyset red-haired man who wore a Harley-Davidson bandana and held a camera helmet under an arm. The other popped the lid on a can of Mountain Dew. His face was wide at the top and narrow near his chin, and his too-thin mustache reminded me of rodent whiskers. Both were in their late twenties.

I smiled at them. The cameraman nodded back. Rat Man didn't acknowledge me.

I climbed into the plane and Scud followed close behind. He gave two hard slaps on the back of my container and said, "That's gonna weigh the whole plane down."

"Shut up."

"I love it," he said. "She already sounds like a wife."

◇◇◇

We got eight points, or made eight separate formations, on that dive before breaking off at twenty-five hundred feet. Considering Scud was on the dive and none of us women had weight vests, I thought we did a decent job matching fall rates. At break-off, Scud held onto my wrist a beat longer than he should have. He snuck a kiss pass. Before turning and flying away to open his parachute, he kissed me. If the girls noticed, I thought we might get flack for it on the ground. Then I realized any girl who jumped with that clown got kissed.

My ride under the Manta was pathetic. A lightweight jumper like me was nothing under its huge surface area. I buried my right toggle, pulling it fully down to my hip, even wrapping some steering line around my hand to get more pull—a maneuver that would have put me into an aggressive spiral under my Sabre—but the Manta only responded with a slow, flat turn to the right. I gazed toward the Gulf of Mexico only a few miles away, and remembered my student jumps under a Manta. Huge parachutes didn't bother me then. I was too excited about skydiving to notice how slow they were.

Back then, I was in college. My boyfriend broke up with me because I spent more weekends at the DZ than I spent with him. I figured it was better in the end; any man who understood me would take the whole package, parachute and all. The summer I graduated, Jack signed for the whole package.

When Annette came along, I quit. It was bad enough missing time with her while I was working. I wouldn't miss our weekends too. That was five years ago. Last year, I finally started jumping again. Missing my husband and daughter, I'd returned to my surrogate family at the drop zone.

A gust pushed me forward and snapped me back to what I was doing—setting up to land. The Manta was docile when I turned into the wind. Once there, I got almost no forward penetration. Slowly, I sank toward the grassy landing field. I missed the higher speed, swooping landings I got with my own gear. When I touched down, I scooped what seemed like acres of canopy nylon into a bundle and made my way toward the hangar.

The cameraman I'd seen earlier loafed at the picnic table with his buddy, smoking. They held their cigarettes away from my gear when I got closer.

"Rick says you're another space geek," the cameraman said.

I smiled. "Small world." I gave my name and new-in-town story, none of which seemed news to him.

"I'm Hank, but around here they call me Big Red. You a contractor or civil servant?"

It certainly hadn't taken long for the NASA lie to bite me in the ass.

If I answered contractor I feared he would ask which one, so I told him I was a civil servant and tried not to sound edgy.

"On-site, then. Which building?"

I'd clicked past a map of the center on-line, with its myriad of buildings and roads, but I hadn't thought to study it.

"I was only there once, for my interview. Can't even remember the building." I gave him a puzzled look, not entirely fabricated, and tried to remember the pictures I'd seen. "It was kind of impersonal and bland…with hardly any windows."

Big Red laughed. "That's half the buildings at the center. The place is huge."

I imagined so.

Big Red's rat-like friend watched our exchange, expressionless. I wondered if a personality waited, dormant, beneath his flesh-like exoskeleton.

"Well, my last name's Powell. Hank Powell. When you get settled, look me up on the Global and maybe we can meet for lunch. I'm in Building Fifteen."

I promised I would, and continued into the hangar, wondering what a Global was.

◇◇◇

Later, I made two more jumps with the same group. When Beth went home, I jumped a three-way with Scud and Linda. We paid for Big Red's slot so he'd videotape it. Afterward, Scud left, and we didn't have enough people to make a load. Big Red dubbed copies of our dive onto DVDs for Linda and me. It had our dirt dive on it too. I figured Karen Lyons could at least get a look at Linda and Scud.

On the monotonous drive back to Houston, I tried Jeannie from my cell phone, but only got her answering machine. No such luck when I tried Richard.

He picked up on the first ring. "Got anything?"

"I didn't meet anybody with Kidnapper or Pedophile written on his forehead, no."

I ran through the names of everyone I'd met and waited while Richard scribbled his notes.

"Where are you now?" he asked.

"I just passed Lake Jackson." I glanced in the rearview mirror at the single car way behind me. No one was in front. "This feels like Siberia."

"Sorry for the long drive."

"I have an idea about that, actually. They're having a boogie this weekend, like a festival for skydivers. The place'll be packed. I'm going to get a tent and camp at the DZ like everybody else."

It's not uncommon. Camping's free and saves a long morning drive. Jumpers can drink all they want when the beer light goes on because nobody has to drive home.

"It'll be a great excuse to plant myself here."

He mumbled that it would be okay.

I hadn't been asking for permission, but I let it go.

"Where can I find a sporting goods store? I need a sleeping bag and a tent." I hesitated. "At your expense, of course."

He told me the exit to use and I thought putting seventy miles between Richard and me for the rest of the trip was a fine idea.

"What about you?" I knew from our breakfast meeting he'd planned to talk to Karen Lyons' neighbors.

"Only a small lead," he said. "An old-timer two doors down says the street's been quiet since Eric left. Apparently, Eric drives a diesel pick-up. Truck used to wake the guy when Eric left for work every morning. Neighbor says he hasn't heard the truck for a week. That's consistent with the last time Eric visited Casey. This fellow didn't wake up Saturday night. I don't think Eric was anywhere near the place."

"If it was Eric, surely he'd use a different car."

"Of course." Richard paused. "I said it was a small thing."

I remembered Richard wanted pictures so I mentioned the video Big Red had made. I said I'd leave it at the desk at the hotel. That brilliant plan of avoidance was the best idea I'd had all day.

"I'll pick up a disposable camera tonight when I'm out getting supplies," I added. "Tomorrow I'll set up camp. I'll call with any news."

After we hung up, I imagined Karen hunched over a cup of cold coffee at her kitchen table, willing the phone to ring. And I wondered if the person who stole her son did it for money or revenge, or maybe to explore a sick, twisted fantasy. I worried Casey might already be dead. Then I shuddered, realizing we might never know.

◇◇◇

I fell asleep that night with a *People* magazine draped over my chest, and I never knew it until the bedside phone in my hotel room clanged the following morning and scared me out of my wits. I scrambled upright under my covers and the phone rang again before I remembered where I was. It rang a third time before I found it in the pitch-black room.

"Hello?" I groaned, squinting at the digital clock.

It was Richard.

"Guess whose body turned up in the San Jacinto River."

I leaned closer to the clock. 6:20 a.m.

Then Richard's words registered. And they resonated in my skull so violently I thought the room was shaking.

Chapter Seven

"You there?" Richard asked.

"They found Casey," I said, thinking immediately of his mother.

"No," he said flatly. "Eric."

I collapsed back onto my pillow. At least it wasn't Casey. Then I felt horrible for preferring any one person's murder over another's.

"A fisherman found him an hour ago. Eric's father phoned me."

I imagined that call. "How awful for his parents."

"And awful for his ex," Richard added. "She was sure Eric took Casey. At least she could believe her baby was being cared for. If Eric's dead, who has their son? Is he even alive? She's terrified."

I pushed myself out of bed and stumbled toward the coffee pot, flipping light switches and stretching the phone cord as I went. At the sink, I filled the pot with tap water. "How'd it… happen?"

"Shot twice in the chest. Police are shifting gears now, treating this as a stranger abduction. Mr. and Mrs. Lyons told Karen what we're doing. I'll share your video and list of names with her today."

"What can I do?"

He exhaled. "Put this news in a separate place in your mind. Show up smiling at the drop zone today. See what you can learn."

It seemed impossible.

"Good luck," I said, and we hung up.

I dropped the handset into its cradle and stood by the bed. Something else was wrong. The room wasn't quiet.

Soft, rhythmic taps at my window meant it was raining.

I walked to the window and separated the drapes. Droplets stuck to the other side of the glass. I focused past them, on the wide Texas sky. It was gray in all directions. Below me, shrubs in the hotel's landscaping leaned in the wind.

I hoped conditions were better near the Gulf. When the DZ opened in a few hours, I'd call and ask. Bad weather meant no skydiving. No looking for clues.

Since it was too wet and windy to run Tuesday's route, I used a treadmill in the hotel's fitness room and thought about what to do. By mile two, I decided to visit Gulf Coast Skydiving, no matter the weather. Staying at the hotel would do nothing for Casey. It might improve my standing with Bowman, if I could concentrate long enough to get some work finished, but impressing Bowman wasn't high on my list.

During mile three, I changed my mind. Showing up at a drop zone in the rain would be suspicious. How would I explain it?

By the time mile four rolled around, I had a side stitch, but no plan. I toweled off and stalked to my room.

It was only seven thirty, and I didn't expect anyone to show up at the drop zone until ten or eleven. That left hours.

I showered and dressed and called Jeannie at work.

"Got your message yesterday," she said. "Gimme the scoop."

I heard a second call ringing on her phone.

"Wanna get that?"

"I'm already taking a call," she said. "The scoop?"

"I made a few jumps at that drop zone yesterday. Met some good looking men."

"Yummy!" I could hear the smile in her voice.

"Everyone was nice, though. No one seemed creepy or weird."

"The M&M jar on your desk is empty," she said.

"Thank you so much for your rapt attention. There's back-up candy, but just for that, I'm not telling where."

I imagined her pouty mouth. Lip liner, ColorStay gloss, and all. "What am I missing at work?"

"Oh. Bad news." She lowered her voice. "Bowman's panties are in a bunch. When are you coming back?"

"I was thinking Monday. Why? What'd he say?"

"He didn't mention you by name, but in our staff meeting he reviewed leave policies from the handbook. He talked about 'proper channels' and 'misuse,' particularly of discretionary leave."

"That would be me."

"Well, you can't tell him the truth."

I didn't answer.

"Don't worry. We'll think of something."

"Why can't I tell the truth?" I sighed. "Maybe I can patch this up if I call and explain why Richard asked me—"

"Em. Come on. You didn't tell him Monday. You won't tell him today. If he finds out this is about another kid, he'll push you back into counseling."

She was right, and I didn't like it. Bowman would hang my past over my head. After my family died, I'd swallowed a bottle of pills. Some mistakes follow us because we can't forgive ourselves. Others linger because jerks like Bowman won't let us forget.

"Emily? You've thought of that, right?"

In fact, I hadn't.

"Of course I have."

"Now you're pissy."

"I've worked at BioTek for seven years. Four patents, and how many publications? I had one bad year. A long time ago, I might add...and he still treats me like a time bomb. I should quit."

"Please don't do that. I couldn't hack it without you." She paused. "Say, did I mention your M&M bowl's empty?"

Her levity cheered me a little. She'd earned some chocolate. "Top left drawer."

"You're awesome."

"I try."

"How's Cole, anyway? Is it weird?"

"Weird for me. Who knows what goes through his mind? Haven't seen him since yesterday morning when he gave me a map and a car and basically said 'see ya.'"

"I don't think it's good for you to be around him. But, I admire your trying to find that kid." She changed to an authoritative tone. "Purchasing said it'll be here Friday."

"Gotcha," I laughed. "I'll call you at home later."

Busted again.

Chapter Eight

No matter how much time passed, some people would always see me as the unstable, depressed woman I was after my family died. Sometimes, even years later, the ghost of that woman still rattled chains in my heart. It seemed Bowman heard them too.

I hadn't eaten yet, and needed to. I took my journal to the hotel restaurant and paged through it during breakfast.

◇◇◇

April 10—10:30 a.m.
Conference, coffee break

I skipped yesterday's morning session to meet Keith and Nora at the airport for brunch. Nora could hardly look at me without bursting into tears and gushing thanks. Mattie sat through lunch, cute as a button, munching tater tots and smearing ketchup on his face. I have to wonder about that kid. Three weeks away from his parents and none the worse for wear.

I said goodbye to them at the security checkpoint and called home to assess the damage. So far, it's surprisingly minor. Jack's biggest lapse has been sending a peanut butter and marshmallow sandwich to daycare for Annette's lunch.

When the last session finished yesterday, I walked to the Cineplex and caught a movie. Some would say that's a bad use of time in a new, exciting town, but to those people I say: you don't have a toddler. It was great to see a movie on the big screen with a giant bag of overpriced popcorn. A DVD in our living room with a slightly burned bag of the microwave stuff isn't the same. I hardly missed the company of unfolded laundry and an overflowing toy box at all.

Tomorrow I'll catch a 5:20 flight back to Cleveland. It would be so nice to walk into a clean home, but I'm afraid it will be a successful three days for Jack if our house is still standing and he brought the right child home from daycare.

April 11—10:25 p.m.
Home again

This is funny. Jack thinks I'll sleep with him. When I unpacked my underwear, he winked at me and told me I wouldn't need them. A while ago he gave me a dopey grin and asked if I was "ready for bed."

Sure, after I pick up the living room. Pack a lunch for Annette. Move the clothes from the washer to the dryer. Put away bath toys. Pay the gas bill. And unload the dishwasher. All while he watches sports highlights on ESPN.

It must be nice to live in a self-cleaning house, watch sports, and think you'll get lucky at the next commercial break. I'm not sure if he's expecting I-Missed-You sex or Thank-You sex. The Thank-You variety in these circumstances would seem unlikely, but he did keep Annette clothed and fed.

It's so wonderful to be home with her! I hugged her so hard tonight I thought I'd squish all the goo out of the poor kid. There's no better feeling in the world than a hug from my baby!

But the sex? Not happenin'. The only thing that could turn me on is the sight of Jack with a mop and a bottle of Mr. Clean.

April 12 – 12:05 a.m.
Home again II

...or, the sight of him turning off sports, jumping up from the couch, and chasing me around the kitchen table.

I pushed him off at first. I mean, really—the nerve. But, let's be reasonable. What he had in mind was more fun than housework. I made it twice around the table before I slipped and he caught me. He spun me around and started kissing my neck. I accused him of trying to get out of trouble. He said he was trying to get into trouble. Then there was more kissing, less of the socks, less of the shirts, way more laundry on my floor...And to summarize: Welcome home to ME!

I give it a 9.5. Technical merit was certainly there but I think he might have been trying to wrap it up in time to watch an interview with the Indians' coach.

Now he's sleeping, but I'm wired. I checked voicemail and e-mail.

1. Detective Cole sent a photo line-up to the local FBI office. I'm supposed to go tomorrow morning. That's intimidating. He explained that because Mattie was kidnapped and taken across state lines, the FBI is investigating. The truck we saw on the surveillance tape was registered to a body shop, but no employees resembled my computer sketches. Detective Cole said after they put some "heat on"—his words—during questioning, one employee admitted loaning the truck to his cousin. They later discovered the cousin did resemble my sketch. Thus, the photo line-up.

2. I won the eBay auction for the baby jogger. It shipped yesterday and should arrive by the weekend. I browsed for guitars, but held back. Must. Wean. Self. Off. eBay.

◇◇◇

Baskets of overflowing laundry on the couch and a dirty plastic lunch box on the kitchen counter would be a welcome sight now. Even Jack on our couch, wielding his remote, would be a blessing. I'd die a happy woman to have him chase me around the table one more time, the way he did that night.

And sweet Annette. What I wouldn't give to trip over her toys or wipe peanut butter off my silk blouses again.

When I think about these things too long, I get into a funk. But Dr. Raleigh used to say it was healthy to remember, that I needed to let myself do that. So I do, several times a day—I can't help it—but not for too long. For example, the stinging in my eyes at the breakfast table meant it was time to close my journal and think about something different for a while.

Marie answered the phone when I called the drop zone later that morning. Skies down south were overcast, but she thought the clouds might burn off by afternoon. What I saw from my hotel window made me skeptical anything would burn off that day, but I decided to make the trip anyway. In the best case, I could spend the afternoon jumping and looking for clues. In the worst, maybe I'd get more names for the list Richard was taking to Karen.

Chapter Nine

On the coast, the sky was a charcoal dome. Rain assaulted the roof and windshield of my borrowed car to the point the wipers had trouble keeping up. The dirt drive leading through the tiny airport had deteriorated to mud. Clumps of it thudded against the undercarriage of the car.

I thought back to the Sheltons. Mattie's kidnapper walked free, thanks to a botched trial. When I'd finally put the pieces together, I accused Richard of being part of that mess. Though he'd never admitted it, he'd never denied it either.

The hangar's sliding door was open enough for a person to squeeze through. I parked next to two other cars, as close to the building as I could, and dashed for shelter.

Inside, the little Cessna seemed enormous. I wiped my wet forehead on a damp sleeve and pulled open the office door. Marie peeked from behind a computer monitor to greet me. Her smile was strained. An open and partially disassembled computer case was on the table beside her. I was surprised to find Big Red's friend in the office too, kneeling over an open tandem rig on the floor.

Rick popped up from behind the counter and grinned when he saw me.

"This is Craig Clement," he said. "Newest hire, meet newest regular." He winked at me when he said that last part.

Craig nodded wordlessly and returned his attention to the parachute cells spread before him. He not only had the face of a rat, but was so quiet and unobtrusive, I could imagine him sneaking around like one in the dark.

"Son of a gun," Marie muttered. She smacked her mouse on the desk. "I hate this machine."

She eyed the disassembled computer suspiciously, like a creature might crawl out.

"What are you trying to do?" I moved closer.

Craig rose onto his knees and looked from the fabric he was folding toward Marie. He opened his mouth to say something, but Marie spoke first.

"I bought a RAID card and another hard drive to back up the computer, but I'm doing something wrong. When it boots up, it doesn't find the second drive." She stared at the instructions in front of her like she was missing something obvious.

Rick shoved a stack of papers into an accordion file. "That's the reason I leave the techno mumbo-jumbo to the little woman. Sure, she's got brains. But how 'bout my good looks?"

He flashed me his cheesy grin.

For once, I was thankful for Peter Bowman's anal-retentive micromanagement style. BioTek scientists were responsible for our own data archival and backups, and he routinely audited our files. I knew I could help Marie. A bonus would be getting a glimpse at her computer files in the process.

"I'm glad you're backing up," I said. "One power surge in weather like this...you could be in a world of hurt."

I lifted the instructions and looked them over. "What would you say to a free balloon jump Saturday in exchange for this hardware installation?"

Rick answered before she could. "Sold. To the good looking red head with brains and nice legs."

"Good riddance," Marie said into the open computer case. She crossed the room to a table stacked with several boxes and began pulling out sacks of party supplies. I took her seat and plotted my first theft since high school. Back then, it was a lipstick from the corner drug store. Today, it was files.

"We're getting ready for the weekend," Marie said. "We've got plates, cups, and utensils for the barbecue. We've got kegs. Cameras and videotapes are handled. Stereo equipment's handled. There's extra soap and shampoo for campers—this'll be our first boogie since we got our indoor plumbing…"

She sounded like a bride planning reception details. I glanced at Rick. He made gabbing gestures with his fingers pointed toward his ear.

Craig kneeled over the canopy and arranged its navy and gray cells. He seemed oblivious.

Installing the new card and hard drive into the Hanes' computer didn't take any time. They tracked their finances with Quicken, like I did. But what really popped out at me was an Access database called Clientele. Would I find Casey's abductor there? Richard could never have foreseen this windfall.

I opened a web browser and brought up the Weather Channel's homepage, then minimized it.

"You a tandem master, Craig?" I aimed for distraction.

"Tandem and Accelerated Freefall," Marie bragged. "And a rigger."

Craig didn't seem one for words. He kept on with his work without looking at us. I wondered if he found us just as boring.

Rick ducked into the rigger's loft and returned with my repacked equipment.

"If I'd known you were going to jump yesterday," Marie said, "I'd have loaned you my one-twenty." She shot a frown at Rick. In her mind, evidently, he'd been rude to put me under the enormous Manta.

"Slow ride's better than no ride." I tried to give a reassuring smile. But I was nervous. Marie's financial data was open on my screen. My hands were leaving wet marks on her mouse and keyboard.

I copied the Quicken data into a webmail application, all the while considering what it would be like to pee with no privacy in jail. I addressed an e-mail to myself from my own webmail account, pasted in the financial files, and pressed Send.

Craig stood and stretched, then walked toward me.

I changed to my decoy screen and told him things looked good for the computer, but bad for the forecast, and when he came around to inspect my screen, we looked at cloud coverage on a Weather Channel map of southern Texas.

He went back to close the tandem rig, and I e-mailed myself the drop zone's clientele database.

When I was satisfied with the file transfer, I pronounced Project Free Balloon Jump a success and collected my gear.

Rick and Marie asked me to come back the next day if the weather broke. Craig only gave a weak wave in my general direction as if to say "don't let the door hit you in the ass."

Yeah, you have a good day too, Prince Charming. I hoisted my gear onto a shoulder and headed back to the rain.

Chapter Ten

An hour later, Richard tossed a Best Buy bag onto the bed in my hotel room.

"I can't believe you stole files."

"Hello to you, too." I pecked the miniature keys of my laptop. It was open on a small desk, wedged between a telephone and two empty Coke cans. I knew Richard was shaking his head but I refused to look at him. "Got some good stuff today," I said. "I'm feeling very Nancy Drew. Very James Bond."

When I finished what I was typing, I leaned back in my chair and waited for him to admit interest. His eyes were red, the skin beneath them sunken and gray.

Finally, he caved. "Well?"

I described the clientele and financial files I'd found at the drop zone. "I've got the customers, their contact info, and notes about them on the thumb drive." I nodded toward the drive beside me on the table. Richard lifted it and dropped it into his shirt pocket.

"The financial part is trickier. That's where you come in."

We installed the Quicken software he'd brought and used it to open the files I'd e-mailed myself. Soon we were paging through screens of spreadsheets and accounts for Gulf Coast Skydiving. Several people on the list appeared to carry a declining balance. I figured Rick and Marie might offer discounted tickets to people who bought jumps in bulk.

"Let's figure out who's on the staff," Richard said.

I ran a report to categorize payroll expenditures for the last six months. Richard scribbled names on hotel stationery. He asked me to do individual reports for everyone on the list so we could figure out how long each had worked there. Most had been around for years. Craig Clement had come on board two months ago.

A few hours later, we'd made a comprehensive list of employees and regular skydivers. We even knew how often each group worked or jumped. It was time to call it a day.

"If somebody there is involved," I said, "I'd think it would be a jumper, not staff. Why would a staff member need a jump ticket?"

"Good question. Another thing you can find out."

I slumped. My list of things to do and watch and find out at the drop zone was getting longer by the day.

By the time Richard left, it was mid-afternoon. I was convincing myself to buckle down and do the work I'd promised Bowman when my cell phone rang.

The number for BioTek's main line was on the display. I was glad Jeannie was thinking of me, and it was like her to call at the perfect time.

But when I answered, I heard, "Glad I caught you. Pete Bowman calling."

Well, shit.

He was brief, making clear in Bowman-esque terms that I was expected back at the office on Monday. There were meetings to attend and butts to kiss, his included.

"I'd like to see your reports," he said. "Please e-mail them."

The reports I'd been putting off ever since I got to Houston.

"Of course. Sure."

He clicked off the line, and in the silence that followed, I had the feeling he'd called about more than my reports. Either he was suspicious or I was paranoid. Maybe both. Jack would have said I was over-analyzing.

It was two o'clock in the afternoon and I'd skipped lunch. Too tired to face the world, I called in a pizza. I told myself that after I ate, I would work on Bowman's stuff for the rest of the afternoon until it was finished.

While waiting for the heart attack in a box, I picked up my old journal again and flung myself over the bed. I was closing in on the tough parts.

◇◇◇

April 12—8:45 p.m.

Had quite a scare at the office today but have calmed down a bit since. Jeannie and I were at my desk, waiting for the Columbus group to tie in for our 1:00 telecon. She was annihilating my M&Ms, yammering on about Sexy Henry. My phone rang, I answered on speaker, but instead of Columbus, it was a lunatic threatening me about Nora's case! He said, "You've got an important meeting coming up, Emily. Be a smart girl when you see those photos." Then he hung up. Just like that.

Jeannie said, "Does shit like that actually happen in real life?" And then she smiled and said that was a good joke, I had her going, and she shook a finger at me like...shame on me and she'd be getting even soon. I lost it right there. Bowman walked by right before Jeannie closed my door.

Who was that? How does he know who I am? And, how does he know where I work, or that I was planning to look at a photo line up of the man I saw with Mattie?

We reported it to the police. I called Detective Cole in Austin and filled him in too. I feel better now. Jack's more upset than I am.

I decided not to tell Nora. This would only make her feel responsible in some twisted way, and she doesn't need that on top of everything else.

April 13—Bus ride

Heading back to office. Photo line up was exciting. I identified the guy from the restaurant: Wesley Reed.

I mentioned that crank call to the agent who helped me. She said I should certainly keep my guard up, but she suspects it was an empty scare tactic. How much time before I can know for sure?

April 13—Rant

I'm not sure if all moms feel this way, but it seems this way to me. You ask your husband to watch your daughter—*his* daughter, too—so you can get some me-time. He agrees. You're happy. And when you come home, your absence has created way more work than if you'd never left in the first place.

All I wanted was dinner with Nora. A nice restaurant meal with my friend to catch up on how she's doing, how Mattie's doing, what's going on with their case.

I got dinner all right. Its price was a 22-ounce container of Johnson & Johnson's baby powder completely emptied all over Annette's room. While Jack was absorbed in his sports channel, Annette got into her diaper supplies.

Powder on picture frames. The bookcase. The Little People farm. Skydiving Snoopy. Mickey Mouse clock. Dresser. Window sills. Stuffed animals. Puzzles. Valences. Bed. Mini-blinds.

I will kill him.

Windex, Pledge, blah blah blah…I finally got around to the Hoover and that's where the story gets creepy. I opened Annette's closet door to sweep—the powder was even in the closet—and found an earring on the floor. Not mine. Maybe it's something Annette pocketed on one of our walks. But I can't help feeling spooked, considering.

April 15—Annette's bedside, keeping watch

I got to work this morning and the day instantly collapsed. Message light blinking, signature folder waiting, 27 e-mails. What did I do first? I opened my damned office mail and my heart has been in my throat since.

I ripped open a cardboard mailer, reached inside, and pulled out a tiny dress. It was Annette's—the one with ladybugs embroidered on the lapels. There was a message pinned to the front:

"You don't listen very well."

I heard my heart beating in my ears. It was deafening.

I grabbed my keys and my cell phone and bee-lined to daycare. Who did I call first? Jack? Daycare? The police? Shit. I don't even remember.

She is safe here now, sleeping in her bed. How can I ever leave her again?

◇◇◇

I hadn't opened that journal for years. Couldn't bear to. And now my hands shook the same way they did the day I clutched Annette's dress in my office.

I rolled onto my side and pulled a pillow into my chest. Another episode of the *If Onlys* was coming on. If only I'd believed the threats. If only we'd stayed home that weekend. If only I'd been with them.

I closed my eyes and remembered Annette's small face, her chestnut eyes, and the feel of her wispy, straw-colored hair sliding through my fingers. The way her smile matched Jack's, the way both of them could grin their way back into my good graces. Their dimples matched. Thinking back, it was their dimples that got me every time.

I fell asleep then, and dreamed of my family, of my reunion with them. This time it was in a supermarket. They were walking through the produce section as if nothing ever happened. No time had passed; Annette was as petite as ever. She asked Jack if she could have some blueberries. It wasn't odd that she could talk. What confused me was their casual mannerisms, their easy-going banter, their peace. I was astonished to find them alive and asked what had happened? Where had they been? Why hadn't they told me? They looked at each other and shrugged as if the answers were things they'd simply forgotten to tell me, and then they both turned their attention to the leafy greens, casual as you please. Like they'd honestly meant to tell me they weren't dead, but they hadn't gotten around to it yet, and did I feel like having a salad with dinner? Then the things that happened afterward flashed through my mind—the pills, Dr. Raleigh, my loneliness in our empty house—and I realized that if Jack and Annette were still alive, then I must have dreamed those other things too. So, everything was okay. It was all a bad dream.

Chapter Eleven

Thursday the weather relented but landing fields were damp. Humidity closed tight around me like wet clothes, and the whole place smelled like earthworms. There would be soggy landings, but nobody cared.

The place was absolutely packed. Skydivers from greater Houston and western Louisiana had swarmed the drop zone, getting ready for the big weekend. Finally, I'd get a chance to meet Rick's client base. I'd brought the disposable camera. At the end of the day, there'd be pictures to show Karen Lyons.

"Why work hard on the ground for something that's free in the air?" Scud's lines were flung over his shoulder as he sorted the cells of his Batwing. He'd sneaked another kiss pass, this time with Linda.

"Consider yourself lucky," Marie told Linda, with a little pout. "When you've been married twenty years, any kiss'll do."

We were in the hangar, packing after our second jump. Scud laid down his gear and wrapped Marie in a conciliatory hug; he even managed to cop a feel on her ass.

"I'm so hungry!" I said. I caught myself separating my canopy cells a bit violently.

Scud looked up. "Easy, baby. Plenty of Scud to go around."

Marie laughed.

Craig Clement passed us without comment and went out the back door toward the landing field. He took a quick look around and peeled to the left, toward an overflow parking area beyond the side of the building. I said I was going to watch the last load fly down, and followed Craig outside.

He disappeared behind the far side of the hangar. I peeked around its corner and watched him go to a mud-splattered pick-up with a beautiful Yellow Lab tied up in back. The day before, when I'd come in the rain, there'd been no trucks in the lot, so I doubted it was his.

He pulled a small pouch from his pocket and unfolded it. It was a napkin. For a moment, he stood by the dog and let it eat whatever was inside. I felt stupid tailing a guy feeding a dog. But when the morsels were gone, Craig stepped toward the cab and glanced around the lot. I ducked behind the enormous aluminum wall and waited out of sight.

When I checked again, he was in the passenger seat, one leg dangling out the door, rifling through the glove box. He pulled out some papers and leafed through them, then reached in his pocket and produced a phone.

Marie's voice came over the loud speaker. Load four was on a ten-minute call and she asked Craig to come to the office. I backtracked toward the crowd and heard the faint thud of a truck door slam behind me.

My packing spot was gone. The floor was covered wall-to-wall with gear in various stages of assembly and my rig had been moved to the sidelines. I didn't mind being bumped; it was time for lunch anyway. I knelt by my gear bag and fished for my car keys. And, suddenly, I had the uneasy feeling I was being watched.

I turned, and Vince was standing in the open hangar door.

He still looked good in jeans and a cowboy hat, but this time it wasn't the man that grabbed my attention. It was the Burger King sacks he was holding. He shook them subtly, like a child using treats to entice a cat. When he raised his eyebrows at me, the question was obvious. *Interested?*

"I'll give you fifty bucks for whatever's in those sacks," I said.

He smiled.

"Ain't for sale," he said with his slight drawl, "But I might share." He wandered out the front of the hangar toward the soggy grass lot.

He never looked back. Where was he taking that food?

I followed him, still in my jumpsuit, and tried to unzip it and pull my arms out while hurrying after him.

"Glad to hear it," I shouted to his back, struggling out of a sleeve. "The sides of my stomach are stuck together."

"Said I *might* share," he called back over his shoulder, and then he disappeared behind the corner of the hangar into the overflow parking area Craig was in moments earlier.

I tried to step out of my jumpsuit while keeping pace with Vince and his fast food, but I tripped and stumbled into the side of the hangar. My shoulder whacked its giant metal panel and made a thunderous *bong*. Thank God he was out of view.

I freed myself from the suit and rounded the corner.

Vince was opening the tailgate to the same truck Craig had searched.

He jumped into the back and sat on the bed's plastic liner. His guitar waited there in an open case, next to the Yellow Lab. The dog had been lounging on a mound of old towels but now feverishly eyed the same sacks that drew me.

"I can't believe you left your Martin in the sun. And next to four dirty paws...Aren't you afraid—"

"Cindy loves music as much as I do," he said with a dismissive wave. "In fact, we think a girl should sing for her supper." His lips curved into a smile and he nodded toward the guitar.

Was he serious?

Cindy gave a friendly tail thump and sniffed the Burger King bags hard.

Vince reached into a bag and tossed her a couple fries, unwrapped a Whopper, and took an ungentlemanly huge bite. I looked from him to the guitar, and finally to the dog, who focused intently on Vince's food.

Vince ate his burger as if sitting there all alone.

"Cat got your tongue?" He finished up a bite.

He squinted at me, the shadow from his cowboy hat not quite shielding his eyes from the noon sun. Looking at him too long felt a little bit like flirting. I glanced away and planted a hand on my hip.

"Come on," he said. "Play us a song. Have lunch with me." He punctuated the last sentence with another enormous bite of Whopper. A mayonnaise-coated chunk of tomato fell into his lap. Cindy took care of it.

"You want me to play a song for you, and then you'll share?"

Still chewing, he only nodded. Cindy looked back and forth between us, panting.

"How about lunch first?" I said.

He held out his carton of fries and I grabbed more than a polite ration.

"There. Now please sing. Don't be difficult."

He smiled again. I tossed my jumpsuit onto the floor of the truck bed and climbed up. I tried to scratch Cindy behind her ears, but she'd only sniff my hands, searching for a handout.

I wiped my hands on my shorts as best I could and picked up his guitar. Perched on the side of the truck, I made an unfortunate discovery in Vince's rear window—my reflection. I was in desperate need of a hairbrush and make-up. Beyond my pitiful image was Vince's glove compartment. I wondered what Craig had been looking for.

"What'll it be?"

Vince wadded his burger wrapper and shoved it into an empty sack. "Another ballad."

He leaned back onto Cindy's abdomen and used her as a pillow. Then he pulled his hat fully over his face, stretched his legs, and crossed them at the ankles. He reached up with one hand to scratch Cindy's chin, nuzzled very near his own, and I noticed the second fast food sack clutched in his other hand.

I sang Patsy Cline's "Leavin' On Your Mind" while load four droned overhead, and when I finished, Vince didn't speak or move. Was he rude enough to fall asleep? I played another song. He still didn't move. I nudged him in the ribs with the toe of my sneaker.

"You dead or what?"

He handed up the bag of food without moving off the dog or adjusting his hat. "Hardly. Was hoping you'd do one more."

I returned the guitar to its case and unfolded the sack. "Maybe if you're nice."

He shifted onto an elbow and pushed his hat back into position.

"Hey," I said, "you friends with Craig, the new guy?"

"Don't reckon we're friends, just work together. Why?"

"I saw him out here with Cindy earlier," I said. I decided to leave out "he was nosing through your stuff."

Vince shrugged. "Everybody likes my dog."

He turned his attention to the sky, where canopies circled. For the first time, I noticed lines by his eyes. Laugh lines. Jack once said laugh lines were the mark of trustworthy people.

I asked him what he did at the drop zone.

"Help in the office. Fly for Rick when he's in a pinch."

"A pilot?" I'd seen Vince's name on the payroll, but it hadn't occurred to me he was a pilot.

He nodded. "Only part-time. I'm trying to get a construction business off the ground."

I reached for a napkin. "Takes guts. Good for you."

He picked up the empty lunch sacks and squirted water from a sports bottle into a dish for Cindy. He snapped his guitar case shut and moved it into the cab of the truck, out of the sun. I was disappointed when he pulled his rig from the front seat. Lunch was over.

Then he said, "Wanna jump?" And it was like being asked to dance.

◇◇◇

Afterward, Linda took our picture with my disposable camera. Ours was the first photograph taken on my Spy Roll.

Marie asked for Vince's help so he left and I mingled. A few jumpers were visiting from nearby drop zones, but several were regulars I was meeting for the first time. I wormed my way into as many skydives with the locals as I could. By dinnertime, I'd managed four more jumps. I took a post-dive photo with each of my groups and no one seemed to think anything of it. One girl asked me to develop doubles and send her a copy.

I called Richard on my cell and we made plans for the film hand-off. I drove north to a Super Wal-Mart he described and dropped the camera at its one-hour photo counter, using Richard's name and number on the deposit envelope. He'd pick up the photos and take them to Karen.

I returned to the DZ and set up camp. For the next several hours, I loafed at bonfires and nursed beers. I listened to campers schmooze and bullshit, and worked on telling the regulars apart from the visitors.

Shortly after nine, my cell phone rang.

"She recognizes one of the women," Richard said. "She knows the face, but not the name."

I couldn't believe something had come of my first roll of film. Even more surprising, I realized, was that it implicated a woman.

"What now?"

"Meet me at the Wal-Mart," he said. "You have to tell me who she is."

Chapter Twelve

Wal-Mart. One place I did not foresee a sleuthing rendezvous, but there I was.

At ten o'clock on a Thursday night, the parking lot was as busy as noon on Saturday. A mammoth SUV hogged the center of a lane, laying claim to a spot when another was vacant three spaces behind it.

I made my way inside, where I was greeted by a middle-aged man in a blue vest and dopey octopus hat. A small McDonald's occupied a front corner of the store, and when I walked inside, Richard was leaning against the restaurant's wall waiting for me.

"Let's sit." He steered me toward a table. The photo envelope was in his hand.

"Hi, Richard. Good to see you too."

He shot me a look of flat irritation as I slid into my side of a booth.

He removed the photos from their envelope. The picture on top of the stack included the group I'd jumped with right after my dive with Vince. Scud and Marie had jumped into the shot for fun, but I didn't remember the names of the others. I reached for my handbag. My logbook was there, and I'd written down all the names earlier. I flipped to the entry, ready to match forgotten names with faces, when Richard surprised me.

"This one, right here," he said, tapping the glossy print. "Karen recognizes this woman. Who is she?"

I frowned. The name wasn't in my book, and I'd never even thought to ask it. In the background of the shot, between Scud and Marie's heads, a woman was walking across the landing field. Richard must have read my confusion.

"What is it?" He leaned in close, hungry for information I didn't have.

"I don't know her name," I said, shaking my head. "She was our pilot."

An obese woman in a muumuu and flip-flops lumbered past us with a loaded tray, and two chunky school-agers followed several paces behind her. Richard slumped backward into the hard plastic booth. At first I thought he was reeling from disappointment. Then he bit his lower lip and started nodding.

"That actually makes sense," he said, mostly to himself. "Here's the thing. Eric worked for a local petrochemical plant. Sometimes the job took him away from home for extended periods."

I kept my mouth shut and let him go on.

"Karen was a stay-at-home mom, so sometimes she and Casey traveled with him." He did his salesman nod. I nodded back to show I was following.

"They traveled on the company jet." He looked hard at me. "Who flies the company jet?"

How the hell should I know? I wondered. And then, mercifully, the light came on. I grabbed the photo off the table and pointed to the woman in question.

"*She* does?" I said. "She flies for Eric's company?"

"Karen recognized this woman from the airstrip Eric's company uses."

I digested that.

"If this woman flew the Lyons family around, she'd know about Casey," I said.

Richard pulled a pen from his shirt pocket and grabbed a napkin from the tabletop dispenser. He scribbled a note.

"Easy enough for her to get their address," he said.

One of the kids with Muumuu Woman shuffled past us on untied sneakers to get a few paper cups full of ketchup.

I lowered my voice. "What would she want with their child? Nobody asked for ransom money."

He clicked his pen shut and shook his head.

"Oh my God!" I whispered. "Do you think this woman had something to do with Eric's murder?"

Richard shrugged. Questions were coming too fast for both of us.

He rubbed the bridge of his nose and closed his eyes, concentrating.

A moment later, they snapped open. "I need her name. Some background."

"Okay," I said. That would be easy to get from the chatty crowd at the DZ.

Richard continued, "It's been six days. You know what they say about missing kids and the first twenty-four hours, right?"

"Their odds plummet after the first day."

"Casey's been gone for six days. Finding out this pilot's name and story might not be enough."

"What are you saying?"

He regarded me briefly. "How comfortable would you be searching through the drop zone office?"

My stomach lurched.

"Define 'searching through.'"

The look on his face said it all. He wasn't going to define "searching through." I felt bile rise into my throat.

"If I were to search the office, Richard, what would I be looking for, exactly?"

"Maybe the name 'Lyons' on some paperwork...evidence of a baby being around the place...something fishy in the day planner. Just look for stuff," he concluded vaguely. "Interesting stuff."

I conjured more images of a jail cell.

"How many offices have you searched in your time, Richard?"

He shrugged. "Dozens."

"Any tips?"

He grinned. "Don't get caught."

I exhaled. One question remained.

"When am I supposed to search?"

Richard gave the tabletop a two-handed smack I read as our conversation-closer.

"Tonight I guess."

Tonight he guessed. Great.

Chapter Thirteen

That night I lay awake in my tent, waiting for the middle of the night to come, unsure when exactly that was. I had one o'clock in mind, but at that hour, some folks were still loafing by fires. So I pushed it back to two. By then, the airport was silent, except for an occasional exchange between frogs.

I rolled onto my stomach and unzipped a few inches of the window panel in my tent. No one was around.

Pop-up campers and tents were set up around the field. A platinum moon, mostly full, illuminated the acreage stretched around me. I pulled on sneakers and let myself out of the tent. Remnants of campfire smoke hung in the air.

Moisture soaked the toes of my shoes and made my feet cold. The hangar door was slightly ajar so campers could use the showers and restrooms. I ducked inside, where the Cessna was parked for the night. Tomorrow a rented Otter would take its place for the weekend.

Vagrant jumpers slept on the hangar's carpeted floor, in the shadow of the plane. I tip-toed around air mattresses and sleeping bags and stalked toward the office, careful not to step on anyone.

I eased the door open and stepped inside. Thin rays of light escaped from the restrooms at the far end of the office; their doors were cracked open. The only other illumination came from the giant blinking light on the old, cassette-style answering machine.

The place was stone silent. I scanned the deserted, shadowy office with my hand still on the doorknob and felt like a common thief and first-rate fool.

A hasty sweep of the countertop revealed nothing in the message pads or ledger. I opened drawers, rifled through notebooks, and thumbed through receipts, but none of the paperwork stood out as a possible link to Casey.

Beside the phone, old copies of *Parachutist* magazine were wedged between a bookend and a small metal box serving as its counterpart. When I reached for the box, something rustled behind me.

I pulled my hand back and whirled. It was only Rick's cat, nosing through a dish of kitty chow. My pulse quickened and pounded behind my forehead. Its rhythm sounded like "Id-i-ot, Id-i-ot, Id-i-ot."

I caught my breath and went back to the box, which turned out to be a stash of jellybeans. I helped myself to one and snapped it shut.

The last place to check was the rigger's loft. I'd left my own gear there for the night to spare some room in my cramped little tent.

I crossed the office and slipped inside the narrow loft. There was no way I'd flip any light switches. The best I could do to get some light was to prop the door open with a waste paper basket. A reasonable person would have remembered a flashlight.

The workbench ran along one wall. Three rigs in various stages of assembly waited on its wooden surface. Tools were meticulously arranged on a pegboard suspended over the bench. A few manufacturers' guides were opened to dog-eared pages. My own rig hung on the opposite wall, behind a queue of student rigs, all neatly aligned, ready for tomorrow.

I pulled open a drawer and found some outdated flight logs and a pack of gum. The drawer beneath it had a stapler and a canister of Pringles.

A TV and VCR monopolized a tabletop beside the far wall, next to a computer and a stack of blank DVDs. The loft was doubling as an editing room. Archived DVDs and VHS tapes filled a row of overhead shelves. I fingered the tapes one at a time, turning my head sideways to try to read their labels, but it was too dark.

I stepped toward the computer.

"Looking for something?" Someone spoke from the shadows behind me.

My pulse quickened again. How could anyone have come in so noiselessly?

I faced the doorway, but couldn't tell who was there. He leaned on the doorframe, one foot crossed over the other, and his shadow spanned the loft like a long, bony hand.

"I was in for a bathroom stop," I said. "And I was…curious, I guess."

The man stepped back into the dim office, still looking at me. The subtle change in lighting revealed the rat face of Craig Clement.

"The loft is for employees only."

"Got it," I said. "Sorry."

I offered an awkward wave and left, brushing past him because he wouldn't move out of my way. I treaded around the sleepers in the hangar and made my way through dewy grass back to my tent, fervently wishing it were all steel with a door to lock. The best I could do was zip myself inside.

I sat on my sleeping bag and second-guessed myself. Why had I agreed to come to Texas in the first place? Four days had passed, we had a sketchy lead at best, and now things were getting freaky.

Chapter Fourteen

When my watch beeped at five, my head was thick with the kind of fatigue I remembered from college all-nighters. There was no way I was going on the first load, even though it meant passing up my free balloon jump. I stumbled to the hangar, drank coffee, and ate eggs and sausage links while making excuses. A young skydiver named Donna, who'd recently gotten her A license, was trying to talk Rick into a cheaper gear rental. I remembered my early jumps, when enthusiasm for the sport outweighed my budget. I told Donna I'd be glad to share my rig. She said I "rocked."

The morning was chilly, so I stayed in the sweatshirt and sweatpants I'd slept in and found an empty lawn chair facing the landing field. I watched the balloon jumpers and Cessna loads and looked for the pilot from my picture, but didn't find her. Someone was filling in, and it wasn't Vince. That was lucky, considering how rough I looked.

Later that morning, I'd just warmed up another cup of coffee when a curvaceous middle-aged blond in leather pants and a tight sweater gingerly crossed the soggy parking lot in unsteady high-heeled boots. She draped an arm casually around Rick as he led her toward the hangar, apparently welcoming her in the same benign, flirtatious way he'd greeted me. Even from a distance, I could see the familiar lacquered red fingernails and overdone lip-gloss. Jeannie!

Right then, Scud sidled up and patted my behind. I was mortified he might have felt the same little jiggle I did. He followed my gaze to the parking lot and locked onto Jeannie.

"Mm, mm," was all he said.

I wanted to leap into her arms and hug her. But instead I turned for the office before she spotted me. Explaining how we knew each other could be tricky. It'd be better to find her later, on my own.

◇◇◇

Rick and Jeannie weren't in the parking lot or the packing area. I wandered out back to the landing field, but they weren't there either. When I passed the training room adjoining the hangar, the morning's ground school class was inside. Students were lined up beside a wooden Cessna mock-up, practicing exits and PLFs—parachute landing falls.

Finally, I found them standing off to the side, watching. It looked like Rick was explaining the drills to Jeannie. When he left, I sneaked up behind her and leaned toward her ear.

"Gonna give it a go?"

She turned, startled. "Jeez, Emily. You scared the crap out of me!"

My sweatshirt protected me from the slap she levied on my shoulder.

"You didn't tell me you were coming," I said. "I'd have baked a cake."

She smiled. "You look like shit. Where's your make-up?"

I ignored her.

She pulled a pack of Salem Lights from her handbag.

"Can't smoke in here." I led her outside.

She promptly lit up.

"What are you doing here?"

"Checking on you." She took a drag on her cigarette and exhaled, careful to blow the smoke away from me. "So what's the skinny?"

Jeannie had to repeat the question, because my attention was elsewhere. Behind her, Craig and the pilot from my Spy Cam were filling up the Cessna at the fuel station beyond the runway. They talked with their backs to us, but I'd seen enough to recognize the woman. Jeannie followed my gaze.

"That woman's a pilot here," I said. "The missing kid's mom recognized her from her ex-husband's company. The guy's staff here too. I pissed him off last night when he caught me snooping."

She looked from them to me, eyebrows raised, and flung her cigarette into the damp grass where she smashed it under the toe of her boot.

I described my mucked up search and how Craig had caught me. "He gives me the creeps. Those two together spell trouble."

Craig turned from the pump station to walk back to the hangar and Jeannie and I looked away. Jumpers headed toward the runway and I spotted Donna with my beautiful Mirage strapped to her back.

"There goes my baby," I said.

Jeannie gave a questioning look.

"My gear. The girl over there with the spiky hair is borrowing my gear."

Jeannie studied the brightly colored jumpsuits and rigs.

"Tell me the truth, Em. Could I do that?"

I laughed. "Probably, sweetie. But it would mess up your hair."

She flipped me off with an expertly manicured middle finger and sashayed to the office without a look back, off to do God knows what.

◇◇◇

Foot traffic was picking up and I recognized several jumpers, but I didn't spot Vince. I'd changed into decent clothes and applied rudimentary make-up in case there was a sighting.

I chatted with a small group of jumpers in the landing area. Someone nearby called out, "Jump run!"

The Cessna was passing ten thousand feet overhead and looked like an aluminum fly ball in low orbit. I held a hand over my eyes to block the sun and craned my neck. This was Donna's load.

When a dark speck peeled off from the silver speck, it meant jumpers were away. We couldn't make them out as individuals until about thirty seconds later, when they tracked away from their formation to open. Soon after, like Technicolor popcorn kernels, canopies snapped open, making sounds like miniature thunderclaps.

A voice in the crowd called, "Cutaway!"

Sure enough, someone had chopped. Jettisoned from its harness-container, a discarded main tumbled over itself, looking more like a sheet in the spin cycle than a parachute. It wasn't until I saw a solid yellow reserve inflate that I realized the cutaway parachute was mine.

Around me, skydivers and spectators excitedly pointed to the sky and speculated, but the sight of a fully inflated reserve, obviously piloted by a conscious jumper, greatly diminished the original wave of alarm. Still, I was uneasy. I didn't like the coincidence of a malfunction on the morning following my first real lead.

Rick emerged from the office with his keys and headed for his pick-up truck. Donna would need a lift back to the airport. She was following the cutaway main canopy instead of steering toward the landing field. She knew that if she lost sight of my expensive equipment, it might be gone for good. I jogged to catch up with Rick, explained it was my gear, and asked to tag along. We climbed into the cab and he drove the length of his bumpy, muddy landing field until we came to a barbed-wire fence bordering a neighboring farm. An A-shaped stepladder straddled the wires, telling me more than one skydiver had landed there before. Donna was already on the ground when we got to her. She was unhurt, gathering up gear.

I used the ladder to cross the fence and sank into soft earth when I stepped down. Rick followed me. "What happened?" he asked Donna. "You okay?"

She frowned. "Line twists. Lots of them. More than I could kick out of, so I had to chop."

I wasn't sure what type of malfunction I'd been expecting her to report, but it definitely wasn't line twists.

"I'm sorry I cut away your main, Emily." She looked distraught. "I tried hard to fix it but it was taking too long and I started to get low and—"

I hugged her. "I'm glad you're okay."

Rick waited for her to finish daisy chaining the lines and helped her out of the rig. A few yards past her, I gathered up the cutaway main. The three of us climbed the ladder back to Rick's side of the fence, and Rick placed the rig and main in his truck bed before turning to her.

"Was that your first mal?"

She hesitated. Skydivers don't admit first anythings. It means they have to buy beer for everyone else.

He put an arm around her. "That's what I thought. Looks like you're buying tonight, beautiful."

At least he made her smile.

I was too bothered by the line twists to smile. I'd packed the rig myself and I don't pack messes. I had the sudden, horrible feeling someone had tampered with it.

It wouldn't have been difficult to do. After all, if I could get into the loft overnight, anyone could. I thought about Craig's strange behavior in the office the night before and shuddered. He was staff, and a rigger. He could go in the loft and open a rig in full view of anyone and no one would give it a passing thought. I berated myself for not locking the gear in my car.

Whoever messed with my gear had to know why I was there. But how could that be? And why not sabotage my reserve too?

I decided it might be a stall tactic. I'd be tied up for a while, awaiting another repack. Maybe I was closer to a discovery than I thought. Maybe someone was buying time.

Chapter Fifteen

Everyone flocked to Donna. She'd been unlucky enough to have her first malfunction on a day the drop zone was thick with curious on-lookers. I scanned faces in the crowd gathered around her and watched as she good-naturedly answered all the questions. Donna's cutaway bothered me far more than it bothered her.

I lifted my rig, lighter without the main, from the back of Rick's truck and headed for the loft to find Billy. Yellow nylon from the deployed reserve overflowed from my arms and hung down to my knees.

Marie was last to leave the office to check on Donna. When the door swung behind her, I caught it with my foot and managed to squeeze inside before any fabric got pinched in the door. Instead of Billy, Craig was in the loft, hunched over the workbench, dialing his cell phone. I stepped backward, out of sight, and listened.

"Monday morning at two," he said quietly. "I'll be in touch." Then his phone snapped closed.

Silently, I placed my gear on the office floor and slunk away, wondering what I'd overheard. Maybe Richard could help make sense of it. My own phone was in my tent, and I went to get it. Scud stopped me in the hangar.

"Guess who's in ground school," he said. "The diva from this morning. Remember? The one with the sexy boots?" He laughed like he couldn't imagine what Jeannie had been thinking.

I smiled to myself and walked on to my tent. I knew exactly what she'd been thinking: *Screw you, Emily.* I'd chosen as my best friend the only woman in the world willing to jump from a plane for spite.

"Touché," I muttered, and slipped inside my tent. Hearing no one else around, I dialed Richard.

I started with Craig's mysterious four-second phone call and worked backward through Donna's malfunction and then to my midnight search. I was almost to the part about how Craig caught me when Richard interrupted.

"Did you say flight logs?"

I pictured the notebooks in the workbench drawer. "They looked like flight logs."

"Did you read them?"

"It was too dark."

"I'd like to know what was in those logs. Might have something to do with that pilot."

During my pilfering, I'd neglected to study the most obvious items I'd found. What was wrong with me?

"I'll handle it." If I had to steal them, copy them, or sneak in and memorize them, I'd get the information from the logs. Richard didn't have to ask. It was my mistake. I owed this to Casey.

We said goodbye and I returned to the office to take care of my gear. I found the main, crudely folded, laying along the wall of the carpeted packing area and figured Rick had moved it from the truck for me. I scooped it up and returned to the loft, feeling better prepared to face Craig.

Who, it turned out, had company.

Billy and two people I hadn't met were with him, standing beside a collection of disassembled gear, inspecting pieces and nodding and pointing. Craig pulled a block of folded fabric from a box. As soon as it was free, it separated and expanded like a gas. Layers of beautiful crisp nylon, all shades of purple, cascaded over the bench.

It looked like the riggers were about to assemble a new parachute system. I figured the likely owner was the tan and athletic man hovering near the crisp, new canopy. A woman behind him slipped her arms around his waist and kissed the back of his shoulder, her blond hair gently falling down her back in a wispy French braid. She was the pilot Karen Lyons had recognized.

Billy noticed me first and nodded. "Heard you had a mal."

"Not me." I shifted my gaze to Craig. "My gear."

I watched for something revealing in his expression but his face was bland as ever.

"Emily Locke," I said, extending my hand to the new guy.

He took it warmly and introduced himself as David Meyer. His lovely, potentially criminal girlfriend was Trish Dalton. She shook my hand with a limp, disinterested grip. A diamond tennis bracelet shimmered on her wrist, partially obscuring a dainty tattoo. The tattoo seemed out of place on a preppy woman like her. She wore a crisp polo-style shirt with a Green Bay Packers emblem. The shirt was tucked neatly around her slender waist into carefully pressed khaki shorts.

"You from Wisconsin?" I asked.

Trish forced the type of condescending smile I associate with rich snobs. "Not originally."

I imagined from her accent she might be an oil-snooty, southern belle type.

"She worked at the Wisconsin Jump Center outside of Green Bay for a while," David said.

"How'd you like that DZ?" I asked. "I've never made it up that way."

She shook her head dismissively, and waved off the question with a swat. "Jerks."

I wondered what Trish had against her earlier employer. Before I could probe, she whispered something to David, kissed him on the cheek, and said she'd catch us later. Just like that, she was gone.

I glanced at the drawer where I'd seen the flight logs, and wondered how to get them. With both riggers in the room, and a full complement of gear to assemble for David, it seemed unlikely the room would be vacant any time soon. I told Billy I'd check in with him later about my repack, and left.

◇◇◇

Richard got busy right away running the names Trish Dalton, Trisha Dalton, and Patricia Dalton through his databases. He turned up several matches for women who'd been employed in Texas and Wisconsin and were near my estimate of thirty to thirty-five years old. Converging on the right one would take a while longer. It was the news he'd received from Don Schaffer, the owner of Wisconsin Jump Center, that he most wanted to share. Trish Dalton had been let go. And it wasn't because she was incompetent, insubordinate, or chronically late. Trish had been let go because of unauthorized use of the planes.

I walked alone outside the hangar and mulled it over. Trish flew for Eric Lyons' company. Karen recognized her from company travel. It was likely Trish had crossed paths with Casey on one or more of Eric's trips. Casey was missing. Trish used planes without asking. Had she snatched him and flown him off somewhere?

◇◇◇

A dog barked in the parking lot and I was happy to see Cindy. She thumped her tail at me from her post in the back of Vince's truck. Her tongue lolled in a drooling pant and made her look like she was smiling. Vince's guitar case rested, abandoned, in the back with her again.

I gave Cindy her requisite strokes and lifted the guitar case out of the truck. I tried to think of something witty to say when I found Vince.

It turned out he found me first.

"Tryin' to steal it?"

He walked up from the direction of the hangar, sporting a day of stubble and the same black cowboy hat pulled low over his forehead. Evidently, his wardrobe was limited to jeans and solid colored tees. This one was hunter green and brought out his eyes. When he got closer, I smelled aftershave. I was pretty sure that was new.

"I'm not stealing it," I said. "I'm moving it inside. You don't deserve this guitar."

He took the case from me, letting his palm brush the back of my hand. Then he headed for the hangar. I followed.

"Actually," he said, "I was coming out to get it. Good thing too, because here you are, thieving it again."

We walked to the same corner where I'd found his guitar on my first day. He set it down, crossed his arms, and looked at me.

Trish emerged from around the corner and crossed the packing area on her way to a cooler. I thought she and Vince exchanged a cold look, but it passed so quickly I doubted what I'd seen.

He turned back to me. "Get your gear," he said, simply. "It's time to jump."

"Can't."

I explained about Donna and my disassembled gear.

Vince shook his head. "I came all the way here on my day off to jump with you, and you don't even have a rig. Pitiful."

He picked up his guitar case again. "Guess I should have asked you before hauling this in here."

"You're not...Are you leaving?"

"Yep," he said. "And so are you. Let's go."

I smiled. "Go where? Since when do I take orders from you?"

He winked and gave me a playful nudge toward the parking lot.

◇◇◇

I liked the rugged feel of Vince's pick-up as it hummed down farm roads, past brown fields and rows of giant, round hay bales. Vince drove a little too fast, and I liked that too. At the highway, we passed a billboard advertising fence repairs in both English and Spanish, and headed south to Freeport, an industrial little town apparently centered around natural gas companies. Street names like Glycol Road and Chlorine Road made me think the town was all business, an impression reinforced by a long series of factories and smoke-stacks streaming by my passenger-side window.

At a red light, I stared at the gargantuan steel framework of one of the factories. Its endless maze of pipes and reinforcements struck me as cold and impersonal, and the ugly steam pumping out did nothing to soften my opinion. "You sure know how to impress a girl."

Vince only winked and gunned the truck when the light changed. Palm trees and gulls gave me the notion water was near, even though I couldn't see it anywhere. Then we started up an enormous bridge over the Intracoastal Waterway, and suddenly I saw water for miles.

Flat boats and industrial ships floated motionless in the channel below, and more factories and stacks populated the marshy landscape to the east. Straight ahead, the Gulf of Mexico dominated the view. Massive and infinite, the ocean was royal blue everywhere except for a wide band of white where the sun glinted off its choppy waves. It was the first truly majestic thing I had seen for years.

Vince turned onto a pitted, desolate road that ran parallel to the coast. On our left, one sign said Plant Entrance while another said Beach Access on our right.

He took the right and eventually the road morphed to sand. Vince didn't let off the gas, though, and his tires slipped the same way mine did in snow. "Quintana Beach."

I looked up and down the shoreline and saw only sand, waves, and tread marks. "Where do those tracks go?"

He parked the truck and opened his door. "Let's find out."

I stepped onto damp sand and took a deep breath. The low rumble of the surf and light ocean breeze made the beach all the more beautiful. Vince unchained Cindy and the three of us walked ankle deep in the surf, Vince and I carrying our shoes. He'd brought a faded tennis ball, and Cindy was dying for it. She lunged into the ocean and tirelessly swam into the waves until she sometimes disappeared behind them, all for that stupid little ball. Each time she came back, she shook water all over us. I was beginning to feel the tightness of salt drying to my skin.

"You really came out today to jump with me?"

He pulled the ball back, tossed it high over the waves, and didn't take his eyes off it.

"Yep."

We watched Cindy leap into the frothy tide and paddle until her head was barely visible.

She mouthed the ball and turned back.

"Wow," I said. "You must really like the way I skydive."

He directed an embarrassed smile at the sand.

"Not really," he said, redirecting his attention to the dog. "You're an Average Jane skydiver."

I huffed and playfully shoved his shoulder.

"But I do like the way you sing. Nothing average about that."

I grinned and looked away. The compliment made me uncomfortably self-aware.

"It remains to be seen about your personality," he said.

"I beg your pardon?"

"I don't know you very well yet. You might turn out to be a nut, or a…bore."

"A bore?"

He smiled. "I'm sure there are lots of wonderful singers with no personality."

I moved to slug him again, and he stepped backward and stumbled over his sopping wet dog. The next wave crashed, soaking his jeans with seawater from the knees down. Cindy didn't care. She shoved the ball into his fist and waited, staring at it.

Vince looked from his drenched pants to me, accusingly.

"Women," he muttered to the dog, and tossed the ball.

"Men and dogs," I replied.

Eventually we came to a fishing pier and Cindy doubled back. Vince explained this was a regular walk for them and we'd arrived at the halfway point. It felt nice to be included in their routine.

Before driving back, he asked me to play for him again. It was becoming a regular thing for us and, he joked, was mutually beneficial: He liked my voice. I liked his guitar.

My song ended abruptly when I broke a string.

"Concert's over." I removed the broken string and shoved it in the back pocket of my jeans.

"Naw," he said, and brushed my cheek. "This is only intermission."

Chapter Sixteen

"Guess I'm not supposed to skydive in leather pants," Jeannie said, running her hands over her tightly fitted hips.

I looked her over. "Or high heels."

She lit up again and we walked across the grass to my tent. She stomped her cigarette into the damp ground and we crawled inside, Jeannie taking care to avoid kneeling in the grass. I fished in my bag for a top and shorts to loan her. She'd need them to practice exits and parachute landing falls. I unlaced my only pair of sneakers, handed them over, and slipped into Birkenstock sandals instead. Jack used to call them my Lesbian Shoes. Jeannie just called them ugly. I told her I'd learned Trish Dalton's name and what Richard had determined so far.

"How's Cole treating you, anyway?"

"He's not annoying me as much," I said. "We've only talked about the case, nothing else."

"Got any socks?"

I searched for those too and tossed her a pair.

"You know," I said, "I've been thinking about this case and the first one. When Casey was kidnapped, his mom's security system never sounded."

She worked herself out of the leather pants. "I thought you said Casey's dad had the pass—" she grunted "—code."

"True, but he was later found murdered. We're assuming he wasn't the kidnapper. So, that leaves the question...what happened to Karen's alarm?"

"Shit," she said, finally free of the pants. "Makes you wonder what you pay the security company for."

She pulled my tee over her head and reached for my shorts.

"Jeannie, do you remember...Do you remember the time Jack went to Pittsburgh?"

Her expression hardened and she stopped moving. I could tell by her concerned look she got my meaning.

Shortly after I'd received the threats during my friend Nora's investigation, Jack left for a two-day business trip. His first night away, I was attacked in my sleep. The man who broke into our house straddled me in my bed. I woke up staring at a facemask, with a gloved hand pressed over my mouth and my attacker's body weight pinning me at the hips. I wasn't raped. I wasn't even hurt. The intruder shoved a piece of fabric into my hand, leaned so close to my ear I thought he might bite it, and whispered, "This is how close I can get to your daughter."

The fabric was a swatch of pajamas he'd cut off of Annette while she slept down the hall. He'd come into our house, cut my little girl's pajamas from right over her heart, left her sleeping in her bed, and come to threaten me in mine.

It all happened without triggering my alarm system.

Days later, a phone technician reported signs of tampering at the junction box down the street. A specialist from my home security company tinkered for hours before discovering cut wires in my attic, severed in a spot hidden by insulation. With a disabled audible alarm, temporary interruption to my monitoring service, and no immediately detectable signs of tampering, it was clear I'd been hit by professional criminals.

◇◇◇

Rick and I stood in the landing field and watched Jeannie's orange and brown Manta creep three thousand feet overhead. Rick spoke into a ground-to-air radio used to talk students back to the landing area. He asked Jeannie for a right-hand turn. Her canopy continued straight ahead. He asked for a left-hand turn. She still flew straight. Soon it was obvious Jeannie was freewheeling with a broken radio. Where she'd land was anyone's guess.

"She's headed for Cromwell's place." Rick shook his head. "Lord, keep her."

"Cromwell's place?"

"Our resident Farmer McNasty."

I winced. "Rough on a first-timer. I'll go pick her up."

From the highway, I found the dirt road Rick said would lead to Jeannie and followed it for nearly a mile until it curved behind a leaning wooden barn. An orange and brown parachute emerged from behind the failing structure. The parachute's cells were puffed up, obscuring most of Jeannie's head, but I recognized my shoes. She looked like the Great Pumpkin with legs.

I put the car in park and tapped the horn. She jumped, and the fabric amassed in her arms slipped over and over itself until it rested on the ground in a sloppy heap. When she spotted me, she gathered up the parachute again and hurried to the car, dragging most of the fabric in the dirt. She was near crying.

"Take this stuff off me. We gotta get out of here."

I couldn't help but laugh.

"I don't see what's so damn funny."

I unbuckled her helmet and slid her goggles off her head. I daisy-chained her lines, released her chest strap, and loosened her leg straps. She stepped out of the rig and I placed it in the back seat of my car.

"You shouldn't drag a parachute." I brushed road dust off the nylon. "It could tear."

Jeannie was already in the passenger seat.

"Bite me." She slammed the door.

I slid behind the wheel and looked at her. She was sweating.

"You okay?"

"Just drive."

When we turned onto the highway, Jeannie said, "That was a treat. A guy from the cast of *Deliverance* lives back there." She gestured behind us with her thumb.

"Rick mentioned him," I said. "I came as fast as I could."

"He's a lunatic, Em. Certifiable." She started to imitate him, stabbing a pointed finger in the air. "'You and yer planes. Noise all day and all night with you. This private property! This private! Git off my land!'"

"I am so sorry. Your first skydive and you had a run-in with the local crank." I hesitated. "You *are* going to jump again though, right?"

She pulled down the sun visor to check her hair in its mirror.

"Bet your ass, sister. Right after I get a cigarette."

◇◇◇

Jeannie did make another jump. She was on the sunset load, the last load of the day. When the Otter's wheels left the ground, the beer light went on and the party was officially underway.

A bare-chested man with a nipple ring set up colossal stereo equipment in one corner of the hangar, and as he manipulated plugs and wires, Linda moved rigs and gear bags from their spots in the middle of the carpeted packing area. I gathered she was clearing a dance floor.

I pulled a bottle of Shiner out of a cooler and scanned the crowd, wondering if Vince would come. He'd bowed out after our beach walk, claiming errands to run. On my way outside to check the picnic area, Marie waved to get my attention.

"Give me a hand, hon'?"

She leaned over a long party table and arranged troughs of brisket and baked beans. I helped her lay out plastic cups and Styrofoam plates as jumpers began to congregate near the food.

"Big turn-out," I said. "Any night jumps this weekend?"

She frowned. "Had an accident a few years back. We don't do them anymore." She pinched a sample of the brisket. "Not bad."

I grabbed my own sample and stepped outside. Vince was nowhere in sight, but I did spot Craig. He was demonstrating a freestyle technique to a couple of young jumpers. It occurred to me the loft might be unattended. Maybe I could get the flight logs. If I got caught in there again, I'd say I was checking on my repack.

In the loft, a cameraman was perched on a stool, editing footage. He ran images backward and forward in slow motion and ignored me when I stepped inside and flipped open the reserve closing flap on my rig. I pulled my packing card from its pocket and verified that Billy had been the one to do the repack, not Craig. I checked Billy's seal, and finding it intact, hoisted the parachute over a shoulder. My back was tender from sleeping on the ground the night before. I groaned.

"Sounds like someone's a little out of shape," the cameramen said, barely suppressing a chuckle.

"I prefer 'out of practice.'" On the screen behind him, Big Red's hulking image came into the frame, and I nodded toward it. "We can't all be built like an ox. I bet his job keeps him in shape. Me, I sit at a desk."

The cameraman followed my gaze over his shoulder to the monitor. He shook his head. "Wrong excuse. Big Red has a desk job too. CPS."

I considered the acronym. "Child Protective Services?"

The cameraman nodded. "Meyer too," he said. "You know Meyer?"

I stared at him. "David Meyer?"

"Sure. They work together." He shrugged, and swiveled to the equipment again.

I thought of David Meyer, choosing a career defending children, and of his girlfriend, Trish Dalton, possibly involved in snatching them. Then I hung my gear back on the pegs and prepared for another attempt at stealing the logs.

◇◇◇

I'd just pulled my second beer from a cooler when Vince found me.

"You're not dancing," he said.

I pulled the top off my bottle. "Not much of a dancer."

He turned toward the DJ and they exchanged a nod I didn't like the looks of. The DJ picked up his mike.

"I've got a request to slow it down, folks, so grab a honey, or a hottie, or whatever you can grab, and come out for some smoochie-smoochie on the dance floor." He made kiss noises into the microphone.

Piano notes from Patsy Cline's "Crazy" rang through the hangar, and Vince extended his hand. I hesitated.

"Please don't embarrass me, girl," he said gently. "If you don't dance with me, I'll hear about it for a long, long time."

He closed a hand over mine and pulled me toward him. Then he slipped an arm around the small of my back, and immediately, it seemed, we were dancing.

It was the first time I'd danced since Jack. Vince leaned over me slightly, his chin on the side of my forehead. A faint trace of cologne clung to him.

Holding him, swaying to "Crazy," I wished the old songs were longer. I rested my cheek on his shoulder and let my eyes close, rocking with him wherever he led me. He opened his fingers on my back and drew me nearer until there was no distance left to close. I slid my hand from his shoulder to the place between his shoulder blades. It was a conversation of sorts, only wordless.

When the song ended and I opened my eyes, I was looking straight over Vince's shoulder at Jeannie. She leaned against the wall with a satisfied smirk on her face and raised her drink.

She walked over to us and introduced herself to Vince before I could. Jeannie wanted to tell anyone that would listen that she'd passed her second Accelerated Freefall dive. This time, her radio worked and she'd had a nice stand-up landing in the field behind the hangar.

As she carried on, I spotted Craig across the room and got an idea.

One thing Jeannie excelled at was approaching men. Most flirted with her, but even the ones who didn't flirt seemed unable to ignore her. Craig didn't fall cleanly into either category, but fortunately, another of Jeannie's talents was idle banter.

I had verified the loft was empty and asked Jeannie to keep Craig busy until she saw me again. She was on him like a suction cup, and only one thing went wrong. When I opened the drawer, the flight logs were missing.

Chapter Seventeen

I caught Jeannie's eye from across the room to let her know she could ease up on Craig. Vince was out back at the picnic bench, having a plate of barbecue with Scud and Big Red. I joined them.

"I learned something neat about you tonight," I told Big Red. "I didn't know you were in social work."

He nodded, and bit into a dinner roll.

"Is it as bad as they say?" I asked. "I hear such awful things on the news."

He raised a hand to stop me. "My dear, I'll talk to you about parachutes and pool tables, motorcycles and mackerel, but not about those kids. Not tonight, not on a boogie weekend."

"Sorry," I said. "I have a soft spot for children."

"Got kiddos, Emily?" Scud asked.

I answered carefully. "I did, once. I lost her when she was very young."

I glanced at Vince, worried that finding out this way would feel like a betrayal. He watched me with a wounded quality, but seemed more sympathetic than surprised.

"Anyway," I said, "I'll ask David about it later instead."

Big Red grimaced. "Don't do that. Touchy subject."

"Why?" Scud asked.

Big Red took a swig of Busch, then seemingly chose to abandon his earlier taboo. "He's being investigated."

"Investigated? What for?" Scud asked.

Big Red wiped his mouth with the back of his hand and looked around to make sure David wasn't near.

"Racial discrimination."

I leaned in, incredulous. David seemed friendly enough. Then again, he wouldn't be the first friendly bigot I'd met.

"We got audited this quarter," Big Red continued. "There were a high percentage of cases closed as 'Unable to Locate'—"

"Damn, Red. You already lost me," Scud said through a mouth full of food.

Big Red started over. "Everyone's assigned field cases to investigate. You know, a neighbor calls in that Mom's mistreating Baby, or Dad's using drugs...that sort of thing?"

Scud nodded.

"Sometimes families are missing when we visit. If they think they've been called in, a lot of parents leave for a while. Many take their kids."

We barely noticed Jeannie when she walked up. Big Red was still talking.

"When that happens, we keep going back until we find them. At least three times. We talk to neighbors, check databases...If it all fails, a case might get closed as 'Unable to Locate.'

"The auditor noticed a lot of Unable to Locates in our office, so he went through the records. Nearly all the cases were David's *and* all of them were white kids. On paper it looks like he never really tried, just wrote the cases off and said he couldn't find them...but I know David. He works hard on everything he does."

I watched Vince and Scud weigh this new information against the person they knew as a friend. I wished I knew David better so I could form my own opinion. Jeannie listened and watched, clearly confused.

"That doesn't make sense," I finally said. "If he didn't investigate cases involving white kids, that'd mean leaving them in potentially dangerous homes. If anything, that's reverse discrimination."

Big Red pointed his fork at me. "You'd think so. But the concern would be that David thinks whites can handle their kids and blacks and Hispanics can't. So he works harder on his minority cases and looks the other way with the whites.

"At any rate," he concluded, "Not a good idea to ask David about work right now."

Scud stared at his brisket like he was thinking about something, but he didn't say whatever crossed his mind. Jeannie leaned close to tell me she was turning in. She was sharing my tent.

Vince jangled his keys and said he was heading out too. I walked him to his truck.

When we got there, he opened its door and sighed. "Well. You're not a bore. I've got that much. But…I can see there's plenty still to learn."

He gave a questioning look and didn't say more. It seemed his way of asking me to finish what I'd started at the picnic table.

I braced myself with a deep breath and looked overhead at the stars.

"Her name was Annette," I said, "and she died before her first birthday. My husband was with her." My voice caught. "It was an accident…they were boating."

Tears began to pool, but were too stubborn to fall, and I shifted my gaze downward. I swallowed hard and stared at Vince's front tire with my hands shoved deep in my pockets. He was quiet.

"It was four years ago," I added softly. "She would have started kindergarten this fall. Jack and I would have been married eight years in June."

He took me gently by the shoulders and pulled me toward him. He wrapped his arms around me and cradled my head in one of his hands. I was too weak with memories to return his embrace, but he didn't let go. We stood like that, silently, for what seemed like minutes. Then Vince kissed me lightly on my forehead, and I took more comfort in his gentle touch than I could have found in any words.

Chapter Eighteen

That night I dreamed of Thanksgiving with Jack and Annette. Keith and Nora Shelton dropped by unannounced and brought a sweet potato casserole. Annette and Mattie played side by side on the floor next to the dining room table, ignoring each other, absorbed in their own toys, and I worried because I hadn't set out the nice china. The doorbell rang, and before I could answer it, Vince and Trish let themselves in. Vince wiped his feet, and Trish tracked in dirty snow. Jack shook Vince's hand in the foyer and suddenly Vince was wearing Jack's clothes, sitting in Jack's usual spot on our sofa. I returned to the dining room to find Big Red where Mattie had been. He was reading Annette a book. Behind them, Trish scooped sweet potato casserole onto an unadorned plate, and her fancy bracelet slid down and covered the tattoo on her wrist.

"Your tattoo," I mumbled, and it was the sound of my voice that woke me.

Jeannie breathed deeply and obliviously behind me in the tent. I checked my watch. It was almost six o'clock in the morning. The crickets were obnoxious.

"Wake up." I rolled partly over and gave her a crude shove.

She rolled further away.

I shoved her again. "Wake up," I said. "Get dressed."

"Why?" she complained, half asleep.

"We're going to see Richard. I remember something."

◇◇◇

Jeannie drove. I used the time to delve into my journal. Maybe there was more I hadn't connected. More that I should be able to connect. Maybe.

July 16—Flight 1622

Dr. Raleigh is an old Air Force friend of Dad's. He's a grief counselor at a residential facility near Portland. I'll be there for two months. Dad said he called Raleigh for some objective help, but I think he called because he's not sure what to do about me. I'm not sure what to do about me either.

It's been nine days since Lake Erie swallowed my family. I try to remember what we did together nine days before they died, and I can't. Does that mean I took them for granted? Who doesn't think there will be endless days of games and stories and afternoons at the park with her baby? Of jokes and kisses and morning coffee with her husband?

Jack grew up on the water and knew his way around all sorts of boats. He said himself the rental was a beautiful craft. They had mild weather, calm water, and all Jack's experience on their side. It was supposed to be their special morning together. How could something so family-affirming be the opposite? The lake gave no hint of its intentions.

I left today with my grass too high, my bills unopened, and my laundry on the floor. I might lose my job. I didn't ask for leave—just packed when Dad said pack and left Jeannie to make my excuses. Some of my friends don't even know what happened. How would I tell them? Call them up with the news?

I think Jeannie told Dad about the pills, but she denies it and I won't ask him. Does he think I didn't consider him reason enough to hang on? If Annette swallowed a bottle of pills, I would feel like I'd failed her. Now I feel like I failed my dad.

He had the foresight to know I'd miss the Shelton trial. I'd forgotten. The assistant D.A. arranged a deposition yesterday afternoon. I hope it goes well for them in court. Their nightmare is ending. Mine is nine days old.

I didn't tell anyone where I'm going, not even Jeannie. Just told her I was leaving for a while to get help with putting my mind and heart back together the best way I could.

August 8—Emerson House

Only one nurse here knows my name without looking at a chart, and I still pick up mail from a cubby slot marked for the last person who stayed in my room. I miss home, and I'm afraid to go back.

What does it feel like to drown? A man who drowns knows he's dying. What does a baby know? I think they both know terror—the man, because he understands what's happening, and the baby, because she doesn't. I imagine a father grieving for a baby he can't save, and a baby crying for a father she can't find.

It hurts that Jack and Annette are gone, but it hurts more that they suffered. Ask any woman to imagine—really imagine—her husband helpless to save himself and their baby. Imagine him in the final moments when he becomes aware of an outcome he's powerless to prevent. Ask a mother to imagine her baby sinking below the choppy surface of a vast lake, spitting water, eyes open even while she sinks—her arms stretched upward, reaching for air, her feathery hair pulsing in the murk. A tender, trusting life, delicate and vulnerable, and the loveliest creature her mother ever beheld...Swallowed. I don't understand how anyone recovers from losing a family.

I tell this to my counselors in various forms and different words every day at our sessions. They say my pain will ease with time. I listen and nod and force brave smiles, and I wonder if I'm the only one here who doesn't believe I will heal.

September 14—Homecoming

I take a deep breath after being home for two hours and know this is the hardest day yet. So, I sit down at my kitchen table and write.

My house is full of beautiful things that hurt to look at.

I read a poem taped to the refrigerator. Jack wrote it on our fourth anniversary. It's smudged from the years and I wish I'd framed it instead of taping it to the door. On the table in front of me is a stack of mail the neighbor has collected. On top is a card from *Motor Trend* magazine asking if Jack wants to renew for another year.

I look at the refrigerator again and smile and cry at the kid art she made with her teacher's help at daycare. A finger painting. Random crayon scribbles on yellow construction paper.

In the windowsill is a plaster handprint from last winter. Behind me, her toy box waits in the living room. I have the unworldly sensation that the toys want to know when she's coming back to play, but I don't know how to answer them. Her bath toys are in the tub, and the half-empty bottle of Johnson & Johnson is waiting for her. I don't want to shower there.

In the kitchen, I open the cupboard to find some tea. Instead, I find Annette's Cheerios and graham crackers. I burst into tears and collapse on my floor.

I try to get a grip. I start some laundry. The dryer is full of Jack's clothes. Do I fold them?

His car's in the garage and his sunglasses are still on the dash.

This is supposed to be a busy house. There is supposed to be a little girl pestering me right now to stop writing in my journal and pick her up instead. There is supposed to be a lawn mower humming in the backyard, and when I look out this window, I should see Jack out there wiping sweat off of his forehead. Instead, the only noise I hear is in my mind and the things I look at sting my eyes like the sun.

◇◇◇

"You saw the tattoo in Austin?" Richard asked.

Jeannie and I sat across from him at a Denny's near his office. Our waitress had come twice for our order, but we'd been too preoccupied to choose. My tattered journal was beside me in the booth, touching my leg. I felt strangely unwilling to part with it and ran my finger over its spiral binding.

"The day I found Mattie, I saw that cursive T. The manager at the restaurant had it, and it was in the same place on his wrist."

Jeannie emptied a package of Equal into her coffee. Richard didn't seem to notice his.

"I suppose that could be a coincidence, but—"

I cut him off. "But there's a common thread, missing kids."

He nodded.

"There's more." I pointed out that both Karen Lyons' home security system and mine had failed on the nights of our respective break-ins.

Richard snapped his fingers. "That reminds me. We know how Casey's abductor got in."

I wanted to continue my line of thought but his new information derailed me.

"Karen Lyons' back door is one of those lead glass styles… you know, with the big pane that takes up most of the door?" He outlined a rectangle in the space between us. "A closer look at the door showed how the alarm was bypassed. The kidnapper removed the glass, frame and all."

"What?" Jeannie screwed up her face in disbelief.

"The whole frame," he said again. "He, or they, took out the entire frame and set it aside. The alarm didn't sound because no entry was breached and no glass was broken."

"And since it happened at night," I said, thinking out loud, "She wouldn't have had her motion detectors on. Nobody has those on while they're at home."

"Exactly."

I thought about Karen's security bypass and mine from years ago. Both clever schemes, obviously planned by someone with experience.

"Why take the time to replace the frame before leaving?" Jeannie said. "That doesn't make sense."

I thought about what had happened at my own house. "It makes sense if you want to buy time. When my house was broken into, it took days to figure out how my system was skirted. Similar circumstances here. What if Casey and Mattie's kidnappings are related? Could the same people be responsible?"

"Suppose we go with that," Richard said. "How would a couple in Texas become interested in a boy from Cleveland? It seems random."

"The couple with Mattie thought they were adopting him," I said. "Maybe they were mixed up in underground baby-brokering."

Jeannie smooshed her Equal wrapper into a tight little ball.

"Keith Shelton's a petroleum engineer," I continued. "Texas has hundreds of oil refineries. That could be the Cleveland-Texas connection."

"It doesn't explain how they'd know about his boy," Jeannie said.

"The planes," Richard said. He looked at me. "Emily, the day you found Mattie, didn't his parents fly from Cleveland to Austin on a private plane?"

I thought back, and fragments of that day realigned in my mind.

"It was Keith's company's jet," I said. "His vice president wanted to help them out, so they wouldn't have to wait for a commercial flight. I'd forgotten, but I read it a few days ago—"

"You folks ready?" The waitress was back. We made hasty choices and she lumbered toward the kitchen with our orders.

Richard asked me to finish what I was saying.

"She read it in her old journal," Jeannie answered for me. "When you showed up at work last week, you really stirred the pot, mister." Her tone was borderline sour.

Richard raised his eyebrows, as if this were news to him. I tried to kick Jeannie under the table but got the table base instead.

I waved off her comment. "Forget it."

Richard hesitated. "Stirred the pot how, Jeannie?"

I interrupted. "We are not going to have this conversation."

"As if he doesn't know..." Jeannie muttered into her handbag. She pulled out her cigarettes and dug for a lighter.

"Exactly what conversation are we not going to have?" Richard asked me.

Jeannie found the lighter, lit up, took a drag, and exhaled smoke over one shoulder. She returned her gaze to Richard. "The conversation about how you took a bribe to botch her friend's kidnapping trial."

I was paralyzed with disbelief. Had she really said that out loud?

Richard looked at me, astonished.

"Is that what you think? That I took a bribe to throw the Shelton trial?"

The waitress returned and told Jeannie we were in a non-smoking section. Jeannie shot her a pissy stare that sent her back to the kitchen.

"Do you?" Richard pressed.

I pushed my coffee away and slapped my journal on the table in front of me. I flipped through its pages, looking for the entry. Jeannie laid a hand delicately on my wrist, her way of telling me to calm down. I swatted it away. When I found the page I wanted, I shoved the notebook at Richard and watched him read it.

September 22

Nora dropped by to check on me. They lost the case. When she told me, she seemed to be holding back.

Something was off. I said I couldn't understand how the case was lost after everything I'd said in my deposition. She seemed as shocked by that statement as I was by hers: What deposition?

The assistant D.A. said I no-showed. When his office tried to reschedule, I'd already left for counseling.

A memory snapped into place—a phone call asking to move the meeting. Same time, different office. Something about trying to get a court reporter on short notice. There was one who'd do it, but a different location was better for her. I didn't give it a second thought, just drove to the new address and told my story.

There were three people: the assistant D.A., Reed's attorney, and the court reporter. They went through all the motions. I never suspected anything was other than it seemed. Who the hell were those people?

"They tried to get a retrial," I said when Richard finished reading. "But there were no witnesses to corroborate my story, and everyone knew I was clinically depressed."

Jeannie pointed her cigarette at Richard. "Emily only told one person when and where the real deposition was going to happen."

Richard dropped his gaze to the table.

"Me," he said softly.

"They bribed you to set up the switch, didn't they?" I asked. "And you did it."

It was the first time I'd confronted him to his face.

He stood and reached for his wallet.

"No," he said, sounding beaten down and exhausted. "They didn't bribe me. They threatened me. They knew things about my kids…where they had ball practice and dance lessons, what time they caught the bus. I didn't put too much stock in it until…"

He shook his head.

"Until what?" Jeannie asked.

"Until the boat wreck," I said quietly, finishing for him. For the first time, I realized Jack and Annette's deaths might not have been accidental.

Richard laid a twenty on the table and silently walked away.

Chapter Nineteen

"Emily!" Scud called from the front of the Twin Otter. I could barely hear him over the engines, and wasn't in the mood to try.

I wanted space to think. Privacy to reorganize my memories and move them around until they fit with Richard's new information. History demanded to be set right in my mind.

But instead, I was sandwiched between jumpers on the floor of the gutted plane, sitting underneath a bumper sticker stuck to the wall that said No Farting.

It was Sunday, the last day of the boogie. That night most people would leave, and probably take with them any chance I had to get answers. Trish Dalton was our only lead and I had to learn more about her. So I'd compartmentalized my feelings and manifested on her boyfriend's load.

"Emily!" Scud yelled again. "Get us some extra altitude!"

I checked my altimeter. We were passing through twelve thousand feet, nearing jump run. Skydivers near Scud laughed, but I didn't get the joke. I looked at them, confused.

Scud held his wrist-mounted altimeter overhead and pointed to it like a watch. He yelled again, "More altitude!"

Then he pantomimed raising his shirt to flash me.

I'd heard stories of women skydivers flashing the pilot to get an extra couple thousand feet of air. Whether this actually happened—or worked—I didn't know.

I flipped him off.

Booing and laughter erupted in the fuselage.

I thought about Trish and the similarities between Mattie's abduction and Casey's. My conspiracy theories seemed alternately plausible and insane.

Now there was a new, sickening question. Had Jack and Annette been murdered? The suggestion had me out of my head with grief and rage.

Linda, seated behind me, tapped my shoulder.

"Trish won't go for it when she's flying," she said. "The boys have tried to flash her, but they got nothin' she wants to see."

I turned around and looked past Scud, at the pilot's seat. Vince was flying today, the noise in his headset apparently shielding him from the nonsense. I wondered how many times he'd been flashed.

David was in front of me, near the door. In front of him, Rick was in the spotter's position. Everyone on board was in two neat rows, facing the door in the back of the plane. Each of us was wedged between the legs of the jumper behind us. Our seatbelts, which were actually more like floor-belts, since there were no seats, were all unfastened.

I stared at the back of David's helmet and thought about him and Trish. She wasn't working today. What was she doing instead? David was doing a four-way with Linda, Big Red, and me.

Vince let Rick know it was time for the spot. His group shuffled onto their knees, putting goggles into final positions and double-checking throw-out handles and chest straps.

"Door!" Rick yelled, and those of us near him yelled it again to make sure jumpers behind us heard.

Rick slid the Otter's door overhead like a garage door and frigid, deafening wind rushed inside. The rest of us moved into semi-standing positions and crouched under the low ceiling of the fuselage. Rick gave two heading corrections, both for five degrees left, and when he was satisfied, he climbed out and gripped the bar on the outside of the door while the rest of his group moved swiftly into position. With an efficient "Ready, Set,

Go," they dropped out of sight and the Otter lurched upward with its lighter load.

Our group was next. Big Red and David climbed out immediately, Big Red in the front-float position, David in the rear. I crouched beside Linda in the door, my left hand gripping Big Red's chest strap, my right clutching Linda's shoulder gripper.

She started the count.

On her Go, I left the Otter behind. A big planet holding all my unanswered questions was headed straight for me.

◇◇◇

"So, how long have you known Trish?" I asked David as he drove us into town. He'd volunteered to pick up lunches for the group, and I'd offered to give him a hand.

David did some mental arithmetic.

"Coming up on five months. She moved in after two." He looked at me sideways, like he thought I'd disapprove.

I shrugged. "Who's to argue with love? My friend got engaged on her third date."

"Yeah? How'd that work out?"

I thought of Jeannie's ex-husband, Travis, a fledgling car salesman who turned out to be so stupid he wouldn't have known a credit report if it stuck to the bottom of his shoe. "It didn't. Now she sleeps with men on the third date instead."

He laughed.

I picked up a photograph of David and Trish that was tucked in the dash. I could make out the scripted T on her wrist.

"I noticed Trish's tattoo the other day," I said. "I meant to ask her about it."

"She and her brother got those when their dad died," he said. "Their old man had the same one."

I thought about that.

"What's her brother like? You met him yet?"

David pulled into the parking lot of a strip mall offering Pizza Hut or Subway. He shook his head and seemed to struggle for words.

"He's got problems. In and out of trouble with police..."

He eased into a parking space. I wanted to hear more, but didn't want to interrogate him.

"They say every family has one," I said.

He smiled.

We got out of the car and I followed him toward the Subway.

"Mark's problem is serious," he confided. "Drugs."

He held the door for me at the sandwich shop and I stepped inside. A young Hispanic boy at a booth with his family said, "Coach Dave!"

His parents turned, and David said hello to everyone as we stepped in line. When we were away from the table, he explained how a friend roped him into helping with Little League. I glanced over my shoulder and overheard the boy tell his sister that Coach Dave was the "coolest one." It seemed high praise for a man accused of being a racist.

I couldn't concentrate on the overhead menu. Choices of breads and toppings were ridiculous compared to other matters struggling for attention in my mind. How had David gotten tied up with Trish? What was the deal with her drug-abusing brother? Was the brother the man I remembered from the day I found Mattie?

The wall clock near the cash register caught my eye. It was almost one o'clock. Most folks would leave the drop zone by seven or eight.

David reached into his jacket pocket for the list of orders. When he opened his hand I saw the wadded list and a tube of lip-gloss in his palm.

"Trish's." He shoved the lip-gloss back in the pocket. "She wears this jacket more than I do."

It was a simple brown bomber jacket; the leather had aged beautifully.

"I can see why."

"Gotta watch her though," he added, and pointed to a light spot on one elbow. "She set her arm in grease at the airport. The dry cleaning bill to get that out was huge."

I watched the girl behind the counter spoon meatballs onto a twelve-inch sub.

"Then last week she borrowed it," he continued, "and lost fifty bucks in jump tickets I'd stuffed in the pocket."

Chapter Twenty

I shoved a Subway sack into Jeannie's hand and motioned to an empty corner of the hangar. She followed me and we sat on worn carpet remnants spread over the cool concrete slab. I told her about David's missing jump tickets.

Her eyes widened. She didn't seem to notice she was squeezing her sandwich.

I extracted my own from its clear plastic bag and began to unwrap it. A breeze blew through the open doors and I tucked our napkins under my leg to stop them from blowing away.

"What'd Trish do with that kid?" I asked.

Jeannie looked over her shoulder to be sure no one was near. "That creepy guy, the one who caught you snooping...do you think he's in on it?"

I removed my wrapper and shoved it under my leg with the napkins.

"Craig Clement. I bet she got him this job. Look at the timeline. He gets hired, and two months later Casey's missing. I'm sure they could have planned it in two months."

Jeannie nodded. "I could plan a kidnapping in two months. Easy."

I looked at her. She probably thought she could train for a marathon in two months.

"Then there's David," I said, "Trish moved in with him three months ago, you know."

She raised her eyebrows. "No. I did not know. Add that jewel to the timeline." Jeannie pulled her sub from its bag and started unwrapping its paper.

The wind was blowing annoying wisps of hair around my face. I sighed and readjusted the elastic band that was supposed to be holding it back. "I hear you. But I don't think David's part of it. He wouldn't incriminate himself by mentioning those lost tickets."

I took a bite of my sandwich but was too distracted to taste it.

Jeannie made a quick inspection of the inside of her sub. "Maybe they don't know the police found a ticket."

I stopped chewing.

She continued, "David would think nothing of mentioning it then."

I imagined myself in his position.

"No," I said. "Trish would worry about where she lost those tickets. If he were in it with her, she'd warn him they could be at Casey's house. Then he'd never mention it."

Jeannie shrugged, apparently unconvinced.

"He works with at-risk kids, for crying out loud," I added. "And coaches Little League. Kids love him."

"Women liked Ted Bundy." She bit into her chicken and bacon sandwich.

We ate in silence for a while, thinking.

"What'd she do with Casey?" I asked again, so frustrated I nearly raised my voice.

Jeannie pulled a napkin from the stash under my knee and wiped her mouth. "Sold him, I think. Like that Shelton boy back home."

It was becoming difficult to separate the two cases. The couple in Austin I'd seen in the restaurant with Mattie was about to pay thirty grand to "adopt" him when I intervened. They couldn't be located at trial time. Without them or me, the case against Mattie's kidnapper disintegrated. Of course, I hadn't known that back then. In hindsight, the entire situation reeked of foul play. An uneasy feeling washed over me. I set my food down and closed my eyes.

Jeannie's hand closed over mine. I thought about what Richard said at breakfast and tried to assimilate it with what I remembered of that couple. Their disappearance, at the same time as my own, was beginning to seem too timely to be an unfortunate coincidence.

"Hang in there," Jeannie whispered, and scooted closer. She wrapped an arm around my shoulder. Tears squeezed past my lashes and dropped to my chin.

I leaned into her. "All I can think about anymore is how much I miss my little girl."

Someone shuffled up and stopped in front of us. I wiped my cheeks without looking up from the floor.

Jeannie sighed audibly. "What do you want?"

When there was no answer, I raised my head and was eye-level with hairy legs and a knee brace. Scud was looking down at us. His expression had none of the dalliance or humor I'd come to expect. Instead, he looked at me with what I interpreted as genuine concern.

"Didn't mean to butt in," he said quietly. "I'll catch up with you two later." He paused before leaving and added, "Emily, I'm real sorry about Annette."

He turned, and seemed to gauge who to drop in on next.

When he was gone, Jeannie said, "That was decent of him."

But as I watched him cross the room, I grew paranoid. I dropped my head into my hands.

"What is it?"

I stood, flustered. Napkins began to slide across the floor.

"I never told Scud her name."

"What?" Jeannie scrambled to her feet. She stomped napkins and gathered them into wads.

I left without her and stalked outside toward the dirt road. I needed to walk and think.

Soon, she caught up. "What'd you say?"

"Last night, Scud asked if I had kids. I told him about Annette, but I didn't say her name." I stopped walking and faced her. "Only Vince knows her name. So either Vince is a loudmouth or Scud's an eavesdropper."

Jeannie looked confused. She placed her hands on the outside of my shoulders and made sure she had my attention. "Honey, calm down. Don't work yourself up."

I studied her. "You don't believe me."

I shook her off and started walking again.

She didn't follow. Instead, she called from behind, "you have a lot on your mind. Maybe you told him and forgot."

The Otter's engines hummed overhead to my right. I turned to watch its approach, squinting at sun reflecting off its silver skin. Vince was inside at its controls. Had I overestimated him?

Jeannie was beside me again. "Let's talk about something else, okay?"

I looked from the plane to the horizon.

"Okay?" she asked again, and gave my ponytail a playful tug.

I groaned and began to walk.

"Let's think about Trish some more," she said. "Go over what else you know."

The gravel and dirt crunching under our shoes was louder than the airplane noise now. I didn't feel like talking. But Jeannie never required conversations to be two-sided.

She answered her own question. "Trish flies for the company Casey's dad worked for. She was fired from another job for using planes without permission."

I kicked a stone.

Jeannie continued, "Flight logs are missing...She's probably up to her old tricks, sneaking around with Rick's planes too. Shuttling stolen kids, I bet."

When I didn't respond, she said, "Well?"

"So she's using the planes," I snapped. "So what? Where's she taking them? When's she doing it? *How* is she doing it?"

My struggle to pull it together felt like I was failing the Sheltons, the Lyonses, and worst—maybe even my own husband and daughter.

Her expression morphed to indignation and she stopped. She planted one hand on a hip, and used the other to wave an admonishing finger at me.

"Look. I came down here to make sure you were okay. I helped you with Craig. Then I stood up to Richard. And even Farmer Freak over there," she gestured toward Cromwell's place, "didn't give me as much attitude as you."

I looked past her to Cromwell's farm. Another half-formulated thought swirled in my overloaded brain. When it culminated, the "click" I imagined might well have been audible.

"She's doing it at night."

Jeannie's scowl didn't soften, but she tilted her head. She wanted to hear me out.

I pointed over her shoulder toward Cromwell's land. "Your guy from *Deliverance* was complaining about plane noise, carrying on about how he couldn't get any peace, day or night. Right?"

She nodded.

"But Marie told me they don't do night jumps here anymore."

We stood in the middle of the dusty road and looked at each other, watching pieces fall into place in each other's minds.

◇◇◇

"I suppose it could be other planes from that airport," Richard said, when I brought him up to speed. I'd tugged my cell phone from my pocket as soon as Jeannie and I made amends. We were walking back to the hangar.

"Could be," I said, "But this airstrip looks more like a hobbyist's parking lot than anything else. The only planes in the air all week have been Rick's."

I studied the vacant metal buildings and hangars as we passed them. All were chained shut. One had a faded metal sign bolted to the door: *Man with shotgun guarding premises three nights each week. You guess which nights.*

No lights were on inside any of the buildings, and no cars were outside either. Small planes around them were all tied down. Grass stood tall around their landing gear, telling me they hadn't been moved for a while. What better place for criminals to set up shop?

I told Richard what David said about Trish's brother.

"I'll check the name Mark Dalton and cross-reference it with the restaurant in Austin," he said. "Let's see if Trish's brother is the manager you remember from Mattie's case."

"You got anything on Craig Clement?"

"Not yet. He's tough. I do have a good start on David Meyer, though. He has a government job, so there's a nice paper trail on him."

I filled Richard in about David's troubles at CPS.

"Hard to do much on a Sunday," he said. "I'll call tomorrow when folks are back at work."

I realized tomorrow was Monday. I was supposed to be back at my own desk at eight o'clock. That further soured my mood.

"Anything else?" he asked.

There was something else. Richard had played a part in setting Wesley Reed free and had inadvertently contributed to the catastrophe that broke my family. But his own family had been threatened and I should tell him I understood—even if I wasn't sure I could forgive. But this didn't seem the right time.

"No," I said. "I'll talk to you tomorrow."

I closed my phone and turned to Jeannie. "Got a few problems."

"Don't we all."

"Tomorrow I might get fired. And the boogie's almost over, so tonight we've got no place to stay."

Chapter Twenty-one

That evening there was a lull while the plane got refueled and Vince took a dinner break. It was the first chance I'd had to speak with him alone. We sat on the wooden Cessna mock-up in the training room adjoining the hangar, and he unwrapped a Butterfinger and popped the top on a can of Sprite.

"I fixed that guitar string you broke at the beach," he said.

Windsocks swelled and deflated on their posts in the landing field. The sun crept toward the horizon, but was still high enough to warm my face and arms. Skydivers with nothing else to do tossed a Frisbee. Another group drove golf balls.

"Figure we'll squeeze in one more load, then call it good," he continued. "Wanna get some coffee afterward? I'll even let you play for me."

It sounded better than what I had planned.

"Can I take a rain check? Tonight's not good."

Vince snapped his fingers, like he'd remembered something.

"Right," he said. "Your job."

"What?"

"The new NASA job starts tomorrow. Red mentioned it. Good luck."

Lying to Vince felt unnatural and wrong. I looked at him. He tipped his Sprite to offer a sip. I shook my head.

"I have an early morning too," he said. "Taking the Otter back to Tulsa."

I wanted to get at what was nagging me, but felt like a big fat hypocrite. Even if Vince had broken my confidence, it would be minor compared to the pack of lies I'd told. Or, more accurately, the pack of truths I'd withheld.

I asked anyway.

"Vince, last night in the parking lot...Did you mention our talk to anybody?"

"Of course not," he said. "Why?"

I believed him.

"It's nothing," I said. Speculating about how Scud knew Annette's name might make me look like a head case. "All that stuff's private to me, that's all."

He placed a hand on my back and made small, comforting circles before patting it lightly and drawing away.

Someone outside ran to catch the Frisbee, reached too far, and tripped. He rolled in the grass and rebounded to his feet.

I could tell without looking that Vince was staring at me.

"I'm not starting a job at NASA tomorrow," I said. "I don't even live here. I came to help a friend, and soon I'll go home."

I waited, my hands in my lap, legs dangling over the edge of the make-believe airplane door. I stared at the floor and waited for what he might say or do.

Finally, he asked, "Where's home?"

His voice was quiet. I thought I heard it catch.

The door to the packing area swung open on our right. Marie charged in.

"There you are!" I thought she'd come to put Vince back to work. It turned out she was looking for me.

"I'm putting an eight-way together for the sunset load," she said. "You in?"

I looked at Vince and imagined the questions he must have, what he must think of me.

I nodded to answer Marie's question and slid off the mock-up. Vince stepped down too.

"Ready, big guy?" she asked him. "Load ten's on a thirty minute call."

He chucked his empty can into a metal trash barrel and its clang was harsh and angry.

We followed Marie to the picnic bench outside where the other six jumpers for her eight-way had gathered. Vince walked straight past us, toward the plane.

◇◇◇

An hour later, I sat with Jeannie on the threadbare sofa in the drop zone's office and we flipped through Marie's Yellow Pages. Jeannie wanted to get a motel room near the beach. With the boogie over, Rick and Marie would be locking their doors tonight. If I got caught sleeping at the airport on a weeknight, that would look downright weird. Camping wasn't an option, and the long drive back to a Houston hotel didn't make sense.

I dialed a motel in Freeport. Jeannie wouldn't agree to a non-smoking room, so I booked a room for each of us. Then I phoned Richard to tell him where I'd be. He had news.

"My buddy checked out the restaurant where Mattie was recovered," he said. Richard still had connections in the Austin police department—leftover detective friends from before I more or less got him fired. It hadn't been long after I'd voiced my suspicions that Richard was out of a job.

"There's no employment record for Mark Dalton," he said. "When you were there, the manager was Mark Townsend. A waitress remembers him, *and* the tattoo you described."

"Townsend? But that's—"

"The other pilot's name. I know."

Vince.

Richard went on. "He's in the personnel list you gave me. Vince Townsend, staff since…" Papers rustled on Richard's end. "It'll be three years next month. What do you know about this guy?"

What did I know? For starters, my cover was blown. Could Vince really be related to the tattooed man from the restaurant? It didn't seem to fit.

I forced myself not to think about the sick feeling in my stomach. "Could the name be a coincidence?"

It seemed impossible that Vince could be involved with Trish and Mark and their black-market babies.

"No," Richard said. "I had records faxed over. Walt and Caroline Townsend of Austin, Texas, had two kids—Mark in 1966 and Patricia in 1968. George and Amelia Townsend, also of Austin, had Vincent in1971. Walt and George were brothers, both now deceased."

I struggled to get my head around what the new facts meant for the case.

"Patricia married Jason Dalton in 1996, divorced him in 1999. Social Security records show she kept the name."

Jesus. Why hadn't anyone here mentioned they were cousins? Why hadn't *Vince* mentioned it?

"There's more. Once I had the right name, I ran Mark's criminal history. His drug problems are the tip of the iceberg. He moves around a lot, usually to big cities. Passes his time in ghettos and slums. Seems he uses cocaine and meth to extort information from junkies."

"What information does he want from—" I lowered my voice. "What information does he want from junkies?"

"They tell him where the babies are."

"Excuse me?" Richard's story was rapidly becoming incomprehensible.

"San Antonio PD recently had a man in custody willing to trade information about his seller in exchange for a lighter sentence. According to him, Mark's standing offer in the hood is 'drugs for names.' He wants names of users with small kids."

"Why?"

"I have it from Narcotics, these people get pretty messed up when they use. They'll leave their kids with anyone...strangers... if it means they can leave to get a fix."

The connection eluded me.

"We think Mark Townsend wants babies who won't be missed for a while."

Amazing—but I couldn't see how it fitted into Mattie's abduction. My friends Keith and Nora Shelton had had no drug issues. What about Casey's parents?

Chapter Twenty-two

Shortly after eleven, Jeannie was on her third margarita and I'd switched to Aquafina and taken it To Go. Last I'd seen, she was nestled at the bar with a couple of guys on either side, watching college basketball, eating pretzels, and swearing at the flat screen TV in a hole-in-the-wall bar we'd found on East Broad. There were two men, one Jeannie, but as far as I was concerned, the guys were outnumbered.

I walked the beach alone, my socks shoved in my sneakers, carrying my shoes in one hand as I stepped ankle-deep through frigid waves. Unable to think clearly, doubting my instincts, I trudged over the sand listening to waves and gulls and noise in my head, smelling the stale aroma of dead fish, and wishing I had a jacket.

My thoughts returned to Vince. I'd misjudged the only man I'd allowed myself to care for since Jack. Or, maybe I'd only misjudged a man I thought I could care for eventually. After all, we'd spent so little time together, really, and time spent together under contrived circumstances probably only counted as half of actual time, anyway.

But, while Karen Lyons had identified Trish, and Mark had an incriminating rap sheet, the only case against Vince was that he hadn't mentioned being related to either one. In particular, it seemed strange he hadn't told me his cousin worked at the same drop zone. Then again, he didn't know I knew her. I remembered the cold look they'd exchanged the day Vince came to jump with me. Being on bad terms could explain the omission. If Vince had nothing to do with Trish and Mark's schemes, maybe I hadn't misjudged anything.

Either way, he knew I wasn't who I'd pretended to be, and now I was anxious and preoccupied with whether Trish and Clement knew that too.

Mark Townsend was a real problem. He was solidly linked to Mattie Shelton's abduction, and peripherally linked to Casey's by his relationship with Trish. It was Mark I'd asked for help in the restaurant the day I found Mattie. Mark was the manager who'd delayed the tab to give the police time to arrive. But, when they finally came, the bogus adoption agent was gone. Surely, Mark had arranged that getaway.

Had it also been Mark who'd threatened me? Broken into my house? Played the trick that prevented my deposition from making it to court?

It couldn't all be him. How many were with him? At least enough people to work in two states at the same time, maybe more. I wondered whether I was uncovering a sinister conspiracy or deteriorating into a frantic and paranoid nut.

Later, in my motel room, I drew a bath and undressed, feeling slightly flushed. My clammy skin and warm face could be the work of the margaritas, I told myself, or maybe the result of coming in from chilly night air.

Richard said he hadn't put much stock into the threats he'd received until the boat wreck. Thinking of that again nauseated me, and I felt warmer still. I sat on the edge of the tub and watched it fill, steamy water rushing from the tap, crashing into the basin, filling and filling. I focused on my breathing, tried to get a grip.

One point tormented me, clawing and scratching past Vince and Richard, and Mark and Trish. I knew what it would do to me, and tried to stop it, but couldn't.

Only one casket was laid out at my family's memorial. Annette's tiny body was never recovered. If Mark Townsend's people were behind the boat wreck, was it possible she was alive? Had she been sold over pancakes at some roadside diner as Mattie had so nearly been?

I fell to my knees on the cold, cracked tiles of the motel bathroom and vomited into the toilet. And when my stomach was empty, the tears wouldn't stop.

◇◇◇

I sat on the side of my bed, wrapped in a towel, and stared at Annette through the opaque sleeve of a photo booklet I'd pulled from my wallet. TV noise carried through the wall, and I was jealous that my neighbor could relax and I could not. It was Monday now, 12:09. I kissed her picture and tucked it away.

In a few hours, Vince would take the borrowed plane back to Tulsa. If I met him at the airport, I might be able to figure his role in all this. But my fake job started this morning. That stupid lie ended my tenure at the drop zone. Even though Vince knew the truth, I couldn't show my face there again until the weekend without drawing suspicion from the others.

The phone call I'd overheard Thursday suggested Craig would be up to something, somewhere, in less than two hours. I suspected he and Trish might have a secret flight planned before the Otter's return. With its larger cargo capacity, I reasoned, Trish might find it more desirable than the tiny Cessna. She and Craig could shuttle even more stolen kids.

But how many children could they possibly have at any given time? I looked at the clock again. There was time to find out.

I phoned Richard but got no answer. So I pilfered through my dirty laundry—all my clothes were dirty now. I pulled my only pair of jeans and my warmest sweatshirt from the pile and vowed to find a Laundromat tomorrow. When I stepped into my jeans, the cuffs were still folded from my walk on the beach with Vince. A mental picture of him lobbing the ball for Cindy came to mind, and I shook it off.

As I pulled on my socks and shoes, I felt a little relieved Richard hadn't answered. I was having doubts about including him. He was an ex-cop. I knew he'd involve the police. And I was holding out hope for Vince. I wanted to understand his place in all this before I potentially got him arrested. More importantly, a bust gone wrong would be the last I'd see of Trish and Craig. If they disappeared, so would any chance of ever finding out if my little girl might have survived.

◇◇◇

At the dirt road leading to the airport, I switched off my headlights. Twice, I veered into grass because it was nearly impossible to see. After passing two small metal shacks, I eased behind a larger one. When I was sure my car couldn't be seen from the road, I put it in park and killed the ignition. The silence that enveloped my car was so unnerving I locked my doors.

I peered through my windows. The metal surface of a neglected shack was straight ahead. It was faded and partially rusted, but I knew that from memory only; it was too dark to see those details now. I checked my rearview mirror and the driver and passenger windows and found the same thing everywhere: black.

My GPS watch was strapped to my wrist, my cell phone was set to vibrate, and this time I'd remembered a flashlight. A car passed on the highway and faded into silence. The crickets were calling again, probably warning me to go home.

I stepped from the car and carefully shut my door before leaning on the car to call the motel. Jeannie wasn't back in her room yet. Or, more likely, she was back in her room, but not alone. The voicemail system prompted for a message.

"I'm at the drop zone," I whispered. "Thought I should mention it incase the bogey man gets me. Which one did you end up with?"

Then, regretting that I'd come alone, I tried Richard again. Still no answer.

Something howled. I vaguely recalled that coyotes live in Texas and snapped my phone closed.

The moon formed a thin silver crescent, the shape of a fingernail clipping and just as useless. If there were clouds, I couldn't see them. The road was a straight shot to the hangar, but I was too afraid to risk being seen. So, I pulled my jacket zipper to my chin and turned toward a field I knew was behind me but couldn't see to save my life.

The flashlight might give me away, so I decided to make my way in the dark using my GPS. Grass was waist high and wet with dew. It brushed my jeans and jacket and made them damp. By my estimation, which was really only a hopeful guess, the hangar was a quarter mile ahead. I changed screens on my watch. It was ten after one.

The crunch of tires on gravel sent me to my hands and knees as headlights swept over the field. Through the grass, I watched a vehicle cruise up the dusty road beyond the out buildings faster than any I'd seen all week. Its brake lights flared when it got to the drop zone hangar. I'd gotten my bearings, but I wasn't alone. Nor was I sure what to do.

I waited for the car's lights to turn off before I stood. Mud and vegetation had caked to my palms, and my jeans felt cold on my knees. I continued toward the end of the field.

The overgrowth I'd planned to use for cover ended several hundred feet short of the hangar. Ahead to my left, I could make out its looming shape.

Lights turned on throughout the packing area and office and small strips of illumination escaped from the building's crevices. The giant metal door on the other side rumbled open. Someone was bringing out the plane.

From my hiding spot in the tall grass, I couldn't see the back door sliding open, but the landing field behind it become gradually washed in soft yellow light. When the door was fully opened, the air fell eerily silent again.

I crouched and moved forward. When I came to the edge of the grass, about a hundred feet of clearing separated me from the parking lot. I made a run for it.

Another set of headlights swung onto the dirt road behind me.

I didn't stop running until I reached the far end of the hangar. I rounded the corner and stooped at its base to catch my breath. I peered around the front, and watched a fifteen-foot U-Haul drive around the opposite side of the building, straight to the back. I didn't think I'd been seen.

When I peeked around the rear, the U-Haul was backing up to the hangar near the picnic table and the Coke machine. It stopped, and two men in coveralls stepped out. One went to the back of the truck and raised its door. I couldn't see what was inside. The men disappeared into the hangar, and muffled voices carried out into the field.

The only way to see inside the building would be from a position in the landing field, but it was illuminated now. It would be better to get inside the training room and listen through the wall.

I peered around the corner again. Both exterior doors to the training room were closed. The large, enormous one was out of the question. Its smaller, standard counterpart was about thirty feet away.

I took a deep breath and scurried to it. The doorknob was cold in my hand, and when I twisted it, the knob turned. I pulled it open and ducked inside, working hard to control my breathing.

Inside, I stood paralyzed, grasping the knob behind me. A rapid series of beeps startled me.

It was my stupid watch. The GPS satellite signal had been lost inside the metal building and my watch wanted to make sure all the criminals in the next room knew it. I mashed buttons until one silenced the alarm, then I waited. No one came.

I turned on my flashlight and aimed it toward the wall that separated me from them. Garage equipment and rows of stacked plastic chairs cluttered its entire length. The Cessna mock-up where I'd sat with Vince was to my right. A small window in the interior door let in a little light from the room that housed the Otter and, now, those here to use it.

Voices resonated on the other side of the wall in erratic bursts. I inched closer to the door to listen. Then I froze.

Beside me, a training harness swayed almost imperceptibly. Before I could fully register its significance, a powerful arm closed around me from behind and a hand clamped over my mouth so hard my face felt bruised.

"Don't make a sound," a man whispered. "For your own good."

I kicked backward and tried to scream. His grip tightened. I tried to elbow his ribs, but his grip on me was solid. He shuffled me forward, directly toward the wall, and pressed his weight into me until my cheek was flush with a cool, steel beam and I couldn't move.

He whispered again. "I won't hurt you, but be quiet. Understand?"

I tried to swallow but my mouth was dry. I stared straight ahead and waited.

He took the flashlight from my hand.

"Quiet," he repeated. I nodded, aware I was trembling. A tear fell into the space between my cheek and the steel.

He removed his weight from my head, but not my body. I turned and recognized the rat features of Craig Clement. He stared at me with unspoken warning. Then, still leaning heavily into me, he reached one-handed for something I couldn't see. I feared it was a gun.

Instead he produced some kind of leather wallet and held it in front of my face, pulling it backward slowly until I focused on a headshot of him below the words Federal Bureau of Investigation.

When he released his weight, it was all I could do to keep from collapsing onto the floor.

"I checked you out," he whispered. "You've got nothing to do with NASA."

"I've got nothing to do with any of this—"

He held a finger up.

If Clement was a good guy, who was helping Trish?

He put a hand on each of my shoulders and eased me forward, away from the beam.

"You've got more to do with this than you think," he whispered.

He positioned himself behind me and directed me through the training room.

"I think I know what happened on Lake Erie," he said.

Before I could speak, he put a hand over my mouth again and shushed me. He maneuvered me around hardware and lumber until we were at the outermost wall of the training room. I could vaguely make out the contours of an overhead gantry in front of us. A row of harnesses hung from it. Clement parted them like curtains and nodded for me to step into the shadows beyond.

"Stay here until I come for you. No matter what."

"But—"

"No matter *what.*"

When I was hidden, he pointed to the floor, directing me to sit. Then he passed me the flashlight and let the harness hang freely again, closing me in the dark corner. I sat. The cement floor was frigid under my jeans. I listened for more instructions, but none came. All I could see of him were his sneakers, padding away almost silently.

I pressed the Indiglo button on my watch. One twenty-six. Clement was somewhere in the shadows to my right, presumably back at his listening post by the door. How long had he been here? What was going on in the next room? And what did the FBI know about my family's boat wreck on Lake Erie? I considered creeping over to beg him for answers. Then light spilled into the training room. Clement had opened the door.

Chapter Twenty-three

The door clicked shut behind Clement and sealed the training room in shadows. I expected a commotion on the other side of the door, but heard nothing. What was he doing out there? I couldn't stand it. Could. Not. Stand it!

Using my flashlight, I made my way across the room. Dim light filtered through the window in the interior door separating me from the main area of the hangar. I moved toward that window and straightened slowly, trying to glimpse what was happening inside.

In the packing area, the Otter's nose pointed to my left toward the landing field out back. The door I'd jumped from earlier was practically right in front of me, a set of portable stairs pressed flush against its frame.

The U-Haul, backed up to the hangar's huge open door, held several wooden crates the size of refrigerator boxes inside.

Everything else was as it had been earlier—jumpsuits on hooks, gear on pegs. I spotted a duffle bag at the foot of the portable stairs and heard the office door swing open on the other side of the plane. I ducked and listened.

"What are the drop conditions?" It was a woman.

It sounded like Trish.

"Southeast wind, twenty knots. Gusts to thirty. Seas four to six feet. Hey, give me a hand with this, man."

It was quiet for a moment, then the same voice, a man's, asked, "Trish, where the hell's that boyfriend of yours? No, dude…this one, over here."

A shot of adrenaline hit me like a punch.

Jeannie was right—Trish wasn't working alone. By the sounds of it, she had more help than we'd figured. I remembered our talk and felt like a fool for defending David.

"Son of a bitch," someone muttered. "I cut myself."

"I'll get the kit," Trish said.

Carefully, I stole another glance. A man in coveralls stood near the U-Haul, inspecting his palm. A thin streak of red coursed over the back of his hand. Trish, in jeans and David's bomber jacket, walked toward the office, her back to me, and disappeared behind the nose of the plane. The other man in coveralls stood in the back of the truck, trying to maneuver a dolly under one large crate. A third man sat in the cockpit; the pilot's door wide open at his side. From my vantage point behind him, all I could see were his elbow and shoulder. A clipboard flashed near his arm and disappeared.

Where was Clement? Who were these people? I moved away from the window.

"Suck it up, Decker. We don't have all damn night," someone said. A moment later, he added, "I mean it, Trish. Where is he?"

I peeked through the glass again and watched Trish pass a small metal first aid kit to the bleeding man before pulling a phone from her pocket and flipping it open.

Almost immediately, a series of rings broke the silence in the training room. I pressed a hand over the phone in my pocket and, smothering it, darted away from the door. Then I remembered—my phone was set to vibrate.

I swept my flashlight beam around the room and froze when it revealed a figure standing near the wall. At first, all I could make out was a man's form, and the glint of a phone in his hand. But then I snapped the light toward his face. Scud raised an arm to block his eyes.

I thought I'd be sick.

"She's calling *you*?"

He reached behind his back with his free hand and produced a pistol. He began walking toward me with the gun in his hand, swinging it casually at his side.

"I'm here," he said into the phone. "And heads up, you've got company out there. I'm on my way."

He snapped the phone closed and shoved it in his pocket, never taking his eyes off me.

"Recognized your name right off, but wasn't sure it was you until you mentioned your kid." He stopped for a moment, studied me. "Shame you're so pretty. I hate waste."

He started toward me again. It seemed the closer he got, the faster he walked, despite his limp.

"Sorry, sweetheart. She hates when I'm late." He raised the gun.

As he closed in, I aimed my light straight at his eyes. He flinched, and I rushed forward and tried a front kick. My foot connected with the underside of his forearm and knocked away the gun. It hit the slab with a smack. Scud entangled the leg I'd used to kick and shoved it upward until I fell backward on the concrete. I broke the fall with my hands, but lost my flashlight. It rolled to the base of the metal wall and barely lit the area around us. When I got my feet under me, I saw Scud retrieve the gun from the floor.

Two shots rang out from the main part of the hangar.

I lunged toward Scud before he could take aim and grabbed his hand and wrenched it toward me. I bit the meaty part of his thumb as hard as I could, forcing my teeth into flesh until I tasted the metallic tang of blood. The gun clacked on the concrete beside my knee. I reached for it, but Scud closed a fist over my hair and yanked my head backward so my grasp came up short. I managed to kick the gun and heard it slide toward the Cessna mock-up.

I twisted under his grip until I was off my knees, then reared up and smashed the top of my head into his chin. His teeth crunched. It felt like a hammer had struck my skull.

Another round fired on the other side of the door.

Scud pulled at my jacket and closed me in a headlock from behind. Then, he wrapped a leg around my shin and pushed forward until we both fell to the floor, belly down. The impact forced the air from my lungs. I tried to twist away, and freed my upper body, but he stopped me with another violent jerk on my hair. Then he grabbed my shoulder with fingers that felt like talons and pushed me onto my back, where he pinned me under his weight again.

He kneeled over me and pressed both of his hands into my throat. I thrashed and kicked until my eyes and neck throbbed with pressure.

I dug my nails into his wrists and pried. I couldn't breathe. If only I could reach the gun. A block of wood. Anything.

I had an idea, or at least what would have to pass for one.

Letting go of Scud's wrists was hard to do. As soon as I released, his clutch tightened and I felt faint.

I reached for the seat of my jeans and fumbled for the opening to my back pocket. Snaking my fingers into the fold, I dug until I felt the coil I was looking for, then hooked my finger around it and pulled it to my belly. Above me, Scud's weight shifted as he tried to see what I was doing.

I had Vince's broken high E, the thinnest steel string on a guitar, and I counted on it to deliver a sting. I wound it around my fingers in the narrow space between our bodies. Then I raised it to his wrist and slashed upward and sideways with all the strength I had left.

"Damn it!" He winced enough for me to steal a gulp of air. It was enough.

I adjusted my grip on the string and tried again. This time I thrust my chest and shoulders upward when I felt resistance on the string.

He reeled off me, squeezing his wrist. I drove my foot into his bad knee, smashing with all the strength I had. It buckled, and I scrambled, crawling for the gun a yard away.

I reached for it. Scud gripped my ankle and pulled my leg backward with a determined jerk.

My chest hit the floor as I closed a hand over the pistol's long barrel. I pulled it with me as Scud dragged me backward. Something seared into my calf, and I yelled out from the pain. I collapsed on my side, and glanced toward the door. Surely someone had heard. I wondered if that someone would be on my side or Scud's. He lunged toward me again. I rolled to my back and aimed for his chest.

When I squeezed the trigger, a muffled *fffi* sounded. Scud's shoulder flinched backward and spun him to the floor. He tried to get up. I shot him again.

He collapsed on the slab, motionless.

I scooted to the flashlight, picked it up, and swung the beam to Scud's body. There was a hunting knife on the floor behind him, its awful blade wet with my blood. I turned the beam onto my leg. The denim covering my wound was dark and warm. I held the flashlight beneath my chin and took off my belt. I tied it in a crude knot above the gash and limped toward the door.

Through its window, I saw the men in coveralls disappear around the nose of the plane and heard the thump of the office door closing. In front of me, the Otter's fuselage had been fully loaded with the wooden crates from the truck. They were stacked horizontally, nearly to the plane's ceiling. Only a few square feet of unused space remained in its tail. I decided to find out what Trish was hauling and closed a hand around the doorknob.

But as I pushed the door open, I spotted Clement on the far side of the plane, near the office. He was facedown in a puddle of blood that had spilled from his chest or abdomen, I couldn't tell which. I concentrated on his back and noticed a subtle rise and fall.

I stepped back into the dark training room and pulled my phone from my pocket. It wasn't until I saw the phone in my hand that I realized I was shaking. I told the 9-1-1 operator to send an ambulance to Gulf Coast Skydiving, and added that the police and FBI should come too. I dropped Clement's name and said he'd been shot but was still breathing. Then I hung up. I had to see inside the crates before Trish's people came back.

When I stepped out into the packing area, it was all I could do not to kneel beside Clement and beg for what he knew about my family. But he'd been shot too close to the office. There was no way to get to him without being seen.

I winced when I climbed the portable stairs leading to the Otter's open jumpers' door, but I got inside quickly. I stayed low and fumbled with a latch on the nearest crate. It popped open.

Three others remained. Once opened, maybe I'd know what was going on.

I popped the second latch. Something inside might lead to Casey.

Maybe even to answers about Annette.

The office door swung open. I crouched and froze.

Castors squealed in the packing area, followed by the rhythmic clang of something being wheeled up a loading ramp. I listened while the back door of the U-Haul slid down and was latched into place.

Heavy footsteps reverberated through the room, growing louder as their owner drew near. I squeezed into a narrow gap between the far wall of the fuselage and the wooden boxes that had been crammed inside.

"Decker, what's this?" The speaker seemed suspicious.

My hand went to my pocket. I wondered if I'd dropped something.

"Not mine," Decker answered. "Maybe the Fed's?"

Silence followed.

"Check your shoes."

It hit me: they'd found blood. Had I bled a trail through the Otter? I applied pressure to my leg and waited.

"My bad," I heard. "It's me. Must've walked through it." Then, louder, he added, "Trish! Kurt! All yours."

The portable stairs scraped something as they were pulled away. I started to panic. What if I couldn't get off the plane?

Failing to include Richard was proving to be a very stupid mistake.

An engine started, the one to the moving truck, and my breath quickened as its hum faded.

Then the office door pushed open and smacked shut. A moment later, the plane bobbled as people climbed in through the pilot and co-pilot doors. Trish was talking.

"He said he was here, and now he won't answer his phone. You boys get us on our way, then have a look around. If we don't leave now, we'll miss the drop."

Someone rolled down the jumpers' door on the side of the plane. I felt hot. Burning spasms shot through my calf.

A new engine rumbled. It was the tow tractor, here to pull us to the field. The plane lurched forward and we rolled over a bump. I hoped it wasn't Clement.

When the Otter's engines whirred to life, I checked my watch—1:48 a.m. We accelerated, bumping over pits and mounds on our way down the grass runway. The wheels touched off and the nose inclined, and I expected crates to topple over me, but they didn't. I could look through a window, but not well enough to see below.

We banked hard to the right, and shortly afterward, we banked right again. Trish was heading west.

Chapter Twenty-four

Fifteen minutes later, my main concern was the throbbing, stinging gash in my calf. I needed to stretch and check my leg.

The cabin was unlighted and loud with the humming of twin engines. Trish and Kurt, whoever he was, might have been talking. I couldn't have heard a word over the noise. That was partly good because I didn't think they couldn't hear me scooting around either.

The Otter's cabin was almost twenty feet long with the jumpers' door located near the back. Trish's men had stowed their crates in the usable cabin volume between the cockpit area and the door, but several feet of empty space remained in the tail. Trish and her co-pilot could never see me back there, even if there were light, because the wooden boxes took up most of the cabin's height and width. I'd have to move slowly though, so they'd attribute any resulting trim adjustments to ordinary gusts or turbulence. Thankfully, the Otter was a large enough aircraft that its center of gravity would be unaffected by my maneuvering, as long as I moved smoothly.

I inched through the gap between the side of the fuselage and a row of crates, and headed toward the tail. When I got to the back of the plane I stayed low and stretched. I rolled up my pant leg and twisted to have a look at the back of my calf, but it was impossible to see in the dark. I ran a finger along the wound and was surprised it was only about an inch long.

Its depth worried me more, but I wasn't going to poke around to get an estimate on that. The opening was wet and sticky. At least the bleeding seemed to have slowed. I reapplied the belt and took a moment to think.

If my abbreviated 9-1-1 call was successful in getting police to the airport, authorities could be there now. They'd discover Clement and Scud, and eventually, I assumed, my car. Tags would be traced to Richard, who could have no idea about any of this.

The engines were loud enough I could probably make a call from my spot in the tail without being overheard in the cockpit, but I was reluctant to chance it. I sent a text message to Richard instead and briefly summarized my mess, making sure to include the GPS coordinates from my watch.

Next was 9-1-1, but since texting wouldn't work there I actually placed the call. I repeated my coordinates several times, only to hear some variant of, "I can't hear you, ma'am" or "Are you still there?" I couldn't risk speaking any louder, and eventually gave up. I slipped the phone into my pocket.

My thoughts returned to what I'd overheard about the drop conditions. Whatever we were hauling wasn't going to land with the plane. That presented another problem because somebody had to make the drops. Eventually, Kurt would probably venture to the back of the plane and unload whatever cargo was onboard. When he discovered me, he'd probably try to force me out the door with whatever was in the crates.

I took a deep breath, feeling the total weight of the situation for the first time. My interest in the flight didn't stop at mysterious cargo or its potential link to missing kids. What drove me onto the plane were questions about Jack and Annette. Clement's reference to "what really happened on Lake Erie" confirmed it was more than an accident as I'd believed for the last four years.

Hidden from Trish and Kurt, I scooted into a corner and leaned back to rest while I figured what to do. An object loomed where I'd expected emptiness. I ran a palm over a solid fabric surface and it didn't take long to identify the straps and ribbing of a parachute system. I felt along the floor for goggles or a helmet, but found only the gritty surface of well worn carpet. The parachute was probably insurance for Kurt. If I were standing in an open aircraft door shoving large amounts of contraband overboard, I'd want a rig too.

It solved one problem. I'd use the parachute to get off the plane before I was found. The question was when to do it.

The Otter wasn't pressurized, so we wouldn't exceed twelve or thirteen thousand feet. It wasn't how high we might fly that worried me, it was how low. Lower jumps meant less room for error. Without an altimeter, my GPS offered the only way to know how high we were. Right now, Trish was flying at eleven thousand feet. A momentary sensation of heaviness against the floor told me she was still climbing.

The drop conditions had been said to include four to six foot seas. That meant open water—a perilous skydive in daylight, a deadly one at night.

There was no way to know if the drop would occur in minutes or hours. Either way, I'd have to bail before we got too low or went over open water. The trick would be timing an exit as close to the drop as possible before conditions got any worse. If I could manage that, at least I could get the authorities in the ballpark of Trish's rendezvous point.

I shifted to my knees, careful to stay low, and stared out the window into blackness below. Distant lights, small as crumbs, were aligned in alternately random and ordered patterns, and as I took in what little view the night offered, I felt an adrenaline surge—the bad kind. The kind that told me I'd really screwed up.

Only five night jumps were under my belt, all planned in advance and executed under controlled conditions—full moons, bright landing fields, and lighted altimeters. I'd carried a flashlight to check my canopy, and worn a strobe light to make myself visible to other skydivers and planes. Tonight, every factor I could think of was against me, right down to the unfamiliar rig.

If I could eavesdrop, I might learn something about the drop. Maybe I could determine how much time was left. Maybe they'd talk about the dubious cargo.

On hands and knees, I crawled through the passage I'd used as a hiding place. It opened in a tight space behind Kurt's seat on the right side of the plane. He was directly in front of me, but all I could see of him was the green band of a headset spanning a patch of dark hair.

Beside him, Trish was at the controls, speaking into a microphone attached to her own headset. When her mouth stopped moving, Kurt nodded and moved forward in his seat, reaching for something, I supposed. They were talking all right, but I wouldn't hear any of it.

A duffel bag was wedged in the narrow space between their seats. It was the bag I'd seen on the portable steps leading into the fuselage. I asked myself what sort of things criminals might carry in a bag like that. Drugs? Weapons?

Hell, maybe a clean shirt and stick of deodorant. In any case, I wanted a peek inside the bag. Its contents might clue me in to whatever I'd unwittingly signed up for. But the duffel was too close to them for me to risk taking it, so I backed into my hiding spot again and debated what to do.

Was it more important to figure out what was in the crates, what was in the bag, or to learn the drop location? The way I saw things, I could only do one. Opening a crate or snatching the bag would give me away and I'd have to bail immediately; there'd be no time to search both. If I jumped, I'd never find out where the plane was headed. If I stayed on board until the plane started its descent, I'd have an idea about the drop location, but no idea what Trish was hauling. The questions were infuriating.

Staying onboard seemed riskiest. Kurt might unbuckle anytime and head my way to make the drop. The longer I waited, the closer we got to whatever body of water Trish had in mind. My anxiety over an unplanned night jump was nothing compared to that of opening over water.

I backed my way out of the little corridor. In the tail of the plane, I tried to organize. I zipped the jacket pocket that had my cell phone. Then I maneuvered into the rig, pulling its shoulder straps over my jacket and trying to smooth fabric that wanted to bunch at my sides. No telling what sort of aerodynamic nightmare the unconventional attire would cause in freefall, but I didn't suppose it mattered.

I checked our altitude again. Twelve thousand feet. It occurred to me I could grab a duffel bag in seconds, but had no idea how long it might take to wrestle the lid off a crate. So I decided to go for the bag.

I squeezed through the narrow space that led to the front of the plane. Passage was more challenging with the rig on my back. Each time my foot flexed, no matter how slightly, shooting pain radiated from my calf and I imagined my wound stretching and tearing. I breathed deeply to work through it.

In the cockpit, Trish was watching something out the window to her left. Kurt craned his neck to see, and then, apparently frustrated, turned to the right to look out his own window. His shoulder was only a few feet in front me, and I watched the top of his head press into the window glass. He was looking for something below.

I leaned into the open space behind their seats, closed my hand around the nylon strap of the bag, and eased it backward. I pulled the bag into my hiding spot and pressed backward through the corridor as quickly as I could.

In my spot in back, I double checked my chest strap, cinched my leg straps, and hooked the duffel's nylon handles into the crook of my elbow.

I ran a hand along the crates and let them lead me to the door. My fingers passed over a metal latch, and I hesitated. It was the latch on the lid of the crate I'd opened before take-off. Through the clearance between the tops of the crates and the ceiling of the cabin, I could barely make out Trish and Kurt in the cockpit. I set the duffle bag at my feet and felt along the edge of the lid for the remaining latches. Cupping my hands over them one at a time, I popped them all open.

Kurt shifted, but didn't turn around. I pressed the bottom ridge of the lid upward with the heels of my palms. The wood flexed, but didn't budge. I felt along the perimeter until I found additional latches on the right and left sides and then I flipped those open too.

This time when I pressed upward, the lid rose. I lifted it seven or eight inches, until its ridge touched the ceiling of the cabin, and peered inside. It was too dark to see anything. I held the lid with one hand and reached inside the box with the other, patting its contents with outstretched fingers, trying to figure out what I was touching. Plastic. Plastic wrapped around something hard.

"Hey!"

I looked over the lid. Kurt was out of his seat, sliding toward my passageway.

"Who the hell are you?" he shouted.

Without warning, the plane lurched downward, sending Kurt and me to the ceiling. My shoulder barreled into the corner of the crate lid I'd been supporting. Kurt was unfazed by our sudden weightlessness. He pushed off the ceiling, continuing toward me.

The plane leveled.

My feet found the floor again and the wooden lid collapsed into position, wedging my upper arm. I jerked it loose and grabbed the duffel, pushing its straps into the crook of my elbow.

Kurt rounded the corner to my hiding spot as I struggled to raise the jumpers' door. It was a tough pull at first, but once I started it moving, it rose swiftly. The onslaught of wind stopped Kurt in his tracks. Trish didn't try another drastic maneuver either, now that her buddy had the open sky to contend with.

My face and shoulders were out the door when Kurt's hand closed over my arm and tugged me back. He grappled for the bag.

I crossed my arms over my chest and clenched my shoulder straps, locking the duffel in place. When I leaned out again, I dropped my head and felt Kurt's grip loosen as I somersaulted into the night.

Chapter Twenty-five

It was a wild ride.

My freefall was clumsy because of my awkward body position protecting the duffel bag. After my third or fourth flip, I reached for the pilot chute and tugged it from its pouch on the bottom of Kurt's rig.

The wind grabbed it, extending the bridle, and an instant later the closing pin was out. It was the point in the opening sequence when I'd normally reach for my risers to lessen the opening shock. But this time, I only had one arm to use. My left hand was clenched around my right shoulder strap, locking the duffel in the crook of my arm. Grabbing the right riser alone wasn't enough. When the parachute snapped open, I thought I heard every bone in my back crack. It felt like I'd been jerked halfway back to the plane.

At least the chute had opened.

With the parachute flying level, I released my left hand and raised it overhead. The bag slid to my shoulder. Two-handed again, I reached up and unstowed the toggles, the handles to my steering lines. A quick steering check verified the canopy was good.

The quickest way down would be a hard, continuous turn to one side that would spiral the canopy toward the ground and bleed off altitude. I spotted a reasonable landing place, and when I was approximately over it, I buried my right toggle near my hip and spun toward Earth, round and round toward what looked like a rock quarry. When I got dizzy, I brought the toggle up again and let the canopy fly straight for a while, then spiraled again. Enormous mounds of stone were brightly lit beneath me. Nearby spotlights illuminated a giant American flag that I checked for wind direction. I focused on a wide patch of gravel bordering several mountains of various grades of stones. It would have to do; I turned into the wind and prepared to land.

When my feet touched, I skidded a little on the gravel but didn't fall. The parachute fell behind me with a soft *whoosh*, and the first thing I did was look to see if anyone was around.

The quarry was empty. It was almost three in the morning.

I unfastened my chest strap and loosened the leg straps enough to step out of the gear. Taking off the rig was a physical relief. Under the quarry's bright field lights, I was finally able to get a good look at my leg.

My calf was stained from the back of my knee all the way to my foot. Even the heel of my sneaker was dark red. I removed the belt I'd knotted there and adjusted my pant leg. How did such a small cut produce that much blood? The knife must have gone in deep. I squeezed the sides of the wound together and applied pressure, wondering for a moment whether I could find medical attention. How would explain myself if I did?

The sensible thing would be to call the police. I eased myself to the ground, reapplied my makeshift tourniquet, and considered how to tell them my story.

Kurt's duffel bag started ringing.

I turned and stared at it. It rang again and I pulled it to me.

When I opened the zipper, I found myself staring down into blocks of cash. Thick stacks of hundred dollar bills—more money than I'd ever seen.

Another ring chirped, and I plunged a hand into the sack and shoved them aside, feeling for a phone. My hand closed over it. I pulled it out and flipped it open. Engine noise droned in my ear.

She came straight to the point.

"Where are you, Emily?"

I listened, waited.

"You have something that belongs to me. I'll send someone."

"Did you kill my husband, Trish? My daughter?"

She breathed into the phone, the kind of disgusted sigh that proved my heartache was only a fleeting nuisance to her.

"Make this easy on yourself," she said.

I snapped the phone closed.

Almost instantly, it rang again. Somehow, I wasn't surprised.

She asked again where I was.

"You're starting to sound like a broken record, Trish. Get over yourself. You're not getting this money back."

"Why don't you call your little friend? Ask her what she thinks you should do."

"What?"

"You heard me."

This time, she hung up on me.

Chapter Twenty-six

I immediately dialed the motel. When the desk clerk forwarded my call, I closed my eyes and muttered "please-please-please-please" under my breath while I waited for Jeannie to pick up.

Instead, a man answered. My eyes opened.

"Sorry," I said. "I was trying to reach room one-fourteen?"

"You have the right room," the speaker said. "Blondie's room. When we get our money, you'll get your friend."

I was speechless.

"Thing is," he continued. "You don't have a lot of time."

"Look—"

"Bring the money to this room by eight this morning. The key'll be under the parking block in front. Put the bag on the bed and leave. If the money's all there, your friend'll be back here by nine."

"But how will I—"

"One more thing," he said. "Not a word to the police or Richard Cole."

Christ. Who were these people?

"Cole's son, Tim?" the man said, "Has his swim team practice in a few hours, before school. Be a shame if something nasty happened on his way there."

"At least let me talk to her," I said. "How do I know you haven't already done something?"

His voice faded as he muttered to someone else, "Bring her here."

There was rustling, and Jeannie said, "Em?"

Her voice was strong.

"Jeannie, are you—"

"Edward Kosh," she said plainly, "I saw it on a receipt."

I heard a whack and a moan, followed by more rustling. Something bumped the receiver on other end.

From some distance away, I heard Jeannie shout, "K-O-S—"

Bumping and scuffling came next, then the original voice.

"Eight a.m." he said, and the line went dead.

I dropped Kurt's phone into his bag. My hands were shaking when I zipped it. Just when I'd thought things couldn't get worse.

I'd nearly been killed. Clement was shot and left for dead. The people responsible were the ones who'd murdered Jack and Annette. I didn't feel smart or strong enough to tackle Trish and her gang of lowlifes alone, despite their instructions. Outnumbered and overpowered, I felt as small and insignificant as the little stones piled all around me.

Police would have more questions than answers. So using my own phone, I dialed Richard. My call ended in his voice mailbox again. I summarized everything I knew. Then I sorted the few facts I had.

When Trish had called, she'd addressed me by name, even though she'd never seen me in the plane. Kurt had seen me, but he had no idea who I was.

Then there was Jeannie. I'd only had the sack of cash for fifteen minutes, twenty tops. It wasn't enough time to pull off a kidnapping and arrange a trade.

They must have been watching us. Maybe Scud or Trish got suspicious and sent a goon to follow me. I thought of the beachfront bar Jeannie and I had drinks at earlier and wondered if one of Trish's henchmen were there spying. Was it someone who'd sat with Jeannie at the bar? Bought her a drink? Maybe when I'd left Jeannie, I wasn't alone on the beach like I'd thought. Or, maybe I'd walked past someone hiding in a car in the motel lot.

However they'd done it, it still didn't explain how Trish knew I was on the plane. I chewed on various scenarios and kept returning to the simplest explanation: Scud.

The men who'd loaded the plane would have found him after we left. If he were still alive—and I cursed my naïve, amateur self for not checking—he'd tell them I shot him. Trish would call to explain what happened to the money. They'd realize I was their stowaway, and I'd puzzle over the predicament in a gravel pit in God-knows-where at three o'clock in the morning with a battle-scarred body and so much cash I could spare a few bills for toilet paper.

I palmed a fist of gravel and hurled it into the night. *Scud.*

Headlights approached. I wasn't keen on hitching a ride, but I had no idea where I was, and couldn't exactly call a Yellow Cab. I grabbed the duffel, abandoned the parachute, and struggled up a mild embankment to the roadside, where a beat-up El Camino stopped along side me, exhaust rumbling. I was relieved to see a woman behind the wheel.

Inez, a nineteen-year-old Latina with a disturbing eyebrow piercing, drove us through a series of poorly marked farm roads. We commiserated about her go-nowhere bartending job and the fictitious low-life who'd abandoned me roadside because I wouldn't put out on our second date. Four cigarettes and a king-sized Snickers later, she agreed to sell me her cousin's dumpy, piece-of-crap car for twice its worth. I paid her with Trish's money, and her only reaction to the large stack of bills I counted was a smile wiser than her years. We'd each have explaining to do, but no one could argue either of us got a bad deal.

At the curb in front of her house, she got out of the car and patted its roof as I slid behind her sticky steering wheel. I tried not to stare at her garage door, which was so run down its panels sagged on one side. I offered another hundred-dollar bill for whatever money she had on her, and she dug in her purse and thrust forty-seven bucks through the driver's side window. I took note of her address as I pulled away. If I didn't end up dead or incarcerated, Inez could have the car back later and keep Trish's filthy money.

A few miles up the road, I parked the El Camino in front of a pump at a twenty-four hour gas station where I topped off and found a map. Turned out I was two hundred miles away from Houston, outside Corpus Christi. A flight path from the Houston area over Corpus Christi suggested Trish might have been heading to Mexico. I bit my lip and thought it over while I filled the largest size coffee cup I could find. I took the coffee black, paid with Inez's small bills, and got back in the car to head for Jeannie.

By quarter after five, highway traffic was picking up, but there was still no hint of sunrise. I glanced at drivers I passed, and at those who passed me, and felt like a social outsider. They were listening to morning talk shows on their way to respectable office jobs.

Finally, Richard called me back.

"Clement's alive," he said. "The shooting's all over the news."

A car coming up behind me blinked its headlights and I moved out of its way.

"Thank goodness," I said. "Does the FBI know where Casey is?"

"I don't know what they know. What about you? Are you okay?"

I brought him up to speed.

"I'm staying home til one of my buddies gets off duty. He'll keep an eye on my family," he said. "Then you and I have a date."

"Where?"

He read a street address. "Edward Kosh turned up in the drop zone files you gave me. Don't know about you, but I'd like to stop by and say hello."

Chapter Twenty-seven

Kosh's beachfront paradise was a mere thirty minutes from the drop zone, and ten minutes from my motel, a coincidence that didn't sit well. It wasn't clear whether Jeannie had shouted his name because she thought he could help us or because he was involved, but I assumed the worst.

Richard should have been there waiting for me, but his car was no where in sight, so instead of parking, I slowed the junky El Camino and studied the home of a man I'd never met.

Judging by his house, Edward Kosh didn't do half bad. His home was elevated on stilts, with the living space directly over a carport and outdoor shower stall. Beyond the house, waves lolled on a private beach and morning sun glinted off the sea. Like its neighbors, the home had been built facing the ocean. From my spot on the street, I was actually looking at its back. A couple of newspapers lay forgotten in the driveway and his carport was empty except for a few sea gulls scavenging near the trash cans. Apparently Kosh was already gone for the day, off earning his nice living.

I was partly tempted to climb the steps and peek through his windows, but doing it alone and unarmed with no real assurance the place was actually empty seemed foolish. So a block ahead, I parked and called Richard. When he didn't answer at any of his numbers, I tried to convince myself that he was an ex-cop and could take care of himself. Still, I worried. It wasn't like

Richard to be late or unresponsive, and I doubted any amount of training or experience could adequately prepare a person for a situation like ours.

Unsure what to do without him, I used the waiting time as an opportunity to clean myself up. Otherwise, I knew my tussled hair and bloodstained clothes would eventually draw attention. At a nearby super center, I grabbed the first suitable items in my size with no regard for fashion—a pair of lemon yellow Capri pants, long enough to cover my wound, a peach camisole, and a pale green cardigan. I draped them over an arm and headed toward the pharmacy, thinking the whole time that the gash in my leg must be splitting even wider. On my way, I swiped a backpack off its display hook. Next I found the antibiotic ointment, gauze, and medical tape that I needed most, and finally enough basic toiletries to make myself passable.

After I paid, I used the restroom to clean and bandage my leg and change clothes. I washed my face, made it up, and pulled my hair into a tight bun, the only presentable hairstyle I could manage with a rubber band and a travel-size can of hairspray. When I left the restroom, I was a regular person again. At least, on the outside.

By 7:20, I was back in Kosh's neighborhood, but there was still no word from Richard and no sign of him. One of Kosh's neighbors, a prim woman in a sleek jogging suit, retrieved her empty garbage can from the curb. She followed me with her eyes as I passed.

Again, I parked a block away and tried calling all of Richard's numbers. He didn't answer anywhere and I was coming up on a decision point. The men who had Jeannie expected their money in less than an hour. I'd either have to explore the Edward Kosh angle by myself or return to the hotel to make the exchange for Jeannie. The choice should have been obvious, but I kept going back to our phone call.

Jeannie had wanted me to know something about Edward Kosh badly enough to take a beating for it. Whatever that was, it seemed I owed it to her to visit his house, to at least do *something.* I thought about his nosey neighbor and worried about being seen.

Then I tapped my fingers on the steering wheel, thinking about that neighbor's trash.

She'd been hauling in her garbage can, but I remembered the gulls in Kosh's carport. He hadn't set his own cans out. Then there were the newspapers in his drive—two of them. I grew hopeful. Certainly Kosh knew that Jeannie had leaked his name. Maybe that was the reason his house was empty.

Feeling better about the odds, I decided to give it a shot. I moved both cell phones, mine and Kurt's, and all Trish's cash into my roomy new backpack. A crumpled paper was wedged among the bills. I unfolded it and read what looked like somebody's fast addition problem—a series of four numbers down the left side of the page and corresponding values down the right. Numbers in the first column looked like dates with no slashes to separate the day, month, and year. The second column had three numbers—89, 75, 84—summed at the bottom. The fourth spot was blank; someone had drawn a question mark there.

That's what my whole week was beginning to feel like—a big question mark.

I shoved the paper into my bag and walked to the house, trying not to limp. At the top of the steps, on Kosh's upstairs landing, I deliberately dropped my keys. As I bent to get them, I surveyed his street. No one was watching.

His front door had several panes of ornamental glass. If I could break one, I could reach inside and unlock the door. Nobody would see. The only view of the door was from the deserted beach behind me. I decided to use my sweater to help me shatter a piece of glass without cutting myself, the way I'd seen it done on TV.

Then I stopped. What if there were an alarm?

I cupped my hands over my eyes and pressed my forehead toward the glass. On the other side, about ten feet away, a questioning face looked back at me. A matronly Hispanic woman, holding a squirt bottle of Tilex, came forward and opened the door. She had what looked like a cleaning-products-holster around her broad hips.

I improvised. "May I see Mr. Kosh?"

"He's not here, so sorry." She began to pull the door closed.

I frowned. "That's strange. We're supposed to meet for breakfast."

She shrugged. "Not home."

"If you don't mind," I said, "I'll wait out here. Hopefully he'll be back soon." I leaned against the porch's wooden banister and turned toward the surf. The wind was picking up.

Behind me, she said, "You want to sit?"

I turned. When she nodded to a kitchen barstool, I smiled my thanks and followed her inside. She closed the door behind us, and I surveyed the front rooms. The living room, to the right, was bright with natural light and furnished with white leather and maple pieces. Enormous windows offered a spectacular view of the sea. The kitchen, where I sat, was small and tidy and smelled like citrus cleanser. The only items on the granite countertops, still damp from having been wiped, were a cutlery set and an espresso machine. Ahead, a hallway led to the part of the house that overlooked the street.

I turned around and looked at the door. No alarm system keypad.

"The house looks great," I said. "Mr. Kosh says nice things about you. Ana, right?"

"Teresa."

"Of course, I'm sorry."

She nodded and disappeared into a bathroom down the hall. I heard the shower curtain being pulled back and water running in the tub. It gave me an idea.

I wandered toward the bathroom and found her bent over the tub, the fabric of her slacks stretched tightly around her extended rear end.

"Is there another restroom I could use?"

She pointed to the right without looking up from her scrubbing.

"Thanks," I said, turning toward Kosh's master bedroom. I stepped inside and made a hasty search. The hanging space in the closet was filled with expensive women's clothes. A small portion of one rack had men's suits.

Nothing was under the elaborate king-size sleigh bed, but a jewelry box on the dresser protected an impressive collection of gemstone earrings and pendants. I ran a tentative finger over what must have been thousands of dollars in necklaces, bracelets, and rings. I ducked inside the master bath and flushed the toilet.

On the way back to my designated kitchen stool, I paused. "How long to clean a house this size, Teresa?"

Kosh's home office was straight ahead.

"This house, two hours." She grunted as she stood. "Other houses…not so neat."

Kosh had two computers, a desktop and a laptop, side by side on his desk. I looked from one to the other and wondered which would boot up faster.

"Place looks perfect," I said. "You must have been here two hours already."

She raised the toilet seat and squirted cleanser under the rim. "Almost done. Finish here, sweep floors. Then, next house."

I returned to the kitchen. When a vacuum cleaner started in the master bedroom, I unlocked a living room window. I wanted to come back when Teresa was gone and search Kosh's computers.

I could only hope that the fact I'd seen no sign of an alarm meant there wasn't one installed. *You're an idiot, Emily. Let's just hope you're a lucky one.*

Chapter Twenty-eight

Teresa pushed and pulled the vacuum down the hall, where it sucked up perfumed powder she'd sprinkled on the floor. Gesturing at my watch, I signaled I was giving up on my fake meeting with Kosh and waved goodbye.

Hidden in the carport's shower stall, I waited next to His and Her flip-flops and beach towels until Teresa's ride came at quarter to eight. When the car pulled away, I went back upstairs and let myself in through the open window, closing it behind me.

Trish's money was supposed to be delivered to Jeannie's hotel room in fifteen minutes. I wasn't sure what to do. The money was the only leverage I had. If I gave it back, Trish and her cohorts would disappear. I'd never find out about Casey or how this mess was tied to me. But keeping the money didn't guarantee an explanation either, just more trouble for Jeannie. I remembered Eric Lyons being found in the river and thought about how Craig Clement and I narrowly escaped death hours ago at the drop zone. Even if I turned over the cash, could I really believe they'd let Jeannie go?

I used my cell to dial the motel. I'd say I couldn't get back to Houston in time for the trade, but I was coming as fast as I could.

No one answered in Jeannie's room.

They'd probably left. My instructions were to return the money by eight and then go back at nine for Jeannie. Whoever had her probably didn't want to be there when I showed up. I used Kurt's phone to call the number Trish had phoned from earlier, but Trish didn't answer either.

I went to Kosh's office and powered up his desktop computer. Its files were password protected. I tried the laptop. It had no password protection, which was a surprise, but then something else shocked me more. The screen's wallpaper image was a picture of Trish and Scud.

I stared at their charming, misleading smiles and facts fell into place. Edward Kosh was the skydiver I knew as Scud. The man I'd shot, now maybe dead, for all I knew, back where this mess had begun. The trendy clothes in the closet, expensive jewelry on the dresser…those had to belong to Trish. There was no other explanation.

I thought of David Meyer. Trish had been living with him for months. But why? She was using him, but I couldn't imagine for what.

I decided to take the hard drives, but I needed a screwdriver. I went to the kitchen and pilfered through drawers until I found a can opener with an end piece flat and small enough to do the trick.

The desktop's drive was in my backpack and I was unfastening the last screw on the laptop's access door when I thought I heard a car in the drive downstairs. I peeked behind the drape as the trunk of a gold sedan disappeared into the carport below.

I raced to finish the drive removal, but my fingers would no longer work together. The last screw was difficult to maneuver, but it finally yielded. Car doors slammed under the house as I pulled the access panel away. When I tried to extract the drive, I discovered it was fastened to the inside of the case with four, tinier screws. There was no more time.

I put things back in the approximate place I'd found them and closed myself inside the office closet. It seemed my pounding heart would give me away.

Moments later, the front door opened and keys dropped onto the granite countertop. Voices in the living room were muffled, but there were at least two men. I made out "just twenty minutes" and "watch the street" as one voice got closer.

The door to the bathroom closed. Its overhead fan turned on. I cracked the closet door open so I could hear better.

"Want some eggs?" someone called from the kitchen.

The man in the bathroom shouted that eggs sounded good, and then the same question was asked to someone else.

I didn't hear an answer.

The speaker said again, "Want some eggs, beautiful? Hungry?"

There was a pause, and then he continued, "Come on. Might as well eat something."

His tone was taunting. Suggestive. The toilet flushed on the other side of the wall and the bathroom door squeaked open.

The guy in the hall said, "I got something better than eggs."

An unequivocal reply came from the living room: "Fuck you, pencil dick."

My breath caught. It was Jeannie.

Someone mumbled about hardheaded broads and acid tongues.

The phone on Kosh's desk rang and someone answered on an extension in the front of the house. I heard, "Is it there?" but couldn't make out the rest.

I looked at my watch. 8:00.

They were talking about the money. The men were hiding out with Jeannie while they waited to hear if I'd returned it. I heard them discuss what to do. One said he'd call me.

Shit. Where was my bag? Any minute my phone would ring, and I'd left the ringer on incase Richard called.

I spotted it on the floor beside the desk chair, only a few feet away. But the open office door was a problem.

All I heard were kitchen sounds associated with breakfast. Somebody could be dialing. I stole a glance into the living room, and when I didn't see anyone, I crawled behind the desk and grabbed the backpack, opening the zipper right away. I fumbled for the phones, unsure in my panic which one they'd call. I found mine first and turned off the ringer. Kurt's was buried and I ransacked the bag with two hands before finding it deep in a corner. I managed to find his Ringer Off option. My thumb was still on the key when the phone's LCD screen changed. It was signaling the number of an incoming call.

"She's not answering," I heard from the kitchen. "Should I leave a message?"

"Forget it. She's playing tough."

The LCD on Kurt's phone changed to report one missed call.

"She's smarter than the two of you together," Jeannie said. "If I know Emily, this place is already surrounded by cops."

I'd have been delighted with one. Where was Richard?

I peered around the corner of the desk. Jeannie was now on the pristine leather sofa in the living room. The sight of her almost moved me to tears. Her face was swollen.

She wore yesterday's clothes, now wrinkled. Her coif was disheveled, her make-up gone, and soon there'd be a shiner. No wonder she was ornery.

I pushed the pack over my shoulder and crawled back to the closet. Jeannie spotted me. Her eyes widened. I backed into the closet and pulled the door mostly closed.

"Gotta pee." Jeanne's tone was matter-of-fact.

She was probably already crossing the living room, because the next thing I heard was, "Hey! Sit down!"

"Relax, mister. I promise not to flush myself out to sea."

"Let her go," the other said. "No windows in the bathroom."

Soon, footsteps brushed on the carpet inside the office.

"Em?" she whispered.

"Here," I whispered back, and pressed the closet door open a bit further.

She stared down at me, crouched on the floor under a series of hanging jackets, and I had the feeling she wasn't really seeing me.

"What are you wearing?" she whispered. "You look like a damn sherbet."

"Hey, what's going on back here?" Someone was approaching the hall.

Jeannie pushed the closet door until it was open only a few inches. She stood in front of it with her back to me. I ducked into shadows.

"In here," she said, annoyed. "Seriously. Relax. Swanky beach house. Wanted to look around, that's all."

"Yeah?" he said. "I think you wanted to look for a phone."

I heard body weight drop into the desk chair as a huff of air escaped from its suspension. The bulldog was guarding his phone.

"I hope you're wrong about your friend," he said. "For your own sake."

"How much money did she take?" Jeannie asked. "You mad a girl got your money?" I could hear the smile in her voice.

"You talk a lot, lady. And you're not as funny as you think."

Jeannie sighed. "Yeah, well, you talk a lot too. And you're not as smart as you think."

Chapter Twenty-nine

The office door closed emphatically. I guessed the message to Jeannie was Stay Out.

A TV droned in the front room and I heard snippets of the morning news mixed with the clatter of dishes and forks. A newscaster prattled about an injured FBI agent at Gulf Coast Skydiving. I pictured Jeannie's kidnappers shoveling eggs as they watched the segment. We had to get out of there. I knew our odds would be better if I could get rid of one of the men first.

I pulled the closet door fully shut, and flipped open Kurt's cell phone in the darkness. I pressed the little illuminated buttons and brought up the number for its last missed call. It was the call Jeannie's kidnappers made moments earlier, and by my bad luck, they'd used the landline from this very house. Had a cell phone been used, I could have texted back. Instead, I'd have to actually speak to them and hope not to be discovered.

I pressed Talk, and Kosh's desk phone rang. Even though I expected it, I still jumped at the noise. Someone answered on another extension.

I used as low a voice as I could. "Your money's back in town, but it's not at the motel. There's no way I'll go there alone."

"Where is it?" I heard his voice through the walls and the phone at the same time.

I named an intersection I remembered from my earlier super center run. There was a gas station on the corner. "I hid it in the shrubbery behind the station's dumpster. Now please let Jeannie go."

"It better be there."

"See for yourself." I hung up.

Immediately a dialogue erupted in the living room. One man asked if they should take Jeannie. The other said not to be stupid. The TV switched off, keys jingled, and the front door thumped closed. It was 8:20.

The man who stayed to baby-sit told Jeannie it was his lucky day. I cracked the closet door open to hear better.

"Thanks to your friend, we got some alone time, beautiful. A chance for some fun."

A car door thudded in the carport below us. An engine started.

"I bet the *only* time you have *that* kind of fun is when you're alone," Jeannie said.

I crawled out of the closet toward the window and parted the curtains slightly. The sedan reversed down the drive. I squinted at its front plate and flipped open Kurt's phone.

"A drunk keeps circling the Shell station," I told the 9-1-1 operator. She took my description of the car and its tag number. I figured the cops and Trish's minion would pull up to the station around the same time. Even if my idea didn't work, at least he was out of the house.

"Get off…Hey! Get the hell off me!" Jeannie yelled on the other side of the office door. She thudded into the wall. I scanned the office for something to use as a weapon and grabbed a brass paperweight shaped like a cube.

On the other side of the door, Jeannie's protests grew muffled and more distant as he pushed her down the hall, toward the bedroom.

I opened the door. She was kicking and squirming on Kosh's bed, pinned beneath a stocky man in a sweater and jeans. All I could see of her were flailing legs. I hurried toward them, ready to drive the paperweight into his skull.

When I got to the doorway, Jeannie spotted me, but her attacker's face was buried in her neck. His hand was already inside her blouse. He pulled it free and reached between her legs. I showed Jeannie the paperweight in my hand. She pointed toward the dresser. The pervert had set down his gun.

I tossed the paperweight toward Jeannie's open hand and grabbed the gun.

"Get the hell off her."

The man whirled, and Jeannie hammered him in the face with the brass weight.

He yelled and reached for his forehead. Blood streaked down the back of his hand. Jeannie shoved out from under him. She drove the weight into his crotch and he doubled over.

"You goddamn son of a—" she blasted him in the side of the head, "—*bitch*!"

She hurried toward me, pulling at her blouse until it covered her again. I kept the gun pointed at the bloody figure writhing on the bed and told Jeannie to go in the office and bring my bag.

"Get your own bag," she said, taking the gun from me. I was afraid to let it go, but I did. It wasn't the time to argue.

"You wanted to get naked so bad? Get naked now!" She pointed the gun at her attacker. "Do it."

I went back to the office closet.

"Start with your pants," Jeannie ordered behind me.

I grabbed the bag with Trish's money and took the laptop off the desk.

When I got back, the man was halfway out of his jeans.

"Okay," I said. "Let's go."

"Next, the tightie whities, and make it fast, you little bastard."

I tugged her arm, but it was as if I weren't there.

"Come on. You couldn't wait to take them off a minute ago."

"Let's go," I said again.

She bristled. I wondered if she'd shoot him down naked, right there. His nose, mouth, and cheek were wet with blood and Kosh's expensive silk charmeuse bedding was stained now too. He pulled down his underwear like she said, exposing himself.

Jeannie laughed. "How can he show that thing around?" she asked me. "Take off your ugly sweater and get off the bed."

I whispered. "What are you doing?"

She ignored me.

Completely naked, he slid off the bed and looked at us. His torso and thighs were white, untouched by sun. Blood from his face dripped onto what little chest hair he had. He was still wearing socks.

Jeannie said it was time to go.

We backed out of the hallway and she kept the gun pointed at the naked, bloody guy as he emerged and shuffled to the living room.

"Go out on the porch," Jeannie said, "way over there, on the left." She indicated the corner of the porch furthest away from the front door.

"Lady, I'm naked."

"Asshole, I know."

She fluttered her hand toward the door as if hurrying a slow-poke child, and he went outside onto the porch like she said.

Jeannie followed him out, stopping to turn the lock on the front door as she passed it. I went out behind her, carrying the bag and computer, and hustled down the front steps as fast as I could. The front door closed, and I heard Jeannie's quick steps behind me.

"Hurry!" she ordered. "He might be crazy enough to chase us."

◇◇◇

Jeannie drove while I searched the laptop. There weren't many folders and it wasn't running any software beyond the standard load. I nosed around in the e-mail application but only found spam. Contents of the Deleted Items and Sent Items folders had been purged. The last websites visited were news sites. I found a link to a web mail application, but got no further than its password screen. The laptop was clean.

"There's one," Jeannie said, flicking on the turn signal. I'd told her to find a place with wireless Internet access. She exited the highway and drove toward an upscale bistro situated near a bustling strip mall.

Inside, smells of croissants, quiche, and gourmet coffee were intoxicating. It had been eighteen hours since I'd eaten. Jeannie ordered for us while I found a private table and connected to the Internet.

I opened a search engine and typed Data Retrieval Houston. Several hits had promise. Nine years experience recovering data from damaged hard drives. Express data recovery nationwide. Recover losses due to hardware or software failure. And—my favorite—Recover losses due to human error. Scud's hard drive was next to me, in my pack, and I was determined to find what he was hiding. I scribbled an address and closed the laptop as Jeannie returned with a To Go sack.

My cell phone rang. It was Richard finally calling back.

I flipped open my phone. "*Where* have you been?" Immediately, a series of beeps told me my phone's battery was dying.

"The police have been here forever, asking about the car," he said. "I couldn't call."

Suddenly I remembered. I'd left Richard's car at the airport—now a crime-scene.

"I'm sorry," I said, although somehow the car seemed slightly irrelevant, compared to the rest.

Jeannie pulled out a chair and sat down. She watched me like she expected me to relay everything he said, right then. Instead I mouthed "battery" and pointed to the failing phone.

"It's fine," he said. "At least Tim was safe with cops around the house."

His first thought was for his family's safety. Why hadn't that occurred to me years ago, when I was accusing him of crimes and trying to get him fired?

"I'm sorry," I said again. I meant I was sorry for everything else. For making snap judgments, hurling accusations, and being mean. I wondered if I would ever find the right words.

"After the police left, I got in touch with a contact at CPS and learned what I could about Trish's boyfriend, David Meyer."

I pulled out a chair and sat across from Jeannie, who'd begun to rummage in the backpack. She discreetly peeled a few hundred-dollar bills out of a block and stood to leave.

Richard continued. "An auditor noticed that Meyer closed a lot of field cases by saying that, despite a diligent search, he couldn't find the families. These were all white families, in a county with large Hispanic and black communities. It raised the question—was he favoring some ethnic groups over others? Meyer categorically denied it. The agency followed up by reviewing his time sheets, case notes, and files."

"What'd they find?" I took the lid off my coffee and watched Jeannie head for the door. She left with no explanation.

"A dedicated and thorough investigator. In fact, he logs quite a bit of overtime."

"Was there anything to validate the racism concerns?"

"No. So, they looked at his computer next. It wasn't his files that got their attention, though, it was his log-on history."

"Excuse me?"

"Apparently, Meyer had logged into the system at times they knew he was in the field, away from a computer. There were several times he was logged in twice, from two IP addresses."

I tried to understand. "He obviously couldn't be in two places at the same time. Someone else must use his password. But why would he share that? It could only get him in trouble."

"I asked myself the same thing. Then it came to me. Maybe he unknowingly gave it to his new *live-in girlfriend*."

He let me digest that for a moment.

"I also found out investigators get case assignments on their computers, flagged in order of priority. Priority Ones are urgent, so they're addressed immediately. Investigators have a few days to address Priority Twos. The missing babies he couldn't find? All Priority Twos...the ones that could wait a few days."

"Sorry to be so thick, but—"

"If Trish knew David's caseload, and wanted to snatch a kid, she could do it *days* before Meyer ever even tried to look for the kid. Later, Meyer could look high and low for weeks and never get warm."

"But surely parents would report their missing baby."

He hesitated. "What if she takes out the parents? Anyone who looked into it would have to assume the parents were trying to avoid a CPS interview. It's a nearly perfect crime."

I opened my mouth. The words on my tongue were "it's impossible to believe," but they disintegrated as soon as the thought formed. Eliminating parents, stealing babies. I thought of Eric and Casey Lyons. It wasn't hard to believe at all.

Jeannie hadn't returned by the time the call ended, so I ate without her. Eventually she returned with a yellow plastic sack from which she produced a pre-paid cell phone.

"For you," she said. "Otherwise, when your battery dies we'll be screwed."

I shrugged. "There's always Kurt's phone."

She looked at me like I was an idiot. "They could cancel service anytime."

"So I have to carry three phones?"

She pushed it across the table with a stack of twenties and fifties. "There's a bank in the next parking lot so I got more small bills too. You never know."

That much was true. I unzipped the backpack and dropped the new phone and extra bills inside.

◇◇◇

"Why do I have to do it?" Jeannie asked, as we walked into the offices of the disk recovery people.

On the drive north to Houston, she'd helped herself to my cheap cosmetics and a pair of sunglasses scavenged from Inez's glove box. The glasses disguised her swollen eye well enough for her to appear stylish, maybe even rested. It was another eerily masterful transformation.

"You should do it," I whispered, walking with her toward the counter, "because you're older than me. They'll believe it if you say it."

"I'm not that much—"

"Shh. Here he comes."

A lanky associate in Dockers and a polo shirt stepped up to the counter in front of us. A plastic nametag said BRAD. He didn't look old enough to shave.

"How can I help you this morning?"

Jeannie stepped up to the counter and grimaced. "This is embarrassing."

The technician gave her a dopey grin. "We pass no judgments here at ResusciData." He chuckled.

She produced the hard drive I'd given her.

"I caught my teenager visiting an...inappropriate chat room. When I grounded him from the computer, the little shit password protected our machine. Now I can't use it either. Can you fix it?"

The tech suppressed a smirk. I wondered if he'd done something similar in his formative computer geek years.

"Does the password box come up when you boot the machine or when you try to get into a particular application?"

"When she boots the machine," I answered.

Brad swiveled his head toward me and seemed to notice me for the first time.

"Let's have a look." He took the drive from Jeannie, dropped it into an electrostatic discharge bag, and carried it to a workbench.

"The protection you described is probably in the system's BIOS."

Jeannie looked at me. I couldn't see her eyes behind the dark glasses, but the creases in her forehead and the skeptical twist of her mouth said it all: "Huh?"

"If I install your drive as a secondary drive in another work station," he continued, "we should be able to get to your data that way."

He took a seat on a stool and we watched him use a ribbon cable to connect the drive to an open CPU and turn on the computer.

"Go ahead and have a seat," Brad said. "This shouldn't take too long."

Jeannie and I sat in chairs along the wall. Current issues of *PC Gamer*, *TidBITs,* and *Linux Today* were spread over the surface of an oblong coffee table with uneven legs. Jeannie dug through the magazines and curled her brightly painted lips in disgust.

I relaxed into my chair and stretched my legs. I let my eyes close. It'd been almost thirty hours since I'd slept. My leg throbbed and a headache was coming on. Or maybe I'd had the headache all along but had been too distracted to know.

My cell phone rang. The call was coming from BioTek.

"It's Bowman." I punched Ignore Call, annoyed he was wasting my precious battery.

"Of course, it's him." Jeannie checked her watch with an exaggerated flourish. "While *I* am on vacation today, I'm afraid *you* are three hours late for work."

I rested my head on the wall behind me and closed my eyes, wishing my *life* had a button: Ignore All.

Chapter Thirty

"Quit it." Jeannie didn't look up from her hands. She was picking at a cuticle. Her legs were crossed, the top foot swinging.

"Quit what?"

"Stop staring at me. You're bugging me."

I didn't know I'd fixated on her. I shifted my gaze to the cluttered tabletop and took in the layers of computer magazines. Except for us, ResusciData's waiting room was empty.

"I'm trying to make sense of Richard's theory," I said.

Jeannie stopped swinging her leg and looked up from her nails. This time, I felt her eyes lock onto me. An automatic air freshener mounted on the wall sprayed out a poof of something lemony.

I stood and paced the little room.

Jeannie followed me with her eyes. The way she looked over the top of her sunglasses reminded me of a disapproving teacher.

"Something's wrong with you." She cocked her head, like she was figuring something out. "It's not what Richard said that's got you thinking. It's what Clement said, isn't it? I've been wondering when you'd come back to that."

I lowered my voice. "How could I *not* be thinking about Clement? He all but told me Trish's people had something to do with Jack and Annette. That means we were right...they did kidnap Mattie Shelton. When their threats didn't work, they tried to kill me before I could testify. Except..."

I felt tears welling and wondered if she could see that.

She was careful to keep her voice low too. “Except what?”

“I didn’t go on the boat that morning. Jack wanted me to have time to myself, quiet time to decompress after the threats and the break-in. So, while I was painting my toenails…or reading on the beach…or doing some other selfish, indulgent thing—”

Jeannie dropped her head into her hands. “They went after the boat you rented. Because they expected you to be on board.”

“I think so.”

“But you’re alive. Why not try again?”

I shrugged. “They got what they wanted. I missed the trial.”

She didn’t speak right away.

“I think they got more than they wanted,” I said. “I think they got Annette.”

When I blinked, tears fell down both cheeks. I swiped at them and tried to compose myself, turning my back to the counter so Brad wouldn’t see.

Jeannie seemed confused. “Sweetie, why don’t you—”

“I think they sold her,” I blurted.

I knew I couldn’t keep it together. Not seeing a ladies room, I rushed outside.

Jeannie followed. We stopped at the corner of the building, beyond the lobby windows. If there were people in the parking lot, I didn’t notice.

“Sold her?”

“This is bigger than Trish and Casey Lyons.” My voice sounded far away. Putting words to my fears made my chin quiver. “I think it’s a group, like a ring. Trish Dalton, her brother Mark, Ed Kosh…I think they’re like a cell, part of something bigger.”

Jeannie wiped my cheek. “Slow down.”

“Think about it,” I said. “Cells use people with different skills. People who can fly planes, disable alarms, kidnap hostages…”

Her eyes flashed at the last one. She started to say something, but the glass door to the computer shop swung open, ringing bells that were tied to its handle. Brad poked his head outside. I turned away from him and wiped my eyes and nose.

"Good, you're here," he said. "It's done."

The bells clanged on the glass again.

"He's gone," Jeannie said.

I sniffled, composed myself. She ran a thumb under each of my eyes, her way of fixing me up and taking care of me.

"Guess we should see what he's got," I said.

"That's my girl."

She wrapped an arm around my shoulder and led me inside.

Behind the counter, we looked over Brad's shoulder at a list of directories on the hard drive. I wanted to shove him out of his chair.

"Hey," I said to Jeannie. "Didn't you want to search the hard drive?"

"Thanks," Jeannie said, to me. Then, turning to Brad, she added, "Can I take a quick look in my son's folders?"

She leaned next to Brad and got so close to the screen her shoulder brushed against his. He wheeled his seat backward, to reclaim some personal space, I imagined. Jeannie grabbed his mouse.

"Let's see what he's been up to."

"Okay then," Brad said. "I'll be over here, ringing you up." He faded toward a computer at the far end of the counter.

"Try My Documents," I whispered.

She double-clicked the folder and a new list of folders appeared.

Jeannie read them off quietly, "Mortgage, Gear, Junk, MP3s, Old, Miscellaneous, Work, Financial, Pictures…"

She clicked on the Work folder, but only old resume drafts were inside. Apparently Edward Kosh—Scud—was a building contractor before he hit it big in human trafficking and contraband.

"Try Financial."

The folder contained a variety of Excel Sheets: Interest Payments, Master Card, Home Improvements, and New Car, among others. In a list of such specific records, a nondescript filename caught my eye.

"Click on Transactions," I said. The Date Modified column indicated it was updated only two days ago.

Excel launched and populated a short worksheet. There were no column headers.

Jeannie and I squinted at the data.

"Oh my God," she whispered. "Is this what I—"

"This has to be male or female," I said, pointing at a column of "M"s and "F"s.

"Origin and destination cities too," she whispered. "And are those the *ages* of kids involved? I can't believe this. What's with the question marks?"

"Maybe a child not placed? And that last column…it has to be the person who took each child."

I remembered the paper I'd found in Kurt's duffel.

"Wait," I muttered, unzipping the backpack. Where was that damn paper? I dug through stacks of money looking for it, and two thick bricks cash escaped onto the table. I glanced up in time to catch Brad staring, wide-eyed.

"Long story," I said, and shoved them back in the bag.

Brad grinned. "Is that—"

"For a prank." Jeannie reached over me, into the sack, and extracted a crisp fifty from her recent bank run. "Looks real, huh?" She winked and handed it to him. "Just don't try to spend it."

He walked toward the counter, inspecting the bill and turning it over in his hand. I wasn't sure if he'd been tricked or paid off, and I imagined he was asking himself the same question.

The paper I wanted was nestled along the backpack's liner and I unfolded it and held it near the keyboard.

"Look," I said. "The first two columns on this paper match the ones on the spreadsheet, right down to the question mark. They could be dates, without the year listed."

"Wait a minute." Jeannie leaned forward and looked from the monitor to the paper. "How much money's in your bag there, Em?"

I frowned. "Before I bought the car it was almost two-fifty."

She ran a finger down the smooth surface of the flat screen panel and stopped on the last three numbers. "Eighty-nine, seventy-five, eighty-four...that adds to what? Two forty-eight?"

"I hate math."

"Well, *this* math," she pointed to the numbers on the computer and paper, "is in *that* bag." She flung her finger toward my backpack. "Column seven here is money, if you add some zeroes. And you're hauling around an awful lot of zeroes, lady."

My eyes followed her finger and involuntarily fixated on the bag. I visualized its incredible stash, safely zipped inside. "Why would they risk toting that amount of cash?"

"Money laundering." She answered with conviction but I doubted she had any idea what she was talking about.

I looked at the last column of the spreadsheet again. "Dalton and Kosh are obvious. And I know that name Reed."

She turned back to the screen, as if double-checking me.

"That's the guy I picked out of the photo line-up in Mattie's case. The guy I was supposed to forget. He's the one who went free because my deposition never made it to court."

"I don't know what to say. You did everything you could."

I'd thought so too, but it hadn't been enough. And now more children had been taken from their homes because that trial didn't take Reed off the streets like it should have. At least six kids had been snatched this year, if I could believe what I was reading. And then it hit me.

"Where are the other years?"

"This is the only tab," she said, clicking across the bottom, checking for more data.

"July seventh," I said. "Do a search on 0707 and see what hits." God, please something hit.

Jeannie opened a search window and typed in the characters. The computer found the text string in an Excel worksheet called Old that was in Scud's Junk folder. When the file opened, my eyes went straight to the entry. I fell to my knees next to Jeannie's chair.

My voice sounded far away again, like a distant whisper in my own ears.

"It can't be anything else." I scanned the row of data, reading out loud. "They took her on the seventh. She was ten months old. On the nineteenth, they placed her. That bastard Reed took sixty-five K for my baby."

Even as I explained, my eyes locked on the entry in the destination column: Galveston.

Chapter Thirty-one

Jeannie and I took a few wrong turns on our way to Richard's office, but eventually we found it. I was surprised to discover he shared a suite with a financial planner and a massage therapist.

"Eclectic group," Jeannie said as we followed him down a hallway, past posters of the musculoskeletal system and a shelf of body oils. She carried printouts of the Excel sheets in one hand.

"This is me." Richard peeled off into a side room. He flipped the light switch and I looked around. His furnishings were simple: desk, chairs, and a filing cabinet. The walls were bare. No drapes. A group of cardboard boxes were the only other items in the room.

"Just move in?" Jeannie asked.

Richard shook his head and tossed his keys onto his desk.

"What'd you tell the police?" I asked. We hadn't heard his rundown yet.

"I told them I haven't been to Gulf Coast Skydiving in over a week and I loaned the car to an associate helping me with a case."

Jeannie crossed her arms and circled a stack of waist-high cardboard boxes. "You didn't just move in, but you leave boxes out like this?"

Richard shrugged.

"When they asked me how to contact you," he said, "I gave the number at your motel. You don't carry a cell phone, do you?" He winked at me.

"Richard," Jeannie said, "Has your wife seen this place?" She walked to his desk and sat in his chair. She found a rubberized stress doll, the kind that bends and stretches, and began flexing him in all directions.

"You could get in big trouble if they find out you lied," I said.

Richard didn't say anything right away. I had the uneasy feeling bad news was coming.

"They won't have to dig that far," he said. "Because it's time for you to tell them what happened last night."

"I can't go to the police yet, Richard. Look what we found on the hard drive."

I extended a hand toward Jeannie, meaning for her to pass the printouts. She was busy contorting the desk toy.

I found the printouts myself and brought them to Richard. I only showed him the entries from this year; I wanted his undivided attention when it was time to tell him about Annette. Richard studied the paper and sank into a chair on the visitor side of his desk, since Jeannie had taken over his usual spot.

"If this means what you think," he said, pointing to a row on the spreadsheet, "this entry must be for Casey. Eleven-month-old male, disappeared from Houston on February twelfth."

I looked over his shoulder. "It says he was placed in Tempe on the twenty-first. That's today."

Richard stared into the space in front of him, thinking out loud. "Maybe he's still here in town."

"Richard's right," Jeannie said. "About the first thing, I mean. It's time to come clean about last night and hand all this over. If we wait too long, they might never find Casey. And the FBI needs to hear what you know about the agent that was shot. But, if you two go in now with everything that's happened, you'll be stuck there for days."

Jeannie tapped her model-perfect fingernails on Richard's desk. "I think there's one angle left that we can explore better than the Feds. David Meyer."

"The detectives can question him," Richard said.

"Yes, but he and Emily hit it off. She's more likable than a strange man with a badge."

"Trish and her men won't be back. Not after nearly being busted last night," I said. "Maybe she's right, Richard. David might be the piece that unravels this. He has to know *something* about what Trish was doing, even if he doesn't *know* he knows."

"At least talk to him before you get tied up at a police station," Jeannie said.

Richard stared at her. She'd begun inspecting her bruised cheek in the reflection of a picture frame.

"Stop looking at me like you're surprised I have a brain, Richard."

"I agree with you," he said. "We should see Meyer first."

I nodded toward the printout in his hand. "You see the last line?"

He raised the paper and focused.

I continued, "Eight-month-old female in Houston, taken six days ago. Has she been in the news?"

Richard frowned, "Doesn't ring a bell."

"Well, I think those question marks you see mean the little girl's on the market."

"All the more reason to help the Feds bring these folks down ASAP."

"Not that simple." I passed Richard the paper with Annette's information. He took a moment to scan the dates, then instantly understood.

His eyes were still on the paper when he said, "Galveston."

"I'm afraid to go to the FBI, Richard. I was there when Clement got shot. If he's unconscious, he won't be able to vouch for me. They won't help me unless they believe I'm innocent. That might take days.

"My only chance to figure out who has Annette is to get these people back into town, back into action."

"Never mind these are the same people who tried to kill you."

Jeannie looked at me. "Got an idea?"

"They have a baby to sell. I have a lot of money."

"You're not thinking," Jeannie said. "You can't set up a deal with them. They know you." She gave a dismissive wave. "They know all of us."

"I'm sure we could find a stand-in to do it for the right price," I said. My newfound sack of money seemed able to repeatedly transform major obstacles into trivial afterthoughts.

"How would you contact them?" Richard asked. "The only phone numbers we have are for Kurt's and Trish's cells. I don't care how good your cover story is, calling one of those numbers is sure to tip them off."

He was right. Money wouldn't help with that one.

"Okay," I said, "Back to David Meyer then. If nothing comes from talking to him, I'll have to take my chances with Clement and the FBI. They knew enough about the racketeering to be undercover at the drop zone. Maybe they know who to call when you want to buy a baby. With data from the hard drive, they could set up a sting."

"How do we do the David thing?" Jeannie asked. "Show up at his office? Wait at his house?"

Richard produced his wallet and started leafing through cards. He pulled out a paper and walked toward the phone.

"We don't have time to wait at his house," he said. "I'll ask about a visit to his office."

"See if you can get the IP address for his remote log-ins," I said.

He nodded and dialed. Jeannie stood and walked to me.

"How are you holding up?" she asked quietly.

I couldn't answer without breaking down, so I shook my head. Jeannie put an arm around me. On the phone, Richard asked for the information I wanted, then about stopping by to see David. I thought about Annette's entry on the spreadsheet again and felt my eyes start to sting, but the sound of the phone dropping into its cradle spurred me to keep myself together.

"Meyer called in sick this morning," Richard said. "He's not at work today. They're looking into the IP address."

Jeannie clucked her tongue. "Is it me, or does the timing of that sick day seem a little strange?"

"I don't like it either," Richard said, and grabbed his keys off the desk.

Chapter Thirty-two

Richard said that in his line of work, calling before an interview is like doing a cannonball jump before trying to fish. We had no assurance that just because David Meyer had called in sick he'd actually be home, but Richard was fairly confident that calling ahead would guarantee his absence.

That's how we ended up in the parking lot of David's apartment complex, staring through Richard's windshield at the second-floor landing shared by units twelve and thirteen. David had no idea we were coming, and I had no idea what to say to him.

"Just introduce me," Richard said. "Most people are open to questions when they think it'll help a friend. If he understands why these answers are important to you, hopefully he'll help us."

"Yeah," Jeannie said to him, "until you come to the part about how his two-timing, psycho girlfriend sells black market babies."

She was in the backseat, leaning forward so she wouldn't miss anything. Richard turned off the car.

We crossed a neatly maintained lawn and climbed the steps to David's apartment. Richard knocked. Jeannie was close behind him, staring intently at the door. I looked behind us and surveyed the grassy yard separating us from the parking lot. An abandoned jump rope was coiled near a patch of geraniums below. I thought of Annette, how she might look jumping that rope, and felt inadequate. Maybe I wasn't even picturing her face correctly.

The door swung open and I turned. I'm not sure who was more surprised, Vince or me.

It felt like ages had passed since we'd last spoken. I wondered if that was because of all I'd uncovered since then, or because of the sour note we'd parted on yesterday. He wasn't wearing his cowboy hat and its absence made him seem oddly vulnerable.

He spoke first. "What are you…Is everything okay?"

He addressed the question directly to me, looking past Jeannie and Richard as if they weren't there. A mixture of confusion and concern was on his face, and I wondered how genuine it was. After last night, finding Vince at David and Trish's apartment was unsettling. Maybe David wasn't a patsy after all. And what if the rift between Vince and his cousin was just another cover? I remembered the afternoon I'd watched Clement search around Vince's truck, and wondered if the FBI knew something about him I didn't.

I introduced him to Richard. Vince studied me a moment longer before shifting his gaze. He nodded to Richard and shook his hand, but his usual cordiality was gone and I had to look hard to find traces of the laugh lines I remembered. He nodded to Jeannie without the smile I'd expected, and then held the door for the three of us.

As we entered, David's voice came from the hall. He was asking Vince who'd been at the door, but stopped short when he rounded the corner and found the four of us standing in his entry hall, staring.

"Hi," he said, almost like a question. It occurred to me I was the only person in my trio he was likely to recognize. I apologized for dropping by unannounced, introduced Richard, and explained that David might know something to help with Richard's case.

"I'm the tag-along friend," Jeannie said with a half-hearted wave.

David smiled at her, but it looked stilted. I wondered what we'd interrupted.

"Could I ask a few questions?" Richard's tone was more cordial than usual. "You might have information about a child I'm looking for."

David's eyebrows rose. "A child? Sure."

He gestured for us to sit. Richard and Jeannie took seats near him on the living room sofas. Vince and I remained standing. I wanted to sit—my leg was feeling weaker every moment—but it was more important to stay where I could watch David and Vince's reactions to Richard's questions. Especially Vince's.

"What can I tell you?" David asked. He took a seat opposite Richard and sat on the edge of the sofa cushion, leaning forward so his elbows rested on his thighs.

Richard frowned. "How about the last time you saw Trish?"

David looked at Vince before answering. Vince's posture seemed to straighten at the mention of her name.

"Trish?" David asked, "What does she have to do with a missing kid?"

"I'm trying to figure that out," Richard said. "When's the last time you saw her?"

"Last night."

Richard redirected to Vince. "How about you?"

The look on Vince's face was stern, and he didn't answer right away. He seemed to be exercising enormous self-restraint. His eyes darted from Richard to David, and finally stopped on me. His posture relaxed a little when our eyes met. I'd never seen him stressed before. He seemed weary.

"Do you know something about Trish I need to hear?"

I hesitated. What to do with a question like that.

Richard pressed. "When'd you last see her?"

Vince raised a hand in Richard's direction and kept his eyes on me. He asked me again. "What do you know about Trish?"

It was difficult, but I pulled my gaze off him to steal a glance at David, who had the wide-eyed look of a man afraid to speak.

Vince seemed devastated. "What's she done?" His shoulders fell slightly. "Tell me what she's done."

"What the hell are you talking about?" David asked. "Vince? What aren't you telling me, man?" He stood. "Can somebody please tell me what's going on?"

There was a collective pause while Vince and David waited for answers we couldn't phrase.

"Why aren't you at work today?" Jeannie asked David. I'd nearly forgotten she was there.

David looked at her, irritated. "What?"

"Why aren't you at work today?"

He scoffed. "Took a day off. Things to do." He gave Jeannie a final glance and turned back to Vince. "What's going on, man?"

Jeannie sighed an exaggerated, impatient sigh that indicated she'd crossed over into loose cannon mode.

"I thought," she said to David, "that you were sick."

Richard pursed his lips and shot her a stare.

"How do you know I called in sick?" David looked from Jeannie to Richard. "I don't even know you. Who are you people?"

"I'm sorry for the ambush," I said. "The truth is, Richard knows you called in sick today because he's in touch with CPS."

David ran his hands through his blond hair and clasped his fingers behind his head, elbows to the sides. When he took his seat again, he let his hands fall into his lap.

"Why are you in touch with CPS?" he asked Richard. "Why so interested in me?"

"Who you are, and where you work, matters to me because you live with Trish Dalton."

Vince raised his head.

"I don't know the right way to say this…" I said. "Trish is… involved with—"

"Your girlfriend's a felon," Jeannie said.

I scowled at her.

"A felon?" Vince asked.

"The boy I'm looking for," Richard said, "It looks like Trish was involved in his kidnapping, and a long line of kidnappings before his."

"That's nuts," David said. "What makes you think—"

Richard continued. "Trish flew for the company this boy's father worked for. She had access to information that would facilitate his abduction. We have evidence linking the kidnapper to Gulf Coast Skydiving. And the boy's mother recognized a photo of Trish."

"*Worked* for?" Vince asked.

"Dead," Jeannie announced. "Shot in the chest, dumped in a river."

Vince looked stricken.

David shook his head. "Trish would never—"

"Before you get too deep into defending her," Jeannie added, "you should know she has another man."

I marveled at her utter lack of tact.

David looked at me. "What's she talking about?"

"Jeannie," I said, "could you please not. . ."

David didn't seem to hear. "That's crazy," he said. "You're not making sense."

His ignorance was painful. But, I decided he'd have to hear the facts now and nurse his wounds later.

"She's using you," I said. "She's involved with another man, probably has been since way before she met you. They run this scam together." I looked at Vince. "They sell babies on the black market."

Vince's face grew paler. He looked away, incredulous.

I continued. "I found a computer file. The baby Richard's looking for is being sold today, to somebody in Tempe, Arizona."

Vince's head snapped up. "That's why she took the plane."

His candor jarred me. "What do you know about the plane?"

"I know it's not *here*," he said. "I was supposed to fly it back to Oklahoma this morning. An FBI agent gets shot at our airport last night. The plane is gone. My cousin's missing. It's not too hard to figure she's had a hand in this."

"Why would you conclude that?" David asked.

Vince glared at him, "She's not the woman you think she is."

"You didn't mention the FBI agent earlier," David said. "What do you mean she's not who I think?"

I wondered what Vince and David were discussing before we got there.

Vince checked his watch. "She took the kid to Tempe in the Otter. They must be there by now."

I shook my head. "She didn't take him to Tempe. Somebody else took him, or he's still in Houston."

Vince cocked his head.

I wasn't sure how much to say. Vince's role in this wasn't clear. Just because he looked surprised didn't mean he actually was.

"Emily was on the plane," Jeannie said. "No Casey."

"You were on the plane?"

I looked for help from Richard, but he shrugged. If Vince was part of the operation, he already knew, or would soon find out, what happened on the plane anyway. And if he had no part in it, there was no harm in telling him what happened. I explained about the night before.

When I came to the part about Scud, Vince sat down. He seemed more shocked at Scud's involvement than Trish's. I told him about our struggle in the training room, how I'd been stabbed in the leg, and that I'd shot Scud but didn't think he was dead. Vince said Clement was alone at the drop zone when the ambulance arrived. He walked over to me and raised my pant leg as if he had every right to do so. The fabric around my calf was stained dark red. I hadn't realized my bandage had bled through. Vince peeled back the sticky gauze and the wound brightened with a fresh surge of blood.

"You should have this looked at," he said, kneeling behind me.

"Nasty." Jeannie shuddered. "He's right."

"Scud did that?" David was pale, his face sweaty. Maybe the facts were beginning to settle in his mind. I couldn't bring myself to add that Scud—Edward Kosh—was Trish's Other Man. But the thought reminded me of something.

"David, do you have a computer?" I asked.

He gestured toward the hall. "In my study."

I removed the saturated gauze from my leg and dropped it in David's kitchen trash. He passed me some paper towels for my leg.

"Mind booting up your machine?" I asked. "I'd like to know the IP address of your cable router."

I hobbled behind as David led us to his study.

"Why?" he asked, but didn't argue.

He powered up the computer and waited for it to go through its self-checks.

The desktop icons appeared and I told David where to get the information I wanted. He hunted and pecked at his keyboard and finally a string of numbers came up.

"Richard, do you have that information from CPS?"

The call had come in during our drive from his office. Richard rooted in his pocket and produced a scrap of paper. He read off numbers as the rest of us leaned toward the monitor. The digits matched.

"What's that mean?" David asked.

"Did you ever give Trish your system password?"

He shook his head. I wasn't surprised. Someone as resourceful as Trish could get it herself. I imagined her coming up behind David as he worked, wrapping her arms around him in the same warm hug I'd seen in the rigger's loft. All she'd have to do is watch his painfully slow typing as he logged in.

I faced David. "Sometimes when you were in the field, someone logged onto this machine as you. Other times, when you were logged in at work, a dual log-in occurred from this machine."

Vince asked, "Are you saying Trish logged into David's work account as him?"

I nodded. "David, you've been having trouble locating some families."

He didn't answer, but I could tell by the way his eyes bored into mine that I had his full attention.

"Richard looked into it. Those families were all lower priority cases." I nodded at his computer. "If Trish knew you wouldn't get to those babies for a few days, she could get them first." I hesitated. "At work they think you're discriminating based on race. Many prospective 'buyers' want white babies, so Trish targets white families."

David stared at me like only half of my words were getting through.

"I think she takes the babies and, when necessary, makes the parents disappear," Richard said.

"Records simply show another deadbeat parent skipped town with their kid," I added. "No kidnapping report, no homicide investigation. Her relationship with you was a gold mine."

It was hard to remember as we spouted our theories that this was the first David had heard of Trish's crimes. The poor sap was in love with her. He'd clearly been blindsided.

I didn't get the same vibe from Vince. David swam in disbelief, but Vince looked to be seething with rage. I just wasn't sure where that anger was directed.

Richard scanned the room. "Does Trish keep many personal things here? Files on your computer? A notebook? PDA? We know which cities some kids were moved to, but not their addresses."

All I could think about was Galveston. Four years had passed. Was Annette still there?

"Is it okay if we look around?" Richard asked, too late for Jeannie. She'd opened the closet door and was already inspecting the shelves inside. David seemed too distracted to take offense. He nodded, crestfallen.

I wanted a break. "I'm going out for some air."

I retraced my path to the living room, opened the door, and only made it as far as the front landing. My leg hurt too much to go down any more stairs than I had to. I looked down. The jump rope was gone, probably picked up and carried inside by a little girl who still lived with the right family.

The door opened behind me, but I was too worn out to turn.

"I'm sorry about yesterday," Vince said. I was thankful not to be facing him. "When you said you were down here helping a friend, and had lied about a new job, you left out a few important details."

There was a light quality to his voice. My throat was too tight to answer.

He continued, "I'm not a part of that, you know. I'm nothing like her."

My eyes stung. I told myself it was still too early to trust him enough to explain about Mattie's case and the boat accident. That's when I realized I was still thinking of it as an accident. Like David, I struggled with my own form of denial. I wasn't strong enough yet to think in terms of my husband's murder.

I sniffled and folded my arms, my back still turned. "Why'd you come here today?"

He moved up beside me. I was careful to keep my eyes forward. Vince rested his hands on the railing.

"The short answer is, to find out what David knew." His tone was quiet. He took a breath and started again. "Trish is a time bomb. I know that. I also watch the news. I didn't like what I saw this morning, particularly the part about the missing plane. I called David. He was worried sick because Trish didn't come home last night. He doesn't even *know* her. The woman he sleeps with is an actress and a fraud."

He drummed his thumbs on the balcony railing and continued. "Her brother has a rap sheet a mile long. And she's doing worse things, I think, but has no record at all. Never anything to call her on. To me, that's scarier. You've seen her. Appearances are deceiving."

I remembered her beautiful smile in the picture on Scud's laptop.

"Years go by with no consequences," Vince was saying, almost musing, "and it seems she gets bolder. I hooked her up with Rick and Marie. Figured a new job around nice folks would be a step toward a cleaner life, but..." He didn't bother to finish.

I listened, curious about the references to her earlier crimes. It wasn't clear if he knew exactly what those crimes were, but either way I was disappointed and angry he hadn't intervened somehow. If he'd ever bothered to follow through with his hunches and turn her in at any point along the way, Eric Lyons might be alive. Casey might be home.

"I have a question for you now." He placed a hand lightly on my shoulder, encouraging me turn toward him. I did the best I could, but had no courage for eye contact.

"You know things about Trish I'm learning for the first time," he said. "She's the reason you were at the drop zone this week."

I nodded.

"The time you spent with me, was that to get leads on Trish?"

The shaky breath I heard after his question told me those words hadn't come easily.

I looked up at him. "I didn't know you were related until yesterday."

His expression brightened almost imperceptibly.

I added, "You might have mentioned that earlier."

He smiled then, a genuine smile like the ones I'd enjoyed all week. I feared that in the lightness of the moment, he might try to hug or kiss me, or do some other demonstrative thing to confuse me even more. I copped out and shifted my eyes toward the parking lot again, turning my face away from him. I wasn't feeling the same closure to our conversation.

"I need to know the truth, Vince," I said, my mind still on my little girl. "How much of this did you know? Did you ever cover for her?"

He didn't answer, but I heard the door open behind me. By the time I turned around, the door to David's apartment was closing between us.

Chapter Thirty-three

Jeannie sidled up to me at the balcony railing. She'd come out so quickly after Vince left me there, I wondered if she'd been watching the door. Almost as swiftly, she lit a cigarette.

"I thought you two would be out here forever." She took a draw on her Salem Light. Its tip flared.

She turned her head to exhale and let the cigarette rest between her fingers.

Jeannie's smooth, ivory hands were so beautiful they even made a cigarette look tolerable. I'd watched her smoke enough to know something here was different.

"You're usually a better actress."

She rubbed what must have been a stiff spot on her neck. "I don't know what you're talking about."

"You never wait this long before the second puff. I can tell you're fake-smoking, using it as an excuse to be out here."

She waved the smoldering tip in front of my face. "Am not."

Even outside, the smoky odor was oppressive. "That's obnoxious. What do you want?"

She huffed and dropped the nearly-new cigarette onto the concrete porch, where she used the toe of her shoe to smash it. Then she edged it forward, under the railing, until it fell. We watched it disappear into the shrubbery below.

"What's up with you two?" she finally whispered, nodding toward the door.

I felt my shoulders sag. "I don't have energy for this."

She put a hand on my arm. "I'm not imagining it, am I? Something's going on."

"Maybe there could have been," I said. "That talk we had ended badly. I can't look at him now, much less talk to him."

She brushed a wisp of bangs away from her eyes and studied me for a moment. In her gentle look, I found the unwavering support of a lifelong friend.

"You don't need this today. We should go."

I nodded.

"I'll get Richard." She gave a weak smile and went inside.

I stayed on the balcony, trying unsuccessfully to think about one thing at a time. I rehearsed what I'd say to the police. When I came to the part about Trish's money, I remembered the bag of cash was still on David's sofa. I opened the front door to grab it.

Jeannie and Vince were together in the living room. They looked at me, startled, and the moment was as awkward as if I'd found them naked.

"Richard's wrapping up with David, in the office," Jeannie said.

I looked down, snatched my bag off the sofa, and left.

For the next half-hour, I couldn't speak to Jeannie about it because Richard was with us in the car. We were headed toward the Texas Medical Center, a virtual kingdom of hospitals inside Houston's I-610 loop. An HPD buddy had told Richard where Clement was being treated for his gunshot wound. Jeannie figured we could double up our mission and get my leg fixed too.

We parked in the garage and found our way to the congested emergency room. An old man with an oxygen mask sat beside a father pressing an ice pack onto his son's arm. In the corner, a toddler wailed in long bursts. Another was drooped eerily across his mother's lap. Both children were still in pajamas at one o'clock in the afternoon.

"This looks bad," I said.

"Check in and ask about the wait," Richard said. "There should be time to hit the cafeteria before you get called."

"Time to eat *and* speak to Clement, I'd say." Jeannie cast a sideways glance at a woman coughing into a bloody rag. "Go check in, Em. These people freak me out."

I filled out the requisite paperwork. A chorus of elevator dings echoed in the halls behind me. Persistent crying seemed to carry from all directions in the vast hospital. I wondered about Casey. Wherever he was, was he crying too?

When I finished, we followed signs to the cafeteria and passed an information desk. Richard wanted to ask about Clement, so he got in line behind a group of disoriented visitors and waited. Jeannie and I took the opportunity to visit the nearby gift shop. Balloons and flower arrangements crowded the entrance to the small, over-stuffed store and I almost knocked over a vase of carnations.

"I should get him something," I said. "What do you get for a guy?"

Jeannie surveyed the arrangements and shook her head. "Not flowers. Do they sell any porn here?"

She laughed. I scanned the room for irritated parents.

"You know," she said, turning toward a shelf of candy, "I think he likes you."

I picked up a basket of gourmet coffee samples and walked toward the counter.

"He's FBI, Jeannie. I don't think he's supposed to like anybody."

She met me at the counter and added a pack of Wrigley's to my coffee basket.

"Not Clement, you screwball. Vince."

The clerk rang us up. Jeannie, restless in the smoke-free environment, tore open her gum with particular zeal.

"What were you guys talking about at David's?" I asked.

We turned for the exit and found Richard walking toward us, struggling through a jungle of ribbons hanging from a collection of helium balloons.

"There you are," he said. "I have Clement's room number. Had to say I was his brother."

I stole a glance at Jeannie. Our conversation had been put off again. She folded a piece of spearmint gum onto her tongue and winked.

◇◇◇

After lunch, it seemed nothing had changed in the E.R.'s waiting room except the numbers on its clock. Everything else was as we'd left it, with the notable absence of the lethargic baby and the blood-cougher. I considered that a small victory.

We took an elevator to Clement's floor and asked directions twice before finding the right corridor. A guard was outside his room, sitting in a chair between a food cart and an empty I.V. pole. He stood when he saw us.

"My name's Emily Locke," I said, "Could I see Agent Clement?"

"You a relative?"

I shook my head. "I have information about the case he was working on when he got shot."

"I'd ask him for ya, miss," the guard said, "but the nurse said he's sleeping."

"It's important. Could you please check again? Maybe he woke up."

A middle-aged nurse stopped to join our little hallway group. Her taut lips and darting eyes gave the impression she was more interested in meddling than helping.

"Sorry, miss," the guard said. "Nature of the job. Can't leave my post."

"Is there a problem?" the nurse asked.

I glanced at nicotine-deprived Jeannie, chewing gum at an inhuman rate, and tried to answer before she went toe-to-toe with the nurse on my behalf.

Richard spoke first. "Could you please see if Mr. Clement will accept a visitor?"

She held his gaze a moment, as if establishing her superiority. "Mr. Clement's resting. You can try back later."

Beside me, Jeannie collapsed inexplicably onto the food cart, sending dirty plates, silverware, and cups clanging to the floor. The guard stepped back into the I.V. pole and it hit the wall. A plastic cup bounced several times before rolling to a stop at my feet.

Jeannie stooped to gather forks and plastic cups from the linoleum floor. Dried kernels of leftover corn and the crusts of a few sandwiches lay scattered at our feet.

The nurse watched Jeannie toss a handful of silverware onto the cart, and then shifted her annoyed gaze to Richard and me.

"Maybe you should check again," Richard said.

◇◇◇

When the guard began to scan me with his hand-held metal detector, I passed my bag to Jeannie. There was no point slowing my admittance to Clement's room by answering questions about the money. Richard and Jeannie would wait in the E.R. and ring his room if my name were ever called, assuming it hadn't been lost in the system or I didn't bleed out in the interval.

Any mental fog Clement might have experienced following his rude awakening disappeared when he saw me. He pressed a button on the controller to his bed and raised the head until he was almost sitting. An I.V. was taped to his wrist, and a bedside computer monitor displayed a real-time trace of his heart rhythm. I couldn't see any bandages. Whatever damage had been done was hidden under the bland pattern of his hospital gown.

His face was sallow, but I was struck more by its youth than its color. For the first time, I looked at Clement and saw him for what he was: a young professional, in his late-twenties at most. His dark eyes, that once seemed so shifty, were attentive and eager, despite their fatigue.

He listened with interest as I explained what brought me to Houston.

"I certainly had my eye on you," he said. Even his voice seemed tired. "There's no employment file for you at NASA."

He gave a disapproving look and added, "But you already know that."

"You had me checked out?"

"Had to. You showed up at the drop zone on the heels of a kidnapping, then spent a lot of time in the company of my prime suspect."

I imagined my name scribbled in the margins of Clement's field notes. A mental image of a thick file with notes about his "prime suspect" followed.

"What's Vince's part in this?"

Clement hesitated. "Officially, we can only talk about *your* part in this. But, off the record, near as I can tell, your friend's involvement stops at mistaken identity. We've been chasing this ring for years. Had a lead in Texas, a pilot named Townsend. FAA records showed only one, Vincent, which is the reason I went undercover at his drop zone. His cousin Trish had become Dalton by the time she got her pilot's license, so our FAA search on her maiden name never hit on her. Seems our informant had old intel." He shrugged. "We caught a break. They fly for the same place. In that respect, Vince led us to the pilot we really wanted."

I let it sink in. Relinquishing my doubts about Vince felt wonderful until I realized what a jerk he must have thought I was.

Clement lifted a glass of water from his bedside table and drank gingerly.

"Back to you," he said. "When your NASA story didn't check out, I looked further and learned about your husband and daughter." He paused. "I'm sorry, by the way, for your loss."

I nodded.

Clement continued, "Was it ever suggested to you that their accident was related to your involvement in the Reed trial?"

I thought about Wesley Reed—the man who almost sold Mattie at a roadside diner in Austin. The one who got off because I missed the trial. Having my fears articulated by a government agent put a fresh sting into an old wound. His question made it impossible to tell my story in order. I skipped to the meat.

"My daughter didn't die in that boat wreck, Mr. Clement. She was sold to a couple in Galveston. At least, they were in Galveston four years ago. You have to help me find them."

Clement leaned forward. I wondered if he should be sitting so upright. He shifted his weight, impervious to the pain he must have felt.

"How do you know that?" His brow furrowed and glanced quickly at his bedside table, then back at me. I thought it might have been a habitual search for a notepad.

I started by explaining what happened at the hangar after he was shot.

"Thanks, by the way," he interrupted, "for making the 9-1-1 call. My mom will probably send you cookies and Christmas cards for years."

I smiled. The more we talked, the more normal he seemed. He listened to my story about stowing away on the Otter, and grew intent when I came to the part about hiding behind the crates.

"You see what was in the crates?"

"I tried to find out," I said, "but Kurt came after me before I could tell."

I rubbed my shoulder where it had been smashed under the lid.

"Whatever it was, was really hard," I added.

He frowned. "Weapons, then."

"Excuse me?"

"With this network, it's three things." He counted them on his fingers as he listed them. "Narcotics. Weapons. Human freight."

Human freight. Clement made it sound like a shipment of tomatoes or lumber.

"Drugs and weapons too? But…" I was too confused to finish.

"They operate in cells, and matrix their resources. Trish's cell traffics babies, but that's not all they do."

"Are you saying Trish was making a weapons shipment last night for another arm of her criminal ring?"

"Perhaps," he said. "And maybe another arm of her 'criminal ring' as you say, was placing a baby somewhere for her."

He took another sip of water.

"Infiltrating their system has been no small effort," he added. "I've been with the Bureau six years. This cell's been my whole career, and its parent ring has taken a nice bite into the careers of dozens of other agents."

"I have something you'll want to see then," I said.

The printouts from Scud's hard drive were in my pocket. I unfolded them and passed them to Clement. He took them with the hand that had the I.V., still giving no indication of pain. Where anesthesia was concerned, it seemed new facts in his case were medicine enough.

I walked to his bedside and reviewed the papers with him, describing my suspicions about the columns' significance. Clement's eyes followed my finger over the page.

"This entry is Casey Lyons," I said. "The date matches when he disappeared, and this is his age and gender. This little girl is missing from Houston," I pointed to the row for an eight-month-old female. "It doesn't look like she's been sold yet. Maybe you can find her."

"Look at those cities," he said, more to himself than me. "And the names. I can't believe he actually attributed the crimes." He was looking at the column that associated names like Kosh and Dalton with the kids they took. "It's like they're keeping score."

It was then I realized what I was up against. I wasn't only battling the criminal network Clement had described, which, admittedly, surpassed even my worst fears. But I was keying in on something else. I was in this to find Annette and Casey, but Clement's priority was to bust the ring.

"Is the FBI going to find my daughter, Mr. Clement?"

He looked up from the list.

"I sincerely hope so," he said. "We want to bring all these kids home."

"When will you start following up on this list?"

"I'm sure a parallel effort will begin after I brief my office on this new information." He raised the papers slightly. "My team will want to spend time with you, hear your story. When we have it sorted, we'll reorganize resources and follow up your leads."

"What's that mean? A day? A week?"

Clement cocked his head. "Hard to say at this point. I'm sorry."

I made a decision then to tell Clement about everything I knew, but not about everything I had. Right or wrong, I'd keep that sack of money because it was my only path to Annette.

Chapter Thirty-four

Forty minutes into my exchange with Clement, a doctor entered his room and told me in succinct but polite terms to leave. She was marking on his medical chart before I stood up from my chair.

"Wait," Clement said, as I moved toward the door. "This shouldn't take long."

I glanced at his doctor, but she ignored me and paced to a computer monitor, where she studied an ECG trace and some changing numbers.

"It's fine," I told Clement. "I need to get my leg fixed anyway, and you should rest." I opened the door and turned to say goodbye.

"Stop," he said. "You can't leave."

He shifted in his bed to sit up, but his doctor protested with a silent pat on his shoulder.

"You shot someone last night. You have critical information about a time sensitive investigation."

The doctor turned to appraise me.

Clement continued. "There will be a formal interview, at the very least. Immediately."

"That's fine," I lied. We had two agendas, and we both knew it. "How about I come back as soon as I'm stitched up?"

Clement hesitated. "Technically, I'm on medical leave. And the interview should be video recorded anyway. I'll arrange for you to be taken to the field office. They can handle it there."

"Of course." I checked my watch and frowned. "I've been waiting an hour-and-a-half and the E.R. is packed. Would it be easier if I came back when I'm done and waited for the agent here with you? Hate to eat up half his day by making him sit around, waiting."

Clement didn't answer, but he didn't stop looking at me, either. I wondered how well the FBI might have trained him to read signs of deceit.

"Miss?" the doctor said, nodding to the door.

"See you in a while," I told Clement.

His distrustful expression was cemented on my brain as I walked down the hall. I didn't want to lie, but Annette was more important. I'd risk anything to find her.

I used a pay phone in a waiting room to dial my cell. It was still in the bag I'd given Jeannie. She'd never been one to worry about answering a phone that wasn't hers.

"It's me," I said. "Is Richard with you?"

"Yep."

"Go somewhere he can't hear you. Take the bag."

"Just a sec," she said, "I'm in a hospital and we're not supposed to use cell phones in here. Let me go outside."

"You're good," I told her. "Tell me when you're there."

A few moments later she said, "Alright, I'm at the drop-off curb. How'd it go with the Fed?"

"I'll get to that, but first I need a favor. Dig out Kurt's phone from that bag and find the number for the call that came in from Trish this morning. Should be two calls back, before the one that came from the apartment."

She talked me through her search of the bag and navigation of the phone's menus. Finally, she found the number. I read it back to her.

"Fine. That's done," she said. "What are you doing?"

"Baiting Trish."

She didn't say anything.

"You can't tell anyone, especially Richard. If he gets involved and my idea doesn't work, this could be the second career ruined for him."

"What should I say if he asks who called?"

"Tell him it was somebody from work." An ambulance wailed on Jeannie's end. "Thanks for the number. I'll be there as soon as I make this call. Plant the seed in Richard's head that I need to give my statement to the local FBI field office next. Tell him we could drop him at his office first. Work out a way to borrow his car."

"Roger, wilco," she said. "Good luck."

I pressed and released the pay phone's switch hook. The dial tone sounded ominous. I punched in Trish's number and waited.

"I want to make a trade," I said when she answered. I tried to keep my voice down.

"I'm listening."

"For my daughter and Casey Lyons."

"When?" she asked. Her voice sounded tinny and distant. I was surprised by her cooperation.

"Today."

"No. Later."

I wondered why.

"You've done more on less notice, Trish. Let's get this over with."

"The answer's no. I don't trust you. Your friend's an ex-cop and the airport's dirty with Feds."

"I'm not working with them."

"I don't believe you. This conversation's over."

"Wait," I said. "You need that cash. If you didn't, you wouldn't have bothered to take Jeannie."

She didn't answer. But, she didn't hang up, either.

"You'll get half when I get the kids, the other half when we're away, safe. Deliver them, and disappear."

"It's a set-up."

"It's not." I paused. "You'll manage the logistics. I'll do it however you want, whenever you want."

I steeled myself.

"How will I get the second half?"

"I'll put it in a locker somewhere and give you the key. When I'm away safe with the kids, I'll tell you where the locker is."

"Maybe you won't. You could get the kids and then keep the other half."

"And you could come empty handed, take the first half, and kill me."

She was silent.

"Are we doing this or not?"

"We'll see," she said. "I'll be in touch."

I took the elevator to the first floor and walked to the E.R. waiting room, feeling enveloped in a surreal dream. Annette was alive. ALIVE! If I could pull this off, I'd see her soon. Jeannie was in the chairs, squeezed between a nodding sleeper and a stooped old man in an army cap.

"Where's Richard?" I asked as I walked toward her.

"He left. Said he'd take a cab to work, had plenty to do. He was glad to loan the car so you could go give your statement."

I was relieved the car had been a non-issue, but also mildly disappointed Richard had left me so easily.

Jeannie seemed to read my mind. "You're in capable hands, honey. Don't worry."

I forced a smile. "Capable if I need a make-over."

"I wasn't talking about me."

"Who, then?"

She leaned to peer around me. I turned and followed her gaze. Vince was feeding a bill to a Coke machine down the hall. Even from a distance, I could tell he was tired. He was no less handsome for it, though.

I spun back to Jeannie.

"What's he doing here?"

"I might have called him."

"How? I don't even know his number."

"I got that for you at David's apartment. You're welcome."

"I should kill you."

The old man next to her chuckled. "Don't do that," he said. "She tells good jokes. Kind you can't take home to mama." He chuckled again.

I leveled a stare at Jeannie.

Vince walked up beside me, open soda can in hand. I was too humiliated to look at him. The desk attendant saved me. She called my name.

"About damn time," Jeannie said, loud enough for all to hear. "You want some moral support back there, hon'?"

Despite my irritation, her offer sounded good. I nodded.

She looked from me to Vince. "Take good care of my girl."

The old man smacked his knee and laughed again.

◇◇◇

"Jeannie told me what Trish did to your family," Vince said quietly. We'd been left in my examination area—basically a curtain-lined cubicle with a paper-covered table. "Nothing I've thought to say could possibly be appropriate."

He sat on a stool and let his hands fall loosely into his lap. The grief in his eyes spoke volumes. He understood what Trish had taken. Whether he was sorrier for my loss or for his cousin's part in it, I couldn't guess, but I wanted to collapse in his arms.

I dropped my head. "I'm sorry I thought you could have been part of that."

He stood and crossed the narrow space between the stool and my spot on the exam table. He was wearing the same cologne I remembered from our walk on the beach, something nautical and fresh. I almost trembled when he placed a hand over mine.

"Thank you for coming here," I added. "I thought I'd seen the last of you."

The drape swished open and a nurse pushed in a wheeled cart with assorted, sterile-looking tools on top. Vince gave my hand a press and leaned in so only I could hear.

"You haven't seen the last of me." He brushed my cheek so softly I thought I might have imagined it, then maneuvered out of the way so the nurse could prep my leg.

Twenty minutes later, I'd been stitched and dosed with painkillers and antibiotics. We were waiting for the nurse to return with my prescription when I heard my name bandied somewhere beyond the curtain. It was Jeannie.

An instant later, she slipped into my exam area and whisked my shoes from the floor.

She shoved one in my lap. "Let's go."

"What? Now?" Vince seemed as confused as I was.

"Sorry, cowboy," she told him, thrusting the other shoe onto my foot. "This wagon train's movin' out."

"Jeannie," I protested. "What the hell?"

She grabbed my arm and pulled me, half-shoeless, from the table. "Suits!" she hissed. "Come on!"

I leaned to put on my other shoe and Jeannie stuck her head beyond the curtain and looked both ways. Then she grabbed me by the wrist and levered me into the hall.

"Suits?" Vince asked. He followed us from the room.

"Yeah, suits," she said. "Flashing badges. Get the picture?" She ushered me past him.

I hustled down the hallway with Jeannie on one side and Vince on the other. We struggled to keep up the pace without looking conspicuous. Vince even managed a casual sip from his Coke can.

We turned and followed another hallway until it dead-ended at a bank of elevators. Jeannie scanned the area for a hiding place. I noticed a suited man rounding the corner at the intersection where we'd turned. He paused to check some sort of paper in his hand and then squinted at me. Vince took a step toward the elevators and pushed a button. When the agent looked up, he began walking toward us again, this time faster.

"That's one of them," Jeannie said. "Go."

She pushed me past the elevators, toward a stairwell door, but it was too late. The agent's footsteps quickened. He was nearly to the elevators when Jeannie and I entered the stairwell. I heard the pronounced *oomph* of two bodies colliding, then a crisp, metallic smack. When I looked back, Vince and the agent were standing over a fizzing puddle on the linoleum floor, the Coke can at their feet. Their shirts and pants were spattered.

Jeannie and I raced up the stairs.

"Sorry, man..." Vince was saying.

The stairwell door thudded closed behind us and we continued. When we were between the second and third floors, I heard it swing open again.

Chapter Thirty-five

Below, footsteps gained on us.

"Emily Locke?" the agent yelled up the stairs. "FBI."

At the landing to the third floor, Jeannie looked at me, pointed to her feet, and mouthed "shh." She flung open the door to the third floor, but continued silently up the stairs to the fourth. I followed.

On the next landing, Jeannie eased open the door silently. We stepped into a corridor thick with disinfectant fumes as a nurse eased a gurney into the elevator. I resisted the weight of the closing door, so its sound wouldn't echo into the stairwell. Jeannie strode purposefully down the corridor and I tried to mimic the confidence she exuded, but I was rattled, listening for the stairwell door behind us. We took the first turn and passed signs for Pediatric Dialysis and MRI.

Behind us, someone called to hold the elevator.

"It's him," I whispered. "He's asking which way we went."

We made a right.

A cell phone chimed.

Jeannie stripped my bag from her shoulder and pushed it toward me. "Turn off your damn phone!"

I unzipped the bag and felt around for it, still trying to keep up with Jeannie yet remain low-key.

Ahead, double doors were positioned under a sign that said Laundry. Jeannie made her way to the doors and pressed one open as I flipped open my phone.

"How's it going at the field office?" Richard wanted to know.

No one was in the Laundromat. Commercial dryers, humming and droning as they spun bland linens, made it hard to hear. I walked to the back of the room, next to a series of wheeled, canvas laundry hampers. It was hot and humid in the room and I was already sweating.

"It's...fine," I said. "But, this is a bad time. I'll call you back soon. Promise."

Jeannie took a post by the swinging doors and peered through their narrow glass panes.

"Emily—" Richard began.

I closed my phone. "Any sign of him?"

Jeannie shook her head.

My phone rang again. I pressed the buttons to ignore the call and silence the ringer.

"Shit!" Jeannie said, in a loud whisper. "He's coming!" She whirled toward me, her face stretched in panic.

I scanned the room. "Get in a basket!"

I burrowed through dirty linens piled in an oversized canvas hamper and tried to ignore its smells. Jeannie did the same. When my hole was deep enough that I could hide beneath the basket's rim, I stepped in and pulled dirty hospital gowns and damp towels over myself. Body odor and the musty scent of old moisture made me want to throw up.

Jeannie whimpered. "Eww! I scooped up something wet and chunky!"

"Get *in*." I hoped she'd do it fast.

Soon, only the rhythmic sound of dryers filled the room. I took shallow breaths, worried the rise and fall of my chest might move the mound of linens covering me.

A moment later, the Laundromat door squeaked. It hesitated in the open position. I imagined the agent surveying the washers and dryers, maybe even the laundry hampers. I held my breath. The door squeaked closed.

I exhaled in relief. Unsure how long to wait, I decided to count to sixty. I'd only gotten to two when the door swung open again.

"Oh!" A woman said. "You startled me."

Holy Hell, I thought, he's still in the room. I pictured Jeannie balled up in her neighboring chamber of sweat and vomit and wondered how she was doing.

"Brent Keller," the agent said. "Looking for a missing patient."

In my mind, I could see the badge flashing.

"Here's her picture," Keller said. "Seen her?"

There was a pause.

"Sorry," she said. "'Scuse me, please. Watch your toes."

Castors rolled over the linoleum. The wheels droned louder until a soft-sided hamper ploughed into my hiding spot and sandwiched me between itself and Jeannie's basket. A dryer buzzed.

The next time I thought the room was clear, I upped the count to two hundred.

That time, I only made it to thirty-nine. Jeannie extricated herself first and cursed up such a storm I worried she'd be overheard. I climbed out too and tried to think of a safe exit strategy. I searched carts and dryers and found a set of scrubs for each of us. We pulled them over our clothes.

Jeannie said Keller, wherever he was, would expect us to go downstairs, so we should go up. We went to a higher floor and found a restroom where we could—in Jeannie's words—"clean off this putrid funk." We crossed the building and made our way downstairs. The hospital's vastness worked for us. Eventually, its cavernous walls spit us out on the wrong side of the block, but a passing intern directed us back to our garage.

When I checked my phone, I'd missed four calls from Richard.

"You drive," I told Jeannie. "I need to call him."

"Call him?" she said. "An hour ago, you told me to keep him in the dark."

"An hour ago, I wasn't a fugitive from the law."

We climbed into the car and closed its doors. Jeannie backed out of the parking space. She braked in the aisle and looked at me. "What happened to 'it'll ruin his career'?"

My head fell back onto the headrest. I didn't know what to do. Jeannie let the car coast down the ramp toward the garage's exit.

"If it weren't for you and Vince, I'd be in custody," I said.

She smiled. "Good thing for you, we kick ass."

I shook my head. "That was luck. I can't skirt the FBI forever. I'll be surprised to make it another hour."

She paid the attendant and the gate arm rose. Sunlight flooding in from the street was blinding.

"Which way do I turn?" she asked.

"I don't care," I said. "I need to find a locker."

She took a right out of the garage and drove where traffic pushed her.

"Are you suggesting Richard can help you evade the FBI until you get Annette?"

"I don't think he'd do that. But he'd probably help explain why I ran."

"You can do that yourself."

"What if they trace my call and come for me before I get her? If Richard explained to Clement, maybe the FBI would help me."

"You've lost your mind."

No, I was an amateur—and way over my head. In my panic, I'd evaded any potential backup. Now I could only hope the outcome would be the best for Annette and Casey.

We passed the Museum of Natural Science and the Museum of Fine Arts. Jeannie rounded a corner and we stopped an intersection with the Health Museum on one side and the Children's Museum on another.

At the crosswalk, mothers and youngsters held hands and checked both ways before crossing to the brightly colored building. Some pushed strollers, others pulled wagons. One mom with a baby on her hip bent to recover a dropped bottle.

"Park the car," I said.

"What?"

"Find a meter and park. Look at all those kids. All their gear." I felt a pang, remembering what it was like to haul a stroller and diaper bag everywhere I went. "They've got to have lockers in there."

For a quarter, I rented a small, wall-mounted metal cube. When we were alone, Jeannie stood watch as I pulled $125,000 of thick, cash bricks from my backpack and stacked them inside. The door snapped shut and I removed a key with a cheap plastic handle from the slot and shoved it into the pocket of my Capris.

Outside, we waited to cross the street and Jeannie turned to me and wrinkled her nose.

"We're sending Trish to a children's museum?"

Chapter Thirty-six

"I lied before," I told Richard, once we connected via phone. "I never went to the FBI field office for an interview."

"I know."

"It's because Trish knows where Annette is. She'll trade her for the money. Casey too."

Jeannie and I were laying low in a park near the Houston Zoo. Richard was my second call. First, we'd called Vince to thank him for his help at the hospital and bring him up to speed. He wanted to help and I'd promised to keep him posted.

"Your emotions are clouding your judgment." My low-battery warning interrupted him but Richard's tone came through; his words snapped with the harsh bite of concern. "What you're planning is suicide. She'll never let you walk out of there with those kids."

"I think she's greedy enough to do it."

"Think. She gives you the kids. You give her the money. What's to say she'll let you leave? She'll kill you, take her money, take the kids—probably sell them *again*—and be back in business before dinner."

I explained where I'd hidden half of her money. Richard wasn't persuaded.

"When's this happening?" he asked.

"She'll call me. The only way she'd do it was for me to let her set it up."

"Jesus." He exhaled. "You know I have to tell the FBI."

From my seat at a picnic table, I spotted Jeannie at the playground, surrounded by a gaggle of little girls.

Richard continued. "By the way, I know what you did at the hospital."

"Look, I want to call Clement, but I'm afraid that if I do, the FBI will track me down before I get Annette."

"You need their help."

I nodded. "I know. But I'm afraid to ask for it. They might accidentally tip off Trish. Or maybe arrest me. I don't know what to do."

"Clement wants Trish," Richard said. "And you're talking to her. That should help. Where are you?"

"Hermann Park. We're waiting for her instructions."

"*We*? You didn't trust me or the FBI, but *Jeannie's* competent?"

I looked up in time to see her "shake it all about" with a group of Hoky-Pokying preschoolers.

I shrugged. "She busted me out of the hospital."

"Stay put," he said. "I'll call Clement, see what he says."

Shortly after we hung up, Kurt's phone rang. Trish was ready.

The plan she laid out wasn't what I expected: "Go to Neiman Marcus in the Galleria and tell them you lost a beaded red bag. Get there by 5:30. Bring the money."

It was 4:35 and I didn't know how long it took to get to the Galleria, or where the Neiman Marcus was. Trish didn't stay on the line long enough to ask her.

"Come on!" I waved Jeannie toward the car. She trotted after me, kids waving goodbye as she hurried away. We asked a speed walker for directions. She seemed to answer in slow motion.

We got to the Galleria in a half hour. I recognized some street names—Richmond, West Alabama, Westpark. It was the neighborhood I'd jogged my first morning in Houston.

Traffic near the high-dollar mega mall was a problem. Cars were gridlocked around the block, turn signals blinking. I feared the wait would eat up the time I had left.

"Go ahead," Jeannie said at the corner of Westheimer and Post Oak. "I'll park. Give me your phone. When you have the mysterious handbag, call me. We'll hook up that way."

I pulled Kurt's cell phone out of the bag, lighter with half its cash missing, and handed it to Jeannie.

"No," she said, "You need that one incase Trish calls again. Give me yours."

"I need mine incase Richard calls."

Impatient, she snatched the backpack from me and took out my phone. We saved the critical numbers—mine, Richard's, Trish's, Vince's, and the new pre-paid—into all the models. Jeannie kept my cell and I took the new temporary phone along with Kurt's. Then I let myself out of the car, waited for a Number 33 Metro bus to pass, and crossed the street toward the mall.

At Neiman Marcus, I passed a security guard at the door and was promptly met by a dignified older woman in a non-descript black suit. A shiny gold nametag I couldn't read was pinned to her lapel.

"Is there a lost and found? I left my purse."

She directed me to an elevator bank between Cosmetics and Shoes and suggested I try Customer Service, downstairs. On my way, I glimpsed a sale price of $1300 on a handbag discreetly chained to its display shelf.

When the associate downstairs handed over my "lost" bag, I was struck by its lightness. I stepped behind a Baccarat crystal display and unsnapped the little purse. A note and key were inside.

Leave the mall through the far end of the food court. Exit to the Yellow Garage. I'll know if you're alone. A white Lexus is parked in area LL1, Zone H, two rows from the door. License plate V72 BNT. Use the key to take it north to Huntsville on I-45. Call when you pass Exit 60.

I found a ladies room tucked in the back of the China department, but the elegant, full-length doors inside made it difficult to know for sure that I was alone. I listened for a few moments, and convinced I had no company, closed myself in a stall and called Jeannie to read her the note. She said she'd tell the plan to Richard and Vince.

She'd try to get to the Yellow Garage and watch for the white Lexus, but she was gridlocked in so much traffic she figured I'd get there first.

"If I wait," I said, "it'll look suspicious."

"No, don't do that. Head up the highway like she said and tell me where you exit. We can help you if we know where you are."

I exited Neiman Marcus and found myself on the second of three floors, all open to an elaborate arched skylight that ran the length of the enormous corridor. On my way to the food court, I passed dozens of elite shops: Chanel, Tiffany & Co., Fendi, Cartier, Ralph Lauren, Giorgio Armani, Versace, Coach. At each storefront, I wondered whether someone were watching from inside. Below, a full-size ice skating rink was built right in the middle of the mall with the food court surrounding it on both sides. The blended scent of frying onions and grilled meat dominated the food court, where space was so limited several people ate standing, watching figure skaters spin and jump below.

I took the escalator to the lower level and followed signs to the Yellow Garage. A video arcade on my left pumped out peppy, electronic tunes that faded when I eased open a glass door and stepped outside, into the garage. Cigarette smoke lingered in the space around me, but the only people I saw were motorists jockeying for a place to park. For a moment, I worried that a henchman or sniper, or perhaps Trish herself, might have me in a gun sight. Then I relaxed a little, figuring they wouldn't kill someone who still had half their money. I surveyed the parking area, but found only innocuous rows of cars, a Sparkletts delivery truck, and drivers too preoccupied to notice me.

I wasn't surprised Jeannie hadn't made it. Through a nearby street exit, I could see traffic outside was still bumper-to-bumper.

I paced two rows of cars and found the Lexus with the right plate. Before getting inside, I checked the back seat. Only immaculate leather and pristine floor mats waited behind the tinted glass.

Twenty-five minutes later, I accelerated up the I-610 ramp on my way to I-45. According to Jeannie, Huntsville was seventy miles north of Houston. The drop zone was seventy miles south. I thought about the extensive cross-city travel and wondered what Trish was planning.

Exit Sixty caught me by surprise because it was nowhere close to Huntsville. In fact, I wasn't even out of Houston when I passed its sign.

I called Trish.

"The next exit is Beltway 8," she said. "Take it east. Follow the signs for Bush Intercontinental." Houston's largest airport, the one I'd flown into with Richard.

"Park in Terminal C," she continued. "Wear the sweater that's in your trunk. Put the money in the pillow."

"The pillow?"

"There's a boarding pass in your glove box. Use it to—"

"A boarding pass to go where?"

"It doesn't matter. You're not getting on the plane. Use the boarding pass to get through the security checkpoint in Terminal C. When I'm satisfied you're not armed or wired, I'll be in touch."

"But I don't have—"

She hung up.

"Shit." My driver's license was at the motel in Freeport with the rest of my things. Without it, I'd never get past security.

My palms slipped over the leather-wrapped wheel. Beltway 8 came up quickly, and I took it east like she'd said. Within minutes, I saw signs for the airport. At the first red light, I leaned over the seat, opened the glove box, and removed an envelope. Inside was a ticket to New Orleans *and my driver's license.* Trish's pervasive ways of doing business chilled me. I grew more worried with each new, meticulous detail.

I set the envelope on the seat and called Jeannie.

"Don't go in," she said. "Wait for help."

"If I take too long, she'll know something's up."

"It's a bad idea."

"Tell Richard to make sure the FBI knows what's going on. The airport's packed. I don't think she'd hurt me in front of all these people."

"She's capable of anything. You should wait for the FBI."

I followed overhead signs for Terminal C and tried to stay out of the way of parking lot shuttle busses.

"I won't risk botching this trade. Tell them where I am. I'm sure they can move fast when they want to."

My lane veered to the left and took me under a set of bridges meant for planes, not cars. At the terminal, a long series of identical airplanes waited at the gates, parked in neat rows. I followed signs for short-term parking and drove up a spiral ramp into the garage.

"I'm here," I said. "I'll call you when I get through security."

I parked in the first parking space I saw, marked for compact cars only, and popped the trunk. Inside, a sweater and a flesh-colored pillow in the shape of a half-oval were neatly arranged in a plastic grocery store sack. The pillow had an elastic band that looked like a belt, and when I lifted it and realized what it was, I felt queasy. The tag inside the sweater confirmed my fear: GapMaternity.

I'd worn a similar faux-belly once—maternity stores keep them in dressing rooms so expectant moms can see how the clothes will fit later. What troubled me about Trish's model was the careful stitching and added zipper that concealed a hollowed-out cavity. Grime along the lining and frayed edges near the clasp told me I wasn't the first to wear it.

I returned to the driver's seat, stuffed the cash bundles into the pillow, and zipped it. Satisfied that no one was looking, I pulled off my cardigan and buckled the fake belly over the camisole I was wearing. Then I pulled the maternity sweater over my head, making sure to smooth it over my new baby bump. I locked the car and took the elevator to ground level. Even from a distance, jet fuel and exhaust fumes were unmistakable.

Skycaps at the terminal entrance ignored me because I didn't have a bag to check. I walked straight past customer check-in lines, computerized self-check kiosks, and bag check-in stations and stepped into the security line with a backpack containing two phones and a cardigan. A young mother in front of me collapsed a stroller with one swift stomp on its frame.

"Guess this'll be you soon," she said, bending to lift it. "How much longer?"

"Two months."

She gave a tired smile. "Prepare to haul a lot of stuff."

Behind her, a TSA officer patted down a Muslim passenger at the metal detector. I got nervous watching the officer's blue latex gloves feel the back of a woman's head through her hijab. Then the passenger raised her arms to the side and the gloved hands smoothed over each sleeve one at a time before running down the sides of her body. The gravity of what I was about to do overwhelmed me and it was an effort just to breathe. I acted like I was adjusting my waist band and discreetly moved the strap of my belly-pillow down so that it would overlay on the waistline of my Capris.

At the x-ray machine, I put my shoes into a gray plastic bin and set them on the conveyer belt next to my bag. Then I took a slow, deep breath—careful to be subtle about it—looked straight ahead, and waited to be waved through the metal detector.

The officer on the other side motioned me forward and nothing beeped.

"Raise your arms to the sides, please."

I did what she said and willed myself not to sweat. She ran her hands along each of my arms as she'd done to the passengers before me. Then she ran them straight down my back and over my hips. She felt my ankles. Wordlessly, she nodded me through.

I stepped to the side, put my shoes on, and headed toward my gate with the bag slung over one shoulder. To my right, an enormous longhorn steer head was mounted over the entrance to some kind of ranch-themed gift shop. A phone rang, muffled in the backpack.

"That was good," Trish said. "Now turn around and go back the way you came. Go downstairs to baggage claim."

I looked up and down the wide corridor and didn't see her anywhere. Above me, an overhead walkway extended from the elevators and escalators toward the parking garage I'd come from. A glass half-wall ran the length of the banister, and I could see she wasn't up there either, but a wide concrete pillar spanning both levels near the elevator bank worried me. Anyone could be hiding behind it.

"How much longer?"

"Go to baggage claim. If you do what you're told, you'll have the kids within the hour."

The phone's line went silent. *Within the hour* repeated in my mind. I imagined Annette in my arms and stepped onto the escalator, thankful to not have to limp down the steps.

When the baggage claim area came into view, I counted eleven carousels. Unsure where to go, I dropped into a seat near the Visitor Information desk and watched a kid with light-up shoes chase his sister. A woman next to me complained to her friend that Newark was always a mess. She was chewing some potent spearmint gum. Trish called again.

"See the ladies room in the corner behind Carousel 10?"

I looked around and found it about ten yards ahead on the left.

"Yes."

"See the pay phones?"

Four telephones were directly in front of the restroom next to a stainless steel table built into the floor. None were in use.

"Yes."

"When I hang up, go into the ladies room and leave both of your cell phones in the trashcan in the third stall. I'll know if you call someone, so don't blow it. Go to the pay phones and pick up the one that rings."

"Both of…what'd you say?" How could she *possibly* know about the disposable back-up phone in my bag?

"Both phones. Yours and Kurt's."

"I don't have my phone," I said. "Jeannie does."

"Sure, honey. Leave two phones or the deal's off."

"Call her if you don't believe me. The number's—"

"I have the number." She hung up.

Unsure what to do, I stayed in my seat. Six minutes later Trish called back.

"Your friend's a trash talker." She paused. "Go to the restroom like I said and leave Kurt's phone in the third stall."

The line went silent, and for a moment I felt paralyzed even though I was already hustling. In the restroom, several stalls, including the third, were occupied. When it was vacant, I went inside, chucked the phone into the trash, and backtracked toward the pay phones. I waited nearby until the phone nearest the table rang.

"Stand by," Trish said. "I'm waiting to hear about the phone."

"I did what you said."

She didn't answer.

I watched the ladies room only a few paces away. A mother came out with a little girl in red cowboy boots, towing a miniature bag on wheels. Two women in saris and scarves emerged. A middle-aged woman came out backward, pulling an elderly woman in her wheelchair. Who among them was checking the trash for Kurt's phone?

"Good," Trish said finally. "An envelope is taped to the bottom of the table next to you."

I crouched and looked up at its base. "Got it."

"There's another car key."

I opened the envelope as she spoke.

"This one's a silver Volvo. Take the inter-terminal train to Terminal A and go to its garage. The parking spot's marked on the keychain."

I turned the key over.

"There's also a set of directions. That's where we'll make the exchange."

I closed my eyes. It was really going to happen.

"Finally," she said, "You're being watched at the airport. And after you leave, you should know there's a transponder on the car. No pit stops. Otherwise, deal's off."

Chapter Thirty-seven

I didn't dare stop driving. I imagined Trish at our meeting place, watching a circular blip, my car, creep across a computer screen. Beside her, maybe Casey was chewing on a teething toy or pulling himself up on furniture. I wondered if she'd feed him or change him if he cried.

Annette would be terrified, and I felt responsible. She'd been torn from a second home, and this time she'd remember. How had Trish gotten her, and what had she told her, if anything? The line of thought stopped me. Maybe she'd been taken violently. What if her new parents, like Jack, were murdered during the abduction? I swallowed. Maybe Annette had been bound or blindfolded. Or slapped. I started to cry.

Who had kept her all these years? If she hadn't grown up with the knowledge of having been adopted, then hearing it from me—a stranger to her by now, I realized—would be confusing and scary. She wouldn't believe me. More likely, she'd think *I* was a kidnapper.

Railroad tracks were ahead, beyond a flashing yellow light. Sixty-five minutes had passed since I'd left the airport, and I'd been off the highway for twenty, long enough for the sun to drop to the horizon in my rearview mirror. I turned on my headlights and flipped open the disposable phone Jeannie had given me. Dividing my attention between the road and the display, I sent a quick text message to update her on my location. It would have been easier to just call, but if Trish really did have a transponder on the car, I worried she might also have it bugged. Jeannie would get my message to Richard and the authorities *if* my phone had any juice left.

The uncertainty left too much to chance. I texted Richard too.

Except for the tracks, the only sign of civilization was a leaning barbed-wire fence separating me from empty, overgrown fields. I passed an ancient wooden barn that had toppled sideways next to a sun-bleached old pick-up, left so long ago its bumpers touched the ground. The road began to morph into something made more of dirt than asphalt. I crossed the railroad tracks and checked my odometer.

A quarter-mile later, the driveway I was looking for disappeared to the right into a forest of pines. My directions said to look for two No Trespassing signs nailed to trees on either side of the drive. They were worn and faded, neglected like everything else—including my common sense, I supposed. But what else could I do?

I eased onto the dirt track. The car bumped when its tires rolled off the road and I let it creep slowly, hearing only the crunch of a thick layer of pine needles. Far ahead, the drive curved, and I couldn't see where it ended. The forest swallowed most of the remaining light from the disappearing sun.

Red reflectors glinted some distance ahead and realized I was coming up on a vehicle parked at the driveway's end. When I came around a final patch of trees, I found the car beside a rustic cabin. An elevated porch wrapped around the modest shack, and thick curtains covered its windows. I pulled up beside the other car. The porch light flicked on. Its feeble glow barely extended to the edge of the porch, but I felt like I was under floodlights.

I turned off the engine and took a quick look around. No one was in sight, but several bags of trash had been left beside the porch steps. Beside them, a couple of shovels and a stack of firewood leaned against the porch.

In front of me, a screen door swung open and Trish stepped outside. I was eye-level with her suede boots. I followed her slim figure all the way up, past jeans and a pullover sweater, to a hateful, steady gaze and opened my car door.

The screen door smacked shut behind her and I stepped out of the car into muggy evening air that smelled like damp earth and pines. My shoes sank into the soft ground. Far away, I heard a train whistle.

"Where's my money?" Trish said.

I leaned into the car and got the pillow from my maternity disguise. When I unzipped it showed her a fistful of cash, she nodded.

"What about the kids?" I could hardly breathe, much less speak. I wondered if Annette was really inside the dumpy little cabin.

Trish pulled the screen door open and held it, never taking her eyes off me. Faint sounds of a television program grew louder and softer as light flashed on the door in various hues.

"No," I said. "You bring them out here, to me."

She shrugged and disappeared inside, and the screen door slammed behind her. A moment later, she returned with Casey on her hip. His curls and cheeks were exactly as I remembered from Richard's pictures. I couldn't believe she'd kept her word. My eyes went immediately to the doorway behind her, but Annette wasn't there.

Trish stalked down the front porch steps, the heels of her boots clacking on the wood. Casey looked sleepy, but not mistreated. She thrust him at me. "Here."

The baby clutched my blouse and laid his head on my shoulder. He turned his face into my collar and began to suck his thumb. Maybe anybody was more comforting than Trish.

She stared at me. "Your little girl's a brat. Like her bitchy mother."

I clutched Casey tighter. "Give her to me."

She tossed her head so her blond hair fell behind her shoulders.

"First, the locker key." She extended an open palm.

I dug in my pants pocket for the key and dropped it into her hand. "Once the kids are safe, I'll tell you where to find the rest of the cash."

She turned and walked up the steps. When she got to the door, she held it open, and called inside. There was no answer.

"Come on!" she called again, and a defiant, "No!" came back.

The voice was small but willful. I darted for the stairs, holding Casey close against my chest, and fought to keep my feet from slipping across the saturated ground. My vision was blurred from tears before I reached the porch.

"No!" I heard again, and Trish stomped inside. When I got to the door, she was suddenly back, first tugging at a delicate wrist, then yanking it hard. A crying little girl appeared from behind the door, pushing and writhing with all her might.

"Let her go!" I shoved Trish with my free hand.

She released her grasp, and Annette stared up at me, wide-eyed. Time had sculpted her to look even more like Jack than I remembered. I dropped to my knees.

"Come here, baby." And—miracle of miracles—she did. I pulled her close.

Her skin radiated warmth and her clothes were damp with sweat. I ran a hand over her beautiful cheek. Blond bangs stuck to her forehead in a wet cluster. She was shaking. I kissed her.

"We're leaving," I told her softly, and hoped she'd find something comforting in me.

Dark, full lashes lined her eyes now. I'd missed all the subtle changes that had transformed her from a baby to a child. She nodded with more maturity than I thought a five-year-old would have, then placed a tiny hand on Casey's back. She dropped her head and kissed him on his cheek.

I stood and led her down the steps. She had gorgeous, thick pigtails and her hair was the color of straw, like her dad's.

As we walked from the cabin, she looked over her shoulder. "I don't like that lady. She's mean."

My baby had more courage than I had. I couldn't look back.

"I don't like her either, sweetheart." With a gentle press on her head, I redirected her attention to the car. "Let's get in."

I let her silky pigtail slip through my fingers. It was impossible not to stare at her.

"Are you taking me home?" she asked.

I could only stroke her cheek in response.

The woods flared in a sudden pulse of brightness. Headlights.

I'd been so focused on Annette that I hadn't noticed a car coming from the main road.

I whirled to Trish. "What's going on?"

The lights grew closer, faster, their beams bounding with each dip in the path.

Trish folded her arms across her chest. "You said you'd keep our deal between us," she said. "But I know you lied."

Annette tugged on my hand. "What's happening?"

The vehicle pulled up behind my car and stopped so suddenly the front end dipped. It was a white, full size van with tinted windows. The driver's door flung open.

"The car that took me!" Annette's squeal startled Casey so badly he jumped. I had to use both hands to keep him from falling backward. Annette clutched my leg. I shifted the baby and freed a hand for Annette. She turned her face into my hip.

I recognized the driver; it was Kurt, the man who'd attacked me on the plane the night before. He stepped from the van, pursed his lips in a smug grin, and leaned on the fender.

Trish said, "Tell me the locker location."

"When the kids are safe," I insisted. "Not before."

Annette began to sob.

Trish nodded to Kurt. I followed her gaze, and watched him slide a jacket panel back far enough to reveal a gun. I looked at Trish again.

"Change of plans. Sorry to damper your reunion."

Her eyes flashed at Kurt. I caught a shared smile.

"Give me the kids," Kurt said. He motioned for me to pass the baby.

"Go to hell."

Annette raised her head, chin trembling. Her eyes darted fervently, as if searching for something or someone to make her world good and safe again.

"You and I are going for a walk, Emily," Trish said. "Kurt will baby-sit."

Annette began to cry and pressed into my leg until I nearly stumbled. Soon her sobs grew so hard her whole body shook.

"I'm not going anywhere without her!"

I held her to my side. Casey began to cry.

Trish smirked. "I was very clear about what would happen if you told other people. Remember?" She walked from the porch onto the first step. "We're going for a walk—right now—or I'll have you shot. Here, in front of your daughter."

Kurt produced his gun and Annette, staring at me in apparent confusion, wailed.

Trish continued. "Do you want her to see that, Emily? Want her to feel your blood spatter?" She paused. "Imagine the nightmares."

"Shut up!"

Annette jerked suddenly and released my leg. She buried her face in her hands. Her shoulders shook but there was no sound.

"Oh God," I dropped to the ground. "I didn't mean you, baby."

I used one knee to support Casey, and the other sank into the cold ground. I rubbed Annette's back. She moved her head to my shoulder, and light reflected off her tear-streaked cheeks. She sniffled and wiped her face on my shirt.

I turned my mouth toward her ear. "I love you, sweetheart. Since before you were even born."

Casey was crying so loudly I wondered if she'd heard me. I shifted him and leaned toward her again, wrapping an arm tightly around her wispy frame.

I heard Trish's boots descend the steps.

"Touching," she said, "but enough's enough."

She walked to us, put a hand on Annette's shoulder, and pulled.

"Leave me alone!" Annette swatted her. "Go away!"

Kurt stepped forward to help. Annette kicked him and he swore at her.

I held onto my child with everything I had, but they pulled until I lost one small part of her at a time. Finally, I only had a grip on her tiny arm. When she cried out, I worried it was because of how hard I was squeezing.

Kurt suddenly shoved her away and tried to wrestle Casey from me instead.

Trish wrapped her arms around Annette's body and tried to lift her. I didn't let go.

"Don't let her take me!" Annette yelled.

I reached with my other hand to hold her back, and instantly Casey was gone.

Both children were crying, screaming with every breath, terrified. Then Trish wrenched Annette's arm from me. I lunged after her, and something struck the back of my head.

Chapter Thirty-eight

I woke up on the cold ground with sharp pine needles poking into my neck and cheek. I closed a weak fist over loose earth and blinked. It was hard to focus. I was still in the driveway beside the cars, and my neck hurt too badly to raise my head.

The sallow glow of the porch light outlined silhouettes huddled on the porch. I blinked again and counted. There were three people now, and no sign of the kids.

Dew had soaked my blouse and pants. I started to shiver and wondered how long I'd been out. Long enough for Trish and Kurt, and whoever was with them, to feel comfortable walking away from me. Not long enough for the sky to completely darken. The woods were wrapped in heavier shadows, but I could still make out the trees. I blinked over and over. There was dirt in my eyes.

It was hard to see, but that had less to do with the grit in my eyes than it did with the blow to my head. When I moved it too quickly, objects blurred.

I focused on Trish's silhouette. She'd gathered her hair into a ponytail. I couldn't understand what she was saying, but she gestured wildly and the ponytail bounced when she spoke.

Kurt must have pulverized my neck when he'd hit me. It hurt to move, and I felt dizzy when I tried. I brought a hand to the back of my head and rubbed. My neck was swollen and a knot had already formed. I checked my fingers. No blood.

The Volvo was a couple yards away. I thought about scrambling behind its wheel, but expected I'd be shot before I reached the door.

A more subtle strategy might be to slide under the car, into blackness. Woods were on the other side. Maybe I'd have a chance if I could get that far.

But, even if I disappeared among the pines, what about Annette? If escaping meant losing her, I didn't want to live.

I knew I couldn't get her out alone. Going for help was probably our only chance, but I had no real idea where to go, or how long it might take. Would there be time? I was on foot; they had vehicles—not comforting odds.

I rolled onto my back and took a deep breath to help control the pain. I had to extend my neck to monitor the activity on the porch. It was agony.

I inhaled and braced for another roll. Slowly, I made my way onto my stomach again. I'd closed half the distance to the car and hadn't been detected. Adrenaline was kicking in.

Another roll, and I was staring at the undercarriage, which had less clearance than I'd hoped. I stole my last glance at the porch and maneuvered onto my belly for the last time, figuring it would be easier to scoot under the car that way. I wedged into the warm space underneath the car. It smelled like oil.

Something hissed at me and I froze.

It was a damn cat. If it belonged to Trish, it was probably as evil and pissed off as she was. I turned my head toward the porch again and let it rest on the ground while I caught my breath. Someone new was talking, a man. I inched further under the car, and the cat hissed again.

When I was completely underneath the car, I squinted in the direction of the cat, but it had slunk away. I breathed deeply and tried to do the same.

I squirmed further beneath the car and made my way out the other side. The terrain leading into the woods sloped downward. I hoped the little ridge would hide me. Crouching, I started down the slight hill. I wanted to hurry, but if I stepped too quickly, snapping twigs and crunching pine cones would give me away.

"She's gone!" It was Kurt.

I broke into a run and angled myself toward the main road. Behind me, someone yelled to bring flashlights. "Over there!"

A gun fired. I ducked behind a thick tree and huddled near the ground, panting.

"Hold it, Emily," Trish called into the woods. I heard the wooden storm door smack closed.

"Can you see me?" she shouted. "See who I have?"

I peered around the base of the tree. Trish stood behind Annette on the porch. It looked like she had a hand on my little girl's shoulder. I thought she had a gun in the other. Annette stood mechanically, as if she'd been posed. Her fight was gone, and I became enraged all over again. Trish had broken her.

Trish yelled, "That was a warning shot. The next one won't be. Bullets are cheap."

I sniffled and wiped away tears I hadn't noticed before. These people thought nothing of killing. I thought about Jack's funeral, and remembered his mom kissing the closed casket before the pallbearers carried it to the hearse.

"Send her back inside!" I called. "I'll come out."

Two strong flashlight beams converged in my vicinity and swept the darkness. I pressed into the bark of my tree and stayed low. The porch door slammed again, and I wondered if Annette had really been taken back inside.

Trish screamed toward the forest. "I want my money, God damn you!" She stomped the porch. "Come out!"

I recognized a man's voice calling from the direction of one of the flashlights: "Come on out to the drive now, sweetheart. I know you think she's naughty, but actually…" he swung the beam through the trees around me, "this is very reasonable for her." It was Scud.

A thick band of light passed over my tree and snapped back. He held it there.

"Olly olly oxen free," he said.

The illumination around me broadened when Kurt added his beam.

"Come over here, toward the drive."

Standing made me dizzy, and I used the tree for support. The base of my skull throbbed. I looked toward the cabin to check for Annette. All I could see were the bright lights shining in my face.

"That was a quite a show at the drop zone last night," Scud said. "I like feisty girls, but I gotta tell ya...you did a number on my shoulder. It hurts like a sonofabitch. So now, I'm afraid there's a score to settle."

He dropped his light to the ground in front of me. I stepped forward. Kurt kept his light in my face.

"Don't worry," Scud added. "Won't hurt a bit. I'm a better shot than you."

I raised a hand to shield my eyes. All I could see was mud and leaves up to a yard in front of me, then nothing.

"You're walking too slow," Kurt said. "Move faster, or your prissy little girl comes out and gets a messy anatomy lesson when she watches me shoot you."

I stumbled forward, following Scud's light on the ground. Soon I climbed the little slope toward the driveway and found myself between the van and the car again. I realized with a pang that I'd hardly gotten anywhere.

"Turn around and walk toward the road," Trish said. It sounded like she was near Kurt.

I turned away from the cabin and flashlights and began walking. One set of footsteps receded behind me. I heard someone mounting the porch steps, and finally there was the familiar slap of the storm door.

Ahead, the flashlight beams stretched into the night to show me the way.

"Where are we going?"

No one answered. I listened to the footsteps following me, grinding the dirt a few paces back. Sometimes the steps sounded so close together I thought maybe only one person was there with me. But the beams weren't moving in sync. I heard whispering, but no words.

"What will you do with them?" I said.

The only response was silence.

I stopped and turned. The flashlights stopped moving; they were about three yards away, very close together.

"What happens to the kids?" I was crying. "What happens to Annette?"

I could make out the faint outlines of figures holding the lights and gauged from her stature that one of them was Trish.

"What happens to Annette?" She mocked me. She even added a fake sniffle. "What happens to Annette?" Then her voice hardened. "Who the fuck cares? Turn around and walk."

I fell to my knees. My sobs echoed in the stillness, reverberated in my ears, completely understating my terror and loss.

"There's no time for this shit," Scud said. He wasn't talking to me. "Was that necessary? Look at her. She ain't moving any faster, is she?"

"Why should I move?" I yelled, staring toward them.

Trish lowered her beam and for a moment I could see more clearly. She raised an arm in front of her, and my chest tightened. She was going to shoot me, there in the driveway.

Scud reached across and put his hand on her extended arm. He leaned close to her and whispered. She lowered it.

"Relax, sweetheart," Scud said to me. "You're right. We want money. We get it many ways. Kids…" he paused "Well, frankly, kids don't fetch a good price dead. I won't sugar coat this, 'cause I'm sure you see things for what they are. You won't walk away from this. But Annette will, as long as you tell us where the locker is. Otherwise, she'll die in front of you. You decide."

When he finished, I expected something snide from Trish. Instead, there was only the faint rustle of swaying leaves. I inhaled sharply, and heard the sound of my breathing too. Tears dropped down my cheeks as resignation washed over me. I was helpless against Trish and Scud, but if I revealed the locker location, at least Annette wouldn't be used as a bargaining token anymore. At least she would live.

"Still thinking?" Scud said. "Get up and walk toward the road."

I don't remember how far we walked before Trish spoke up behind me. "Where is it?"

I was ready to answer, but Scud answered first. "A few yards ahead still."

"Yeah, but where?" Trish's voice.

He cast the beam of his flashlight off the left side of the driveway and swung it back and forth until it found an old, abandoned tire.

"There."

"Here's your turn-off." Trish shoved me in the back.

I stumbled, and walked into the woods where they showed me. I wondered how long Jeannie would stay in Texas before going home. At some point she'd have to accept I'd never be found. Trish had done me one favor, even though she hadn't meant to. She'd spared Jeannie's life by separating us.

I shuffled through the woods wherever they told me to go, stepping over fallen branches and ducking under low ones, until I was suddenly told to stop walking. My eyes stung and my cheeks were wet, but I wasn't afraid to die. I was crying because there was so much I'd never explain to my little girl.

Trish and Scud walked ahead of me a few paces and then diverged to either side. I watched them swing their flashlight beams along the ground as if looking for something.

"Right here," Scud said. Trish turned and joined him.

They directed their lights at the ground, into a giant oblong hole with a thick mound of dirt around its edges. My grave.

"Get in," Scud said. "Make it easy on me, I'll make it easy on you."

Chapter Thirty-nine

Trish and Scud pointed their flashlights at the perimeter of the hole.

"Go on," Scud said.

I knelt on the mound of damp earth surrounding the pit, as if to pray, and made the sign of the cross.

"Forget that," Trish said from the blackness behind me. "You can chat in the afterlife."

I scooped blocks of mud into my fists.

Behind me, twigs snapped and her flashlight beam jostled. I kept my head bowed and steadied myself.

Her foot pressed into my back. I slid sideways and hurled a loosely packed ball of mud toward her face. She looked away and shielded her eyes. I knocked the flashlight from her hand. It landed silently in the crude grave.

Before I could stand, she raised her gun. I flung the other handful of dirt at her and dived for her knees. She thudded onto the ground before she could get off a shot, but Scud fired a round and missed.

Trish yelled. "She's right on top of me!"

A car hummed up the main road. I squinted through the trees and thought I saw the flicker of headlights and taillights.

I grabbed a thick shock of her hair and wrenched her head backward. She cried out and pried at my fingers. I used my other hand to rake fingernails over her face until I found her eyes, then

I dug in. She screamed and let go of me, reaching instead for her face. I staggered to my feet and ran toward the road.

Twigs and brush scraped my legs and I lost a shoe in the sticky mud. I knew Scud was close behind me.

A car turned onto the dirt driveway ahead.

I ran toward its lights, but it continued past me.

"Wait! Help!"

The car was going to the cabin.

A shot fired; it was so loud it seemed the gun was right beside my head. Heavy footfalls tramped in the brush behind me. Scud was gaining speed. I tripped in a low spot and caught myself on a tree. The car kept its course.

"Stop!" I screamed again.

Another shot fired, and a sharp crack exploded from a tree in front of me. The car reversed. I dodged behind a tree and stayed low and still.

From the driveway, someone shouted my name.

It was Vince.

I couldn't answer without giving myself away.

"Emily! Are you there?" he called again. "Are you okay? Emily?"

His voice was getting louder. He was coming into the woods to look for me.

"They've got guns!" I shouted.

I sprinted for him.

"This don't concern you, Vince," Scud yelled, and fired again.

As I neared the driveway, I made out the area surrounding Vince's car, but didn't see him. I zigzagged to stay behind trees and finally hid behind one large enough to cover me.

The car, still running, was in the driveway with its lights on. Vince had left the driver's door open, and the interior was illuminated by the dome light. But I couldn't spot Vince anywhere. Was he taking cover on the other side of the car?

In the distance, a helicopter approached and the aggressive chop of its rotors told me it was closing in fast. Within moments a spotlight swept the woods around us. Its aimless ray was off-target, but I hoped it was enough to scare Trish and Scud.

I caught sight of Scud's flashlight beam; he was about twenty feet to my left and inching closer. I stayed low behind my tree.

A gunshot sounded, and Scud toppled to the ground, doubled over. Vince bolted from the shadows and ran to the driver's side of the car.

"Emily!" he shouted. "Get in the car!"

I emerged from the woods about ten feet in front of the car. I was hurrying toward its passenger door when I spotted a figure on the drive. Trish was the same distance behind the car as I was in front of it, and her gun was trained on me. I was trapped in the headlights of the car.

"Drop it," Vince said.

She swung the gun toward him, but his weapon was already raised. Trish wouldn't hesitate to kill him. I worried the same might not be true for Vince.

"This isn't about you," she said to him. "Don't make me do this."

He didn't move.

They stared at each other, weapons drawn, and I had the sensation more was being said silently between them than what I could imagine. Down the road, a shrill chirp sounded, followed by the beginning wails of several sirens.

In a fluid motion, Trish whirled and redirected her aim on me. Vince fired twice. She collapsed in a heap on the edge of the woods.

I started toward the car as he lowered the gun. He turned and reached for me with his other hand. I began to sob when his hand closed around mine.

"When I heard what you were planning," he said, "I called Trish to try to reason with her. Heard the train in the background and figured she was hiding up here. Your text message to Jeannie confirmed my hunch. This was her dad's hunting cabin."

Above, the helicopter was deafening as its spotlight converged on the secluded old shack. Agents onboard would expect Trish and her henchmen to be inside. I panicked; they might not know about the kids. If they opened fire, Annette or Casey could be killed in the siege. I watched the helicopter hover and spin as it jockeyed for the best view. Then I turned to tell Vince why I had to go.

It seemed his body jerked before I heard the round that hit him. A small patch of red appeared below his shoulder, and before he lowered his eyes to look at it, the stain spread to the size of a grapefruit.

I squinted toward the tree line. Vince slid down the side of the car until he was sitting on the ground next to me. He pushed his gun up into my hand.

On the other side of the car, Scud leaned beside a tree, his abdomen dark with blood. His face, once so striking, was cadaverous and pallid in the diffuse headlights. He kept his gun raised, but trembled as if the effort were exhausting. His eyes flashed and locked on mine. Suddenly his aim steadied.

I leveled the gun and fired until it was empty.

Epilogue

In seventh grade, I asked my dad if he ever shot anyone in Vietnam. We were walking through a parking lot, on our way into a grocery store. He tucked his sunglasses into his front pocket and said, "If they shot at me, I shot back." We entered through automatic doors, he picked up the weekend sales flyer, and that was that.

It took twenty years, but I finally appreciated his brevity. Strangely, I gave little thought to having killed Scud.

In the days following the shootings, I spent many hours in interview rooms, dutifully remembering specifics. Then I spent even more hours trying to forget them. Kurt, I was told, bolted when he heard the sirens and helicopter that night. A boat launch a mile further into the woods offered the best explanation of how he'd gotten away. He'd left Casey and Annette alone in the cabin, probably unwilling to jeopardize an escape by slowing himself down. Reinforcements intercepted him a few miles down the shore. Difficult as it was for me to believe, prosecutors considered him a low level offender. They used that as leverage in exchange for information about bigger fish in his organization, namely Trish Dalton. Only a subset of his resulting story interested me, the details about what happened to Jack and Annette.

Claiming no involvement in the crime that destroyed my family, Kurt gave up the few facts he'd gleaned from Trish on the day of the shootings. Jack's boat—the one I should have been on—was ambushed on Lake Erie, far enough off shore that no other boaters saw what happened. His attackers took Annette, who'd be profitable on the black market, before killing Jack and damaging his boat, making the death look accidental. The explanation validated my suspicions and should have provided closure, but instead only made my heartache worse.

Prosecutors were building a case against Trish. Vince's shots had been damaging, but not fatal. He told me bone fragments had damaged his cousin's spinal cord in the lumbar region, leaving her unable to walk and suffering persistent neuropathic pain. After the requisite stay in a guarded hospital room, Trish would be released into federal custody, where it seemed she'd spend the rest of her life as a "special needs inmate." I often wondered if it was better or worse for Vince that she'd lived.

No one I asked would speculate on what Trish's capture meant for their racketeering ring. I concluded from vague, open-ended answers that folks were sparing me the truth. Clement had described the size of the underground organization that he and so many other agents tirelessly worked to bring down. I imagined that when one leader got incarcerated, another probably got promoted to fill the empty seat. Maybe the beast had been wounded, but I figured it was still very much alive.

Jeannie and I made frequent visits to Vince's hospital room. Once, on our way up the elevator with Richard, Jeannie suggested we try her hospital pick-me-up porn idea. She said we'd missed our chance with Clement, but Vince was a better sport anyway.

I'd never heard Richard laugh before. His laughing with us, clowning around that day, felt like amends for things I'd left unsaid, or poorly said, in the aftermath of all I'd misunderstood about him years ago. Before we said goodbye, he passed me an envelope. Karen Lyons had written to thank me for my part in bringing back her son. She included a picture of the two of them. I'd never seen Ms. Lyons before; the dimples I loved so much on Casey were from her.

Four days passed before a DNA test confirmed Annette was mine. Not that I'd had any doubt. In the interim, I couldn't have her, and neither could the Fletchers—the couple she knew as parents. My parental rights were ambiguous without a test result, and the Fletchers were deemed a flight risk. Annette was placed in short-term foster care.

I used the time to put my affairs in order. When I returned to Cleveland, I quit my job at BioTek, which was timed well, because Bowman was probably about to fire me anyway. Jeannie offered me five hundred dollars and a session at her swanky hair salon if I'd take Johnny Paycheck's approach and tell Bowman to "take this job and shove it" during his weekly staff meeting. She'd throw in a manicure if I'd smack my ass on my way out the door. Instead, I wrote a polite letter explaining my unanticipated family changes and expressed regrets for not providing two-weeks' notice. My colleagues took me out to lunch and presented a gift certificate for Toys R Us.

Movers came and loaded the essentials onto a truck. I left the remainder behind, in my house, where Jeannie would live rent-free until my indefinite return. Meanwhile, I'd be in Texas, taking baby steps to forge a relationship with a little girl who might never call me Mom.

When the test results came back, and the Fletchers couldn't produce a signed waiver of my rights, I received full legal and physical custody of Annette. Yet, what joy is in an outcome that breaks your child's heart?

My relationship with the Fletchers was tenuous to say the least, but we shared a genuine interest in what was best for Annette. We attended family counseling together and agreed to cooperate while transitioning our little girl. They'd been told Annette was from an abusive family. The operative who handled their case went so far as to produce falsified medical records. In their desperation to have a child, and their sympathy for mine, they looked the other way when details of their adoption process were sketchy and hurried. The adoption, they said, had been surprisingly quick, but they'd attributed that to the higher "agency fees" they'd paid. Neither seemed the type to knowingly commit a felony. It was obvious the same crime that had broken my heart was now breaking theirs.

Not surprisingly, Kurt was less forthcoming with details of Annette's most recent abduction, but between Betsy Fletcher's story and Annette's account, we formed a reasonable idea about how he'd pulled that off. On the day Annette was kidnapped from their home, Betsy opened the door to a telephone company worker without a thought. He forced himself inside and took Annette, then shoved her into the back of a phone company van waiting in driveway. Betsy ran to grab her cell phone and car keys and tried to follow them as she called 9-1-1, but it wouldn't matter. Annette was switched to a new car a few blocks away. The man who'd snatched her "peeled the pictures off the side of his van" before driving it away. Clement's team figured the only reason Betsy hadn't been shot on sight was because Trish was planning to ransom Annette back after leaving me dead in the woods.

The Fletchers urged me to consider letting Annette make a gradual transition into my care. I supported the sentiment, but told them outright that I wouldn't risk losing her again. If the FBI thought they might flee with her, why should I believe differently?

I rented an apartment two miles from their home and Annette moved in with me. It wasn't the ideal situation for anyone, but I think the Fletchers appreciated my efforts. They sent over many of her favorite things, including a green pair of sneakers and a stuffed giraffe named Georgina. We had dinner as a foursome most nights, at their house or mine, and spent much of our weekend time together too. I resented the ever-present third and fourth wheels, but needed them. I didn't know Annette was afraid of spiders or that she'd only eat spaghetti if there were no meatballs. Without Betsy to translate and explain my daughter to me, our reunion would have been a clumsy mess. We'd both suffered the terror of losing our little girl and, if nothing else, those experiences bonded us in empathy. Eventually, I realized I had nothing to fear in the Fletchers.

"My mommy said there was a mistake when I was a baby," Annette said one afternoon in March. We were playing Crazy Eights. She had a milk mustache and too many cards for her small fingers to manage. A jack flopped onto the kitchen table.

"What kind of mistake?"

"Somebody was supposed to give Mommy a baby who needed a new family. But I didn't need a new family."

I set down my cards.

"That's true," I said. "I've always been your mommy. And I would have come sooner, but I couldn't find you until now. I'm so thankful your mom and dad took such good care of you for me."

She shoved the misplaced card back into her stack and nodded.

"We're both lucky, you know," I continued. "I get to love a beautiful little girl, and you get an extra parent."

She giggled. "A bonus parent."

My telephone rang.

"Oh!" she said. "Can I answer it? I know how."

I smiled, and she picked up the handset.

"Hello?" she said, then listened. She shook her head. "Nope, sorry. My mommy's not here."

I held out my hand and gestured for the phone. It was Vince.

"I'm calling to collect my pizza dinner," he said.

Annette maneuvered onto her knees and leaned forward in her chair, watching me.

I heard guitar strumming on Vince's end. "You promised to take me out for pizza when I learned to play the F chord," he said with laughter in his voice.

"You were medicated when I said that."

"Still. You said it." He strummed the F chord over and over, but it wasn't quite right.

"You're not holding the strings—"

"So, what are you ladies doing later? Because I think it's pizza night."

I covered the mouthpiece. "Do you want to go out for pizza with my friend Vince tonight?"

"Is he bringing his dog?"

Vince chuckled. "You bring your girl, I'll bring mine. We'll get take-out and eat at the park."

"It's your turn," Annette said to me, and pointed at the discard pile.

"Sounds good," I said into the phone. "Talk to you later."

Annette hung up the phone for me. I drew from the deck and discarded.

She took her turn and sighed.

"Sometimes, can we do it the other way, where I live with my mom and dad and visit you?" She put her elbow on the table and leaned her chin into her hand.

I squeezed my lips together.

"Would that make you happy?" I finally asked.

She smiled broadly and her eyes squinted the same way Jack's used to. His laugh lines were the only thing missing.

"Then I suppose we could do that once in a while," I said, unsure and yet strangely certain at the same time about the rightness of her request.

She laid down a card. "Can we especially do that on the nights you cook fish?"

To receive a free catalog of Poisoned Pen Press titles, please contact us in one of the following ways:

Phone: 1-800-421-3976
Facsimile: 1-480-949-1707
Email: info@poisonedpenpress.com
Website: www.poisonedpenpress.com

Poisoned Pen Press
6962 E. First Ave. Ste. 103
Scottsdale, AZ 85251